Sibba licked her suddenly dry lips and stepped away from Cal's hand and any muddled thinking about mutual attraction.

She had not missed a target since she was six. Even her father used to say that she was a natural. She had never taken him just at his word and had practiced until she became excellent. Her men needed her to succeed.

She swallowed hard and regained control. "I look forward to demonstrating why my men chose me as their leader."

He captured her hand and raised it toward his mouth. His warm breath caressed her palm. A brief tremor pulsed up her arm. "Shall we seal our bargain with a proper kiss, my lady?"

"I trust you to honor your word." She pulled away from him and resisted the irrational urge to cradle her palm to her cheek.

Author Note

In 2022, my journey to the Scottish island of South Uist took an unexpected detour and we had to go via Barra due to ferry problems, spending the night on Barra. As I looked out over the white sands at the steel-gray crashing waves, I wondered about Vikings. Once actually on the Uists, I visited a number of archaeological sites, including the roundhouses at Cladh Hallan, some of the oldest (and longest inhabited) dwellings in the UK, and wondered about those inhabitants and how they coped with the invaders from the north. The result of my musings is Cal and Sibba's story. I do hope you enjoy it as much as I enjoyed writing it.

As ever, thank you for reading my stories. If you'd like to get in touch, I love getting comments from readers and can be reached at michelle@michellestyles.co.uk or through my publisher or Facebook or X, @michellelstyles.

TEMPTED BY HER FORBIDDEN WARRIOR

MICHELLE STYLES

Harlequin
HISTORICAL

Harlequin®
HISTORICAL

ISBN-13: 978-1-335-53977-9

Tempted by Her Forbidden Warrior

Harlequin Enterprises ULC
22 Adelaide St. West, 41st Floor
Toronto, Ontario M5H 4E3, Canada
www.Harlequin.com

Printed in U.S.A.

Recycling programs
for this product may
not exist in your area.

Born and raised near San Francisco, California, **Michelle Styles** currently lives near Hadrian's Wall with her husband and a menagerie of pets in an Edwardian bungalow with a large and somewhat overgrown garden. An avid reader, she became hooked on historical romances after discovering Georgette Heyer, Anya Seton and Victoria Holt. Her website is michellestyles.co.uk and she's on X and Facebook.

Books by Michelle Styles

Harlequin Historical

Saved by the Viking Warrior
Taming His Viking Woman
Summer of the Viking
Sold to the Viking Warrior
The Warrior's Viking Bride
Sent as the Viking's Bride
A Viking Heir to Bind Them

Vows and Vikings

A Deal with Her Rebel Viking
Betrothed to the Enemy Viking
To Wed a Viking Warrior

Sons of Sigurd

Conveniently Wed to the Viking

Visit the Author Profile page at Harlequin.com for more titles.

To Michelle Smart, because friends
who are also good writers are beyond price

Chapter One

Early May 843 AD,
Suthereyjar, Lochlann

Formerly part of the Dal Raita Confederacy but now
controlled by the Norse

Modern-day
South Uist, Scotland

'Land. Port side!' came the cry from the helmsman.

'Nearly there. Good.' Sibba Norrsdottar shaded her eyes against the sunlight dancing on the dark blue waves.

The curve of silver sand with the green hills beyond gave a promise of fertile land and safe anchorage. Such a contrast with the overworked land of her youth where rain washed away the seed and the game had become scarce. The wedding between Bedwyr—the High King of Suthereyjar and the small isles—and Gettir the Sea King's only child, Rindr, would ensure some sort of peace and stability returned to Lochlann, a peace which had been broken when the sea wolves of Barra had ambushed and murdered her father.

The muscles in her neck and back loosened. Just around the headland and then safety. Before they departed, she'd given the excuse to the Sea King that they were taking the northern route because her father had been ambushed. No doubt when they did arrive, the other captains would again laugh at her caution, but the excuse would continue to be accepted without question, and the true reason—her discovery of her brother's secret affair with the Sea King's daughter—would remain hidden.

Sibba glanced down to where her twin brother sat, head in hands in the bottom of the boat, groaning about the unfairness of life and the horridness of dictatorial sisters, rather than pulling his oar.

At least his eyes had stopped spitting daggers and his mouth screaming obscenities at her as they had done when she ordered the ship away from the harbour. Once he realised she'd irrevocably set her course, he'd lapsed into groans, heartfelt sighs and staring up to the sky, appearing resigned to the situation. It could be hard to tell with Haakon these days. When they were younger, he used to follow her lead, requesting her help when their father set him tasks like shooting arrows at a far-off loaf of bread or learning the basics of swordplay. But now they were grown, Haakon demonstrated a worrying lack of common sense, self-preservation, and—more importantly—preservation of the men she now commanded.

He simply did not understand that she had acted quickly and decisively in the only way she knew. As any good big sister would do. Just as he did not truly understand why she had challenged for the leadership of the felag, beating him and two other warriors in the process. Good leaders had to be willing to make hard choices quickly, but Haakon struggled with the simple ones, her father used to say, shaking his head. And she knew how to make those choices, better than any man.

'Can we trust him to keep his mouth shut? Would he not be better gagged and trussed until we know what is going on with the wedding?' her helmsman said, interrupting her thoughts and gesturing to where Haakon now lay, face to the startling blue sky, complaining about the unfairness of being thirsty.

'Haakon understands the necessity of keeping his liaison secret.' She forced her back to be straight and made sure her voice carried to all parts of the dragon-prow longship. 'If anyone—Gael or Northerner—asks, we travelled by the northern route because I feared the sea wolves on Barra after what happened to my father. Nothing to do with missing the wedding or who the bride is. Same excuse I gave her father and mother when I asked permission to depart.'

'One day you will go too far, sister,' Haakon called out, suddenly sitting up. 'Gettir and his wife are no fools. He will have guessed before we cleared the harbour.'

'Now he decides I exist. Now at the journey's end he deigns to speak to me.' She dipped a cup in the bucket of weak ale and made her way to her brother. 'Drink and give me one good reason why you should not be kicked out of the felag. One solitary reason. You endangered every one of us, Haakon.'

Haakon took the cup of ale from her, drained it, and then wiped his mouth with the back of his hand. 'Why did you make me go with you?' He gestured towards the burly helmsman. 'Why did you have me thrown over his shoulder like a sack of grain? I'm a warrior, not a child having a temper tantrum.'

'Why did you try to kidnap Gettir's daughter? His only child? Of all the women, you picked the daughter of one of the most powerful men in the North, a woman who is already betrothed,' she countered, putting her hands on her hips. He appeared to have forgotten his ravings about how he was going to seize the rudder and steer the ship back to rescue his beloved. His beloved! He knew that woman's destiny was different and that the safety of the felag depended on her marrying the High King.

Haakon pushed the hair out of his eyes. 'Rindr is like... like the moon. Perfection in silver. Her voice is like the song of the nightingale I heard in Constantinople. Sweet and melodious.'

'Spare me. You are no skald, Haakon. If you won't pull the oar, answer the questions.' She hunkered down beside him and put her hand on his sleeve. 'Sulking seldom solves anything.'

Her brother frowned. 'We are in love. We belong together. Our eyes met, and we both knew instantly. Not that you would understand, Sibba.' He waved an extravagant hand. 'You never allow any man to touch your heart. Too practical. Hard-headed. Unnatural in a woman. My beloved agrees with me.'

Sibba fought against the urge to scream. There was nothing unnatural about understanding that her duty to the felag came first. And the less said about how her heart had been trampled, the better. 'This hard-headed person saved your life. Had anyone else found you two together, they would have skinned you alive.'

'Is my life saved, though?' Her brother gave a dramatic sigh. 'My love isn't with me, and my life is over.'

'Breath goes in and out of your lungs. A sure sign you live.'

'You must help me, Sibba. Allow me to talk to her before the wedding.'

'Give me one solid reason why I should grant this request.'

'If I can speak to her alone and if this marriage is what Rindr truly desires, I promise I will cease trying to rescue her.' Her brother tilted his head and fluttered his impossibly long lashes. 'All I want is her reassurance.'

Sibba made a noise at the back of throat. Unbridled lust like her brother's current infatuation ruined families and destroyed fortunes. He knew they needed the alliance with the Gaels to give them any hope of fulfilling the oath they had both sworn on their father's funeral pyre. The Northman pirate who had murdered their father needed to be destroyed, and they required help to do it.

'You are always mooning over some girl, until you find another object of your affections,' she said instead of breaking the news that the marriage had most likely taken place the instant Rindr set her daintily clad foot on the shore. Silently she prayed that the High King, with his power, wealth, and command of a huge cohort of warriors, would make Rindr's eyes gleam and her heart flutter faster. When they had spoken last Jul, Rindr's chatter had been of torcs, jewel-encrusted brooches, and finely woven dresses.

'My feelings are deep this time, Sibba.' Her brother thumped his chest. 'I know the difference now. We want to live in a little cottage by the woods, with a stream and a small garden. We won't harm anyone. We want to live our lives in peace.'

'That dream will be a piece of hard cheese,' Sibba said, shaking her head. The idea that Rindr and Haakon would be allowed to live like that was pure fantasy. Rindr's father required a safe anchorage for his fleet to be finally able to attack the Pirate King of Barra, the man who had murdered her father. 'I told you not to eat it. Made you imagine things and lose all common sense. We need allies, not enemies, if we are to truly avenge our father's murder, rather than simply mouthing the words of the vow.'

Haakon's pout increased. 'We discussed it three days ago when she lay in my arms. I am certain I saw the sparks from Sky Cleaver as Thor worked on his thunderbolts. A sign that Thor favours us.'

Sibba kept her face carefully blank. The sky had been full of meteors the other night. She was undecided about their actual meaning, but the exploding lights had made her restless and uncertain about the proposed route that went near Barra and the Wolf King's lair. To puzzle it out, she had gone for a walk and stumbled over the pair intertwined in the moonlight.

'Forget omens from Thor. Soothsayers, runes, and omens are not real.' Sibba took his hands in hers. 'Rindr doesn't mean any harm, but men seem to lose their minds over her. And I've seen it go ill for them. Last Jul—'

Haakon turned the cup round and round in his hand. 'Those men were before me.'

Sibba curled her fists and wished she could stop a habit of a lifetime. 'Think, Haakon. Sparks from Thor's hammer always mean a battle is on the horizon. We will be fighting the Pirate King before the summer is out, and we must have safe anchorage if we want any hope of victory. Rindr will be the weft who ensures the alliance stands.'

Haakon dropped the cup, his eyes alight with a fierce passion. 'Rindr wants to be with me, not with some aged high king who should be taught a lesson about obedience to the North.'

'The Gaels of Suthereyjar have defeated all would-be conquerors, including Thorkell, the Sea King of Barra.'

'Her bridegroom is much older than her. He probably has no understanding about a skald's poetry or decoration of a hall or how the twinkling of the stars makes the night beautiful.' He held out one of his hands. 'And my fingers are smooth, not gnarled. Rindr likes feeling my hands on her.'

Said as if a mutual love of such things rendered their recently sworn duty to Gettir, the safety of their men and indeed their honour unimportant. 'Have you forgotten your oaths that quickly?'

'The Gaels will never listen to a woman about strategy. Rindr told me that.' Haakon's generous mouth turned down in another pout. 'I should be the one heading our felag if you want them to notice us.'

'You lost the archery competition. Badly.'

'But I look like a leader.' He had the sort of good looks which were wasted on a man. Or rather, as their father had once put it, it would have saved a great deal of trouble if Haakon had been the girl and Sibba the boy. Like many things her father had said, his unkind words had a ring of truth. However, he was wrong. Haakon was completely male even if he was not as skilled at the sword or bow as she was, and she enjoyed being a woman.

To her mind, there was no reason why a woman could not be a leader of a felag even if very few women had ever succeeded in doing this. Her father had considered that women's power lay in the gentler pursuits like hospitality, forging connections, and smoothing men's way. After winning control of the felag, Sibba was determined to prove she could handle both the diplomacy and the strategy.

'You might have defeated me, but Rindr is being sold like a piece of meat,' Haakon said, making a lunge for the helm and making the boat swing wildly. 'She begged me to help her. Me. Not you. I intend to give that help with or without your blessing.'

Sibba rolled her eyes heavenwards. 'The last man Gettir

caught sniffing around his daughter had his back flayed. And that was for a peck on the cheek, not what you two were up to.'

Her brother hung his head. 'How was I to know Rindr and I were observed?'

'What would her father have done if he had caught you two together like I did? What would the High King have done—or his son, Calwar, the one who is supposed to be the fiercest warrior the Gaels have ever produced?'

Haakon gathered her hands between his. 'But you will help us? Rindr and I want to be together. We must be together. Our true destiny.'

Sibba inwardly sighed. She loathed having to act the leader, instead of the sympathetic sister. Even if she had private doubts, a part of her did want Haakon and Rindr's love to be genuine and for them to be happy together somewhere without endangering the fellowship. And it would be wrong to give him false hope.

'If I can figure out a way...' she said, trying to let her brother down gently.

'Thank you for your promise, sister.' Haakon gave one of his smiles. 'Bedwyr will not want an unwilling bride. He is a proud man, from all the tales I have heard. Explain it to him or to his son, that warrior Calwar who negotiated the alliance.' He kissed her cheek, all sweetness and light now that he had his way. 'You are good at convincing people. It is why the men follow you instead of me.'

Sibba frowned as the ship rounded the headland. The rest of the fleet should be here, but there were no other ships, not even Rindr's father's ship. And she knew Gettir planned to be based there for the next few months before he attempted an all-out assault on Thorkell's lair as he'd asked for her patience.

'No one is here, my lady,' her helmsman said in an undertone. 'How is that possible?'

A faint prickle crept down the back of her neck. The others were taking the quicker route which went far too close to where Thorkell had attacked and destroyed her father's fleet. Earlier, Gettir had scoffed at her womanish fears but had allowed her to go the longer way as a special favour in memory of her late father and how she'd had discovered the aftermath. She and her crew had only escaped because they were delayed due to a broken sail line. 'No one... But that is impossible. All seven ships should have been here by now.'

'We must have had the tides right,' Haakon declared, rubbing his hands together. 'You worry overmuch, sister. Var is with us. Our luck is in. Rindr remains unmarried. Your promise holds, sister dear.'

Sibba firmed her mouth. Haakon had a funny notion of luck. She saw things going spectacularly wrong. And she'd given her word about rescuing Rindr, counting on the fact that she would have been married long before she and Haakon arrived. Silently Sibba offered up a prayer that she'd be able to keep her word without putting her men in danger.

By the time they had beached the ship and had started to disembark, a small party led by a tall dark-haired man arrived on the flower-strewn dunes above the beach. At some point, the leader had experienced an injury to his mouth causing it to lift slightly. The combination of the neatly clipped beard with his penetrating eyes moving intently over the scene caused her breath to catch. When he spotted her, his lips turned up into a crooked smile. It was as if he glimpsed the dark recesses of her soul and knew her innermost secrets.

'Northmen, do you have a reason to visit these shores?' his deep voice boomed out in highly accented Norse.

Sibba smoothed her gown, before motioning to Haakon to keep quiet and the men to remain silent. She rested her hand on her knife and silently blessed the fact that her favourite nurse had been a Gael and had taught her the language.

'Gael, do you have a reason to be unpleasant to people who come in peace? Whose greatest wish is to celebrate your wedding?'

His brows drew together. 'Not my wedding, my father, the High King Bedwyr's, my lady.'

Sibba inclined her head. 'I stand corrected.'

'Calwar mac Bedwyr, scourge of the North.' He made an elaborate bow. 'You may have heard of me, my lady. And I trust your visit will be short.'

Behind her, her men nosily lowered their shields.

'Given the welcome you appear to offer, perhaps you have misgivings about this marriage,' she said in Gaelic. 'Here I thought you arranged it—a blood alliance to defeat our common enemy. Nothing else would do.'

The scar above his lip quirked upwards. 'A Northwoman who speaks the language of my people, instead of expecting us to speak hers. Unusual. Why have you arrived on your own instead of with the fleet?'

'Your fame as a warrior has reached even our ears. Only a fool would attack such a well-defended place as Suthereyjar,' she continued in Gaelic, pointedly ignoring the fact he'd addressed her in Norse. 'I speak in your tongue so that your men will know what I say. My men have a basic understanding of your language. A necessary requirement, to my mind, if one is to trade peacefully in these waters.'

She gestured towards his men rather than answering his question directly. Until she knew why Rindr wasn't here and wasn't married, she kept quiet about her promise to Haakon. She'd apologise to Haakon later, if necessary, but they would do what Rindr wanted, not what any man in her life dictated.

'You travelled here to be at the wedding, but not with the wedding convoy,' he answered in Gaelic. 'Raises suspicions. Some from the North are unhappy about the proposed blood alliance.'

Sibba forced a smile and held out her hands, palms upwards. 'Gettir gave his permission due to my womanish fears. Ask him when he arrives.'

'I intend on it.'

'A woman speaks for the group while warriors remain silent. What mischief is this, Calwar?' A tonsured priest bustled up, flapping his arms like a great hooded crow.

'Our customs differ from yours,' Sibba said firmly. At her nod, the men beat their swords against their shields. She snapped her fingers, and they ceased. 'Where is Gettir? I wish to speak to him.'

The priest fled, and even Calwar retreated a step. 'Alas, Gettir and his daughter have yet to arrive, but I will ask them when they do. A woman leader is unheard of.'

Silently she counted to ten before she spoke. 'Yet my men obey me.'

His gaze appeared to take in everything about her appearance. Sibba absurdly wished she had worn her more usual sailing clothes instead of changing into her best gown to appease any Gael who might not like the notion of a woman warrior. She always felt like people took her more seriously as a leader when she wore trousers. 'Who are you?' Calwar asked. 'I don't remember you being present at the negotiations.'

She hadn't been there, and neither had Haakon. They had been too busy trying to fix their sole remaining longship, arriving at Rindr's father's hall to the fait accompli. She had discovered Rindr gently weeping and had told Haakon to cheer her up with a song or three, little dreaming of the consequences. Too late to worry about that now.

'Sibba Norrsdottar,' she said, ensuring her voice carried over the dunes to where she was certain the priest skulked. 'My father, Norr the Red, used to be the Lochlann Sea King in the southern isles until Thorkell arranged for his murder last year.'

His hand relaxed slightly on the sword at her father's name. 'I knew your father slightly and was sorry to hear of his untimely death. I understand his felag fell apart, and his warriors scattered.'

'Not all, obviously. We are allies with, but not of, Gettir's felag.'

'Sibba! Sibba! Sibba!' Haakon started the chant, and the others took it up until she raised her hand and stopped it.

Calwar blinked twice. 'I see.'

'What do you have a problem with, Calwar—my leadership or my wish to celebrate this new blood alliance? I speak true.' She paused, remembering the Gaels were Christian and might object to her swearing by Var, the north god of sacred oaths and unbreakable vows. 'I swear on my brother's life.'

Haakon dug his elbow into her side. 'My life? Sibba, you can't, you shouldn't.'

She put a hand on his shoulder. 'I just did.'

'Forgive me if I am wary, my lady of unexpected Northern guests.' Calwar made an elaborate bow, but his eyes remained deadly and focussed on her. 'My people have cause to know the treachery of the North.'

'If we concentrate on past grievances, no one will be able to enjoy the fruits of this unexpected peace.' Sibba raised her chin and concentrated on breathing steadily. If she gave in to her temper and reacted with fury to his provocative words, she stood the chance of losing everything.

One day, she'd teach this arrogant Gael a lesson, but right now she had more pressing concerns. *Patience rewards in unexpected ways* was one of the first and best lessons her father taught Haakon and her.

'Fine words for a woman. Your tongue may be polished, but is your sword?'

The Gael was far from alone in his scepticism. She had mouthed the same words eleven times in the past few weeks.

'A matter between me and my men. But I won my position, rather than being gifted it. And I intend to keep it in the only way I know how—through my skills as a leader.'

'My sister can outshoot any man!' Haakon shouted. 'She won the felag fair and square. I will fight any man who says differently.'

'When I require assistance, brother, I'll request it,' Sibba whispered. 'Until then, still your tongue.'

Haakon put his hand over his mouth.

Calwar frowned. 'I accept you arrive in peace. Make sure you leave in peace.' Said with a grimace, and there was no mistaking the undertone: they were to depart immediately.

'We will remain for the wedding. I wish to toast the bride,' Sibba said, making an elaborate curtsy. No one threatened her or her men like that. 'When the rest of the fleet arrives, the truth will out.' She permitted a smile to cross her face. 'Jump to the wrong conclusion and the entire situation may unravel.'

He tilted his head to one side. 'A threat?'

'An observation. For future reference, I rarely threaten. I keep my promises.'

Her men hit their swords against their shields in agreement, but Sibba snapped her fingers twice. They instantly halted in midthump. She appreciated the gesture, but the darkness had returned to Calwar's face. And she knew he was a hair's breadth from ordering his men to defend the shore against the invaders.

Sibba kept her face carefully blank and ignored the growing tightness of her gut. The fleet would arrive on the next tide. The alternative—that somehow the remainder of the fleet had experienced a grave difficulty and people were now injured or worse—was her mind playing tricks. 'I promised to attend Rindr's wedding,' she said in quiet voice. 'I always strive to keep my promises.'

Calwar drew his brows together and assessed her under hooded lids. His gaze seemed to peer deep down into her soul. Sibba forced her shoulders back and her chin up. 'When should I expect the bride, o lovely and gracious Sibba?'

'A day or two at most, if they altered course like I suggested and went the long way around.' She forced a steadying breath. She knew the reality of her looks—hair the colour of dishwater, eyes a dull grey, and a figure with a shade more curve than she'd like. 'Your father will be married on the day his bride arrives, if that is what he desires.'

Calwar bowed low, but his eyes burned with a barely surpassed fire. 'All that remains then is for me to show you to your temporary accommodation.'

'We will remain on the boat.'

'But I must insist.' His smile showed no warmth. 'You will not mind if I post a guard or two until Gettir arrives.'

Said almost as an afterthought. He did not believe her words of friendship. Would she believe him if the positions were reversed? She sensed the men behind her ready to draw their swords and waggled her fingers behind her back. She heard the soft sound of swords sliding back into their scabbards. 'Do you think we look like raiders?'

'I've given up thinking what a raider looks like. I will not allow anyone to jeopardise this alliance. The safety of my people depends on it.'

'May I confer with your father?' Sibba asked between gritted teeth. If the son refused to see sense, the father surely must. King Bedwyr must have heard about her father and how he desired an alliance with the Gaels to counter the threat from Thorkell in the last months of his life. 'He knew my father, I believe.'

'My father will meet you when the time is right,' Calwar said with a note of great finality.

'You mean when the others arrive.'

'I mean when my father and I decide it is appropriate. If I discover you seek to play me false, Sibba Norrsdottar, it will go ill for you and your merry men.'

Sibba rolled her eyes. Merry men indeed. As if the men who followed her were not seasoned warriors but ones more interested in drinking and skalds' tales. One day he'd learn. Until then, Calwar was another arrogant man who had already made his mind up about her talents and ability to lead a band of warriors.

'I think he guesses something is amiss, Sibba,' Haakon murmured in her ear. 'You must hold to your promise and rescue Rindr whatever happens.'

Sibba pretended to stumble and grabbed his arm. 'You best hope that he doesn't. Calwar is not a man I would care to cross. His reputation as a great warrior precedes him.'

'But…but…'

'We had best hope that Rindr arrives soon, safe and sound.'

'Why?'

'The felag should have arrived before us, and it failed to. Something is very wrong. We are about to get blamed for it.'

Her brother wrinkled his nose and thought for a few heartbeats. 'I never considered that. Should we try to escape?'

She put her finger to her lips. 'Not if you want to help Rindr.'

Calwar gestured towards a small wooden hut which stood on its own at little ways from the bustling ring of houses which surrounded a large wooden hall. About the best that could be said for the hut was it had an earthen roof to ward off the soaking rain which had begun to fall. 'Your home for now. Leave your weapons outside the door. They will come to no harm.'

The knots in Sibba's stomach had developed layer upon layer of further knots, but she forced her face to be serene as if being locked away was not a grave insult. 'Poor hospitality has been the ruin of many a man's ambition. The sea king will not take kindly to his ally being treated like this.'

Calwar's mouth became a thin white line. 'Many men would not dare to say such a thing to me.'

She took a deep breath and lifted her chin. 'There again, I am not a man.'

He stopped, and she was aware that his gaze lingered on her curves. 'Yes, you are most definitely a woman, a woman who proports to lead a group of *peaceful* Northern raiders.'

'Do you require a demonstration of why I was chosen?' she said in a brusquer voice than she intended. 'I look forward to your apology when I best you with bow and arrows.'

He gave a slow smile, captured her hand, and raised it to his mouth. His tongue briefly touched her palm. 'Apologies can be enlightening for both parties.'

The heat in Sibba's cheeks rose. She rapidly pulled her

fingers away from his warm grasp. Unlike Rindr, she had never felt entirely comfortable under a knowing male gaze, and she certainly had never deliberately sought out a flirtation, particularly not after the debacle with her former fiancé. She ducked her head and concentrated on his boots. 'I will take your word for it.'

She turned on her heel, marched into the hut which smelt of decay, disuse and dust and silently promised that he would be the one to apologise.

The sound of his mocking laughter echoed after her. She balled her fists. One day very soon, she would demonstrate to the very irritating Gaelic warrior that she and her concerns needed to be taken seriously.

Chapter Two

The darkened room smelt of tallow, burning herbs, and illness. Cal paused in the doorway and allowed his eyes to adjust. His father, who until three days ago had been more active than most men half his age, lay with his eyes closed and his sword-hand curled into a claw. After his unwelcome intervention earlier, Father Aidan had returned to sit in his usual corner and rattle his rosary beads with great solemnity.

'The situation failed to improve in the time I was seeing to our uninvited guests,' Cal said, forcing a laugh.

Cal doubted the tale the very pretty leader from the North told was the entire truth. When the terms of the blood alliance had been worked out, he had encountered other Northernwomen warriors, and none had had her fragile beauty with a heart-shaped face and strawberry-blond hair. He doubted the woman had ever lifted anything more taxing than a needle, but he'd allow the threadbare deception for now. And she would apologise to him for her veiled threats. Poor hospitality! She was lucky that he had not ordered them chained.

'You should have greater faith,' Father Aidan said with a faint click of his tongue. 'Your father will recover in God's time. The wedding will take place now the Northmen have arrived. God help us all if they fail to live up to their end of the bargain. I know what they did to your late wife's family on Barra.'

'Not the bride, Father Aidan,' Cal said, ignoring the remark about Brigid's former home. He went to stand beside his father, who tried to lever himself up into a sitting position but failed. 'Someone else entirely. Sibba Norrsdottar and her men.'

'She lies. No women can lead warriors,' the priest said, pursing his mouth into a tight bitter plum and allowing his rosary to fall to his lap. 'Putting her forward shows their deceitful nature. You must find the true leader before he has us murdered. It will be Barra all over again. You know the treachery the Wolf King worked there. He guides this woman, I tell you.'

Cal ensured his features were a blank mask. Arguing with the good father wasn't worth it. His gut told him that Sibba was the leader of this small group of men. They obeyed her hand signals without hesitation. 'She speaks Gaelic.'

'Perhaps she was the only one who could.'

'They seemed content to let her claim the mantle.' He watched the priest under hooded eyes. 'I did speak to them in their language. You must get used to a female being a warrior. We are allied with Gettir, the Sea King.'

The priest shuddered. 'Barbaric. Bad enough that Bedwyr is having to marry a young woman from the North. At least this female warrior of yours isn't the bride. Imagine the High King's bride being a warrior in her own right. The heavens would weep.'

Cal shrugged. The good priest would never accept the necessity of making any alliance with the North to ensure the safety of these islands, but then he was only concerned with the state of men's souls rather than the practicalities of keeping people alive. 'She claimed she won her position.'

'Women make many claims. They are all descended from Eve, the temptress.'

Cal frowned. As the confessor to his late wife, the man had been part of the trouble with his marriage, putting ideas in his bride's head about the right way to behave. Having a row standing at the foot of his father's sickbed was something he refused to lower himself to. 'I will keep that in mind.'

'Thorkell Wolf King murdered Norr the Red,' his father croaked from the side of his mouth. 'Not always friend but great warrior. Norr. Respected.'

Cal firmed his mouth. His father still retained his mind. It was his body which had let him down. He wished the marriage to the sea king's daughter had happened a week earlier when his father had seemed healthy and full of life. And he knew he'd heard the name of Sibba's father before. Norr the Red had taken control of most of the shipping lanes in Suthereyjar before he lost his life in a battle with Thorkell last year. Unlike the current king of Barra, Norr had preferred trade to laying waste to farms.

'His daughter arrived for the wedding. With her felag.'

'He makes a mistake to trust that one. She means trouble,' the priest said, shaking his head. 'Best rid yourself of the pestilence while you can, King Bedwyr.'

Cal clung on to the shreds of his temper. Father Aidan had a healing gift, but he had no head for politics. 'Gettir, his daughter and his fabled fleet remain conspicuous by their absence. Sibba Norrsdottar appeared concerned.'

Far too soon for Gettir to have heard about his father's collapse and sudden affliction. Or indeed the whispers that it had been Cal's late wife's dying curse which caused it.

Eighteen months was a long time for a curse, but some people enjoyed making mischief. Gettir still required the safe anchorage, and they still needed assistance in keeping Thorkell at bay.

The priest jerked his head towards where his father lay, breaking his concentration. 'And when they arrive? When they see what Bedwyr has become?'

'We will see they honour the treaty.'

His father's mouth worked up and down before the croaking sound emerged. 'You must... I...can't...'

Cal crossed the floor and took his father's clawed hand lightly in his. When he'd been a boy, his father's hands were always strong and capable; now the fingers could barely curl around his. Deep down he knew what was coming, but he hoped for a miraculous cure.

Even after eighteen months, he often hoped in those first few breaths of waking that he'd find Brigid's death and that of their baby boy to have been some bad dream. He had tried so hard to save her, but she'd slipped away down the cliff and into the waiting sea, screaming that she'd married a coward who would never protect anyone. All because she'd been unable to force him to march on the sea wolf from the other side of Barra, a mission that would have resulted in his death along with everyone else who was fool enough to march.

'You are the sea king's choice, Father. His daughter must marry the High King to ensure the blood alliance never falters— his words, not mine. You remain the High King while you draw breath. Until you regain your strength, you will have my sword defending you. You will rule over these islands for many years to come.'

He stopped and prayed his father would believe it.

His father closed his eyes, and a tear slipped down his cheek. 'Thank you, my son.'

Father Aidan coughed softly, and Cal nodded to him, showing that he understood the message. His father required his rest if he had any hope of regaining his strength.

'I will deal with our unexpected visitors in my own time.'

'Can't afford enemies, son. Make them our friends.' His father's voice had little of its old strength. 'One battle at a time. Your duty. Always.'

He knew how to do his duty without his father's reminder. He gritted his teeth. Make them their friends? Men from the North? He'd sooner trust a snake, but his father's instincts were correct. One common enemy. One battle at a time. He had to figure out a way to bend them to his will.

He spied his late wife's quiver of arrows, lying forgotten in the corner where she must have abandoned it in her last frenzy of activity, a silent rebuke to his refusal to listen to her entreaties to free her childhood home on Barra from the sea wolf Thorkell no matter the cost. She'd taken his refusal badly, and it had sent her on her final spiral. Now he took it as a call to action and a way forward.

Sibba's arrogance about her prowess as an archer would be the start of her undoing. She thought to best him at archery? She'd learn.

The lesson would be quickly administered but well remembered. If she refused to become an ally, she would suffer the consequences.

'It will be done.'

The hut with its piles of broken barrels, mouldy straw, and large patch of mud in the centre failed to improve on closer acquaintance.

Sibba sank down with her back against the rough wall, trying to ease her aching bones and ignore the pounding pain in her head while she kept an eye on the door. She refused to think about Calwar mac Bedwyr or, worse, the warmth which had radiated up her arm when their hands briefly touched. Or how she'd noticed the way his eyes crinkled as if, against all expectation, he found her attractive. She was a leader of a felag, not some giddy maiden who could have her head turned by a fine pair of shoulders and a well-turned calf. She needed to think practically about how she was going to manage to get her men out of this alive.

It bothered her that she kept remembering snippets of Rindr's gossip about Calwar: that his wife had died in tragic circumstances about a year and a half ago; that he rarely smiled because of her; and that Rindr thought he was a man to neither cross nor be married to. She suspected the view was formed because he would not put up with any of Rindr's whims or fancies.

'All will be well,' she whispered. 'It must be.'

'Will it be fine, sister?' Haakon whispered. 'Because from where I sit, we are in a right nest of poisonous snakes with no escape route.'

'Such a turn of phrase, Haakon.' She allowed a handful of straw to trickle through her fingers. 'Do you see any snakes here? Are there any snakes on this island? Does anyone know? I have heard one of their saints drove the snakes out of Eire. I suspect someone has done the same here.'

'You know what I mean,' Haakon mumbled. 'We should have escaped to our boat and returned to the Isle of Man to gather more warriors to avenge this great insult from the Gaels.'

Sibba pressed her lips together. Haakon always had been a poor tafl player. He never understood anything about forward planning or making the most of a bad situation. 'We need the Gaels and their safe anchorage. Our father knew enough not to attack Bedwyr, and his son is even better at defending his lands. In any case, we fight one enemy at a time.'

'What are you saying, sister of mine? We should remain in this blasted hut indefinitely?'

'Gettir and his men were leaving on the next tide. Rindr should have arrived well before us. Yesterday eventide at the latest. There will have been another turning of the tide since we were locked in here,' Sibba said, keeping her voice carefully neutral. The last thing she wanted was for Haakon to panic. 'Something is wrong. I knew something would happen if they went too close to Barra. Thorkell will have been waiting for them like he was with our father. We only survived because we left late due to that broken line and were able to take evasive action.'

'I knew it.' Haakon slapped his hands together. 'The gods sent us here to make it right. I will slay Thorkell. The king will be so pleased that peace is restored that he will allow Rindr and me to marry. I bribed that soothsayer months ago to travel to Barra and foretell Thorkell's death at the hand of a warrior woman.' He paused and rubbed his chin. 'Maybe I should have instructed her to say a murdered man's son instead.'

She pressed her hands against her eyes. Haakon had listened to too many skalds' tales. And that soothsayer simply took his gold and would go nowhere near the Wolf King of Barra. She told him that at the time: Thorkell would never hear a whisper of any rumour, but Haakon refused to believe it, claiming that the soothsayer had given her word.

Haakon's latest boast was preposterous—slay Thorkell? How? The only way would be a direct challenge to his leadership, and to do that Haakon would have to join Thorkell's felag. Besides, the man found a way to get out of every challenge. The last seven challengers had mysteriously died before they raised their sword to Thorkell.

'The gods always punish arrogance, brother. It was arrogant of Gettir to take the southern route. I said so before we departed. I stand by those words.'

'Something must be done, Sibba. You can't turn away from Rindr's plight.'

'I must figure out how to make the Gaels understand, before it is too late.' Sibba rested her head on her knees. 'If only Calwar had allowed me to speak with the king...'

Haakon rose and rattled the door. 'I hate being confined. Reminds me of Constantinople when that prince was sharpening his knives. How long will we be kept in here?'

'Until they learn to take us seriously.' She doubted that the Gaels respected her as a leader. It was a mistake to think that they would. From what she knew of the Gaels, they had little use for women in positions of power. But they might have use for her men now, if her fears about Thorkell attacking Gettir proved to be true. Somehow, she had to find a way to prove to Calwar that she and her men were not the enemy and that she was capable of leading men into battle.

She pressed her hands to her eyes. She should be out there searching for them, instead of being locked away in here. She should have seen the danger and acted before Calwar had locked them away. Her mistake alone, and only she could undo the damage her challenge had done.

'Rindr should have been here and married,' she muttered, going over everything in her mind for the twentieth time. 'Their minds were made up about going to the South and sailing near Barra. I was the foolish one for going to the North and leaving them to that fate.'

'We must rescue her. Take her away from Lochlann,' Haakon said.

'Once we find out what Rindr truly wants, then we act,' her helmsman shouted. 'Listen to your sister.'

'The bride makes the decision, not some man. That includes you, Haakon,' another said.

'I am perfectly capable of speaking my mind, particularly to my twin,' Sibba said, trying to ignore the sudden prickle of unease. The moment she allowed them to start defending her to Haakon, she lost her hard-won control. Her father had given that reason as to why she should wed a capable warrior, when she confided her ambition to lead. She'd written the warning on her heart.

Her men had the grace to hang their heads and quietened.

'But yes, I agree with you. Rindr remains important. If she requires rescuing, we shall ensure it is done. I give my promise.'

Haakon whistled. 'Did you see how old Calwar was? His father must be an old man. How could anyone marry her off to him?'

Sibba put her head in her hands. All too many women would be glad to marry a high king, regardless of how old or infirm he was. The power and the potential for power attracted them, rather than moonlight and stolen kisses.

'Way of the world, brother.'

Haakon scrunched up his face. 'The world needs to change.'

Sibba gritted her teeth. Lovesick madness. One day soon she hoped he'd look back on this time, laugh at his folly and be grateful for his narrow escape, just as he now did about the Byzantine prince's wife.

'Rindr's mother, Nefja, wants the prestige of her only child being married to a high king,' she reminded him.

'From what I understand from the other captains' gossip, the Gaels offered friendship, but egged on by Nefja, Gettir required blood ties before he'd commit to a long-term defence of these islands. Blame her parents, not the Gaels.'

'Not a joking matter, Sibba. Rindr dies and it is all your fault.'

'If you are going to make inane comments, I reserve the right to point out that they are silly and unproductive.'

'Who made you in charge?' Haakon muttered.

'The felag. We took a vote, young Haakon, after Sibba bested you first at archery and then the sword,' the men roared. 'You lost.'

Heavy footsteps stopped outside the door.

Sibba motioned for them to be quiet. The men fell silent instantly. 'We maintain unity in front of outsiders.'

She stood, brushed down her gown and silently directed her men to stand in a horseshoe, ready for whatever was to come, including a fight.

Calwar's silhouetted form filled the doorway as if she had conjured him. Sibba was annoyed with herself that she immediately recognised it. 'I am to take Sibba Norrsdottar for further talks. My father wishes to know more about your concerns regarding his bride...unless someone else would prefer to speak about this.'

He spoke like she would cower or was afraid of meeting King Bedwyr. Bedwyr might have a fierce reputation, but she wasn't frightened of him. Sibba balled her fists, gained control of her temper, and took a step forward.

'I'm happy to speak with your father. I want to speak with him.'

His lip curled. 'Why?'

'Perhaps he will be more accommodating about the sleeping quarters. Perhaps he will see we are no threat.

We are here merely for the wedding. Perhaps he will treat us with legendary Gaelic hospitality.' She forced an accommodating smile and lowered her eyes to the dirty rushes which swirled about on the floor. Anything to make him think she was compliant and not a threat. 'I take it the latest tide has not brought in any new boats.'

'Anything else?' he asked after giving a noncommittal grunt.

'It appears there will be a long wait for any wedding feast. My men's bellies ache.'

'You are the only ones to arrive thus far.' He stepped back from the doorway. Her men started forward, forming a phalanx around her. 'The offer is just for you, Sibba Norrsdottar, not your men. But I will instruct my people to deliver some food to them.'

His people. She frowned, trying to discern the subtext. 'Is there something wrong with the High King?'

'Why are women always capricious? First you wish to speak with my father, and now you accuse me of hiding some problem. Make your choice. Come alone or remain here.'

She signalled to her men to remain. There was some grumbling, but the men appeared to accept her authority. Worse case was the Gaels were splitting them up. She clenched her teeth. 'I give my word, my men are no danger to you. Stop behaving like they are.'

Her men took a step forward. Calwar raised his hand.

'Obey my command if you truly seek friendship with us.'

Sibba rubbed her hand across her face and tried to calm the sudden knotting of her stomach. 'Thing is, I sometimes have trouble obeying commands. Are you saying we, invited guests to your father's wedding, are now prisoners?'

He lowered his brow. 'If you wish to bandy words about, perhaps someone else in your party should speak on your behalf to the king.'

'I merely wanted to ensure my men would be safe,' she said between clenched teeth, hating his arrogance and that she had inadvertently stumbled into a trap. The main thing now was to get their freedom and then to find Rindr. The more she pondered it, the simpler her mistake seemed. Any leader worthy of respect would have seen the potential. If she wasn't careful, she could lose everything.

'You don't have to do this,' Haakon said in a low voice, catching her hand. 'You don't have to do any of this. Once Rindr arrives, I'm sure my darling will speak for us and explain the purity of our hearts.'

She kissed his dear, sweet cheek. She couldn't risk that. Rindr would do what her parents dictated. And she assumed Nefja now knew or suspected about the dalliance. 'Kind, but I know my duty. I knew I would have to do things like this when I vied for the leadership. The High King will hopefully have more manners than his son.'

She heard the sharp intake of breath from her men, but Calwar gave another noncommittal grunt. She balled her fists again and looked forward to Calwar's abject apology. The man needed to be subjected to some humiliation. He would not dare treat a man like this. She needed to figure out how to gain his respect.

Haakon scrunched up his nose. 'Be careful. That's all. We need you, Sibba.'

She patted his shoulder. 'I will be.'

She went out into the gloaming. The rain which had earlier fallen through the hut's roof had stopped. The clearing mist revealed the heather covered hills rising behind the village. The rain had also placed diamonds into the Gael's hair. She had no doubt that many women's hearts fluttered faster when he was near. Thankfully she did not judge a man by the beauty of his face but rather by the strength of his character.

'Does your father understand that something is wrong? That Rindr should have arrived before we did?' she asked, more sharply than she had intended when he directed her away from the imposing hall and towards the practice yard. 'Does your father understand anything? Is he still alive?'

He stopped and looked her up and down. She was uncomfortably aware of her curves, crossed her arms over her bust, and glared back at him.

'I do not want to presume either to know my father's mind nor if you wished someone else to speak with him,' he said finally. 'My father is curious about why you arrived when you did. He wishes to speak with you in due course. But first you and I speak.'

'What is wrong with your father?' she asked.

'He will be able to make the marriage bed, provided the bride is willing.'

Sibba pressed her lips together. It was not what she had asked. 'Does King Bedwyr want a reluctant bride?'

His eyes narrowed. 'Do you have reason to believe Rindr is reluctant?'

'Gettir requires a powerful king for his only child,' she said carefully. 'But has anyone asked Rindr what she wants?'

'You begin to think sensibly. We approach this blood alliance by what is possible, not what is impossible.'

'A compliment from you?'

He shrugged. 'If you require one…'

'I've lived my life perfectly happily without, but I will accept it in the spirit given.'

A sudden smile crossed his features, transforming them into the sort one usually encountered in gods or icons in Constantinople. Sibba knew it would be easy to like this man, and that would be a mistake.

'I'm unused to people from the North. Normally we meet on the battlefield.'

She gave a light laugh and said without stopping to consider, 'And now we meet on the marriage bed.'

'Are we meeting on the marriage bed? Normally there is a sort of negotiation before that happens.'

She caught his dark blue gaze and tumbled in. She belatedly realised that mentioning beds was unwise. Nothing like that existed between them. She'd made that mistake three years ago and had readily gifted her heart to a warrior. Only to learn, in the worst possible way, his interest in her had been about her father's fleet, rather than anything to do with her and her dreams.

'Rindr and King Bedwyr, I mean.' Her voice was too high-pitched and breathless for her liking. She swallowed hard and concentrated on an eagle which circled above the heather hills, hunting. 'There is no other marriage in the offing that I am aware of.'

'Rumours have reached my father that some in the North oppose the proposed marriage and will do all in their power to prevent it.'

A small prickle of sweat beaded down her back. 'I look forward to you admitting that I have told the truth.'

'The truth has many shades, o lady warrior.'

'I have no fears about proving my worth. I'm happy to demonstrate how my skill as an archer won me my felag.'

'An exhibition to prove your worth? Excellent.' The sort of smile a cat gives before it pounces crossed his face.

'Shall we make it worth our while with a wager? A wager between a man and a woman?'

His gaze appeared to linger on her curves. She dismissed the thought as ridiculous. Men were not interested in her in that way: she had too sharp a tongue and refused to simper. Her only value had been who her father was. Now she was overlooked because she was a woman warrior. She had to stop seeing shadows and concentrate on the prize—the ultimate destruction of Thorkell.

'If I win, not only do you admit we came in friendship but I get to speak to Rindr alone before she marries.' The muscles in her neck eased. She could do this in a gown as well as wearing trousers.

The dimple in Calwar's cheek deepened. 'In the unlikely prospect of you winning, yes, that can be arranged. Are you prepared for the alternative?'

She ignored the distinct prickle down her back. The man was overconfident. She wasn't going to lose. Her aim had never failed her. 'What will happen?'

'You and you alone will serve me for a year and a day.'

Sibba wet her lips. The terms were too vague, but the temptation was there. She had yet to meet a man who could best her with the bow. 'Serve you? How?'

'You will find out.' He gave a shrug. 'If you were serious about your skill earlier, then you should accept. Otherwise, reveal your true leader.'

'My men are not included in the bargain.'

'It could make life crowded if they were.' He placed a hand on her shoulder. The warmth from his palm seeped into her body, making her aware of him as a man and that sort of awareness always was a mistake. 'Simply you.'

She licked her suddenly dry lips and stepped away from his hand and any muddled thinking about mutual attraction.

She had not missed a target since she was six. Even her father used to say that she was a natural. She had never taken him just at his word and had practiced until she became excellent. Her men needed her to succeed. They could not stay in that hut, hoping against hope that Rindr's wedding party appeared on some distant tide. But above all, she had given Haakon her word: Rindr would have her choice of marriage partners.

She swallowed hard and regained control. 'I look forward to demonstrating why my men chose me as their leader.'

He captured her hand and raised it to his mouth. His warm breath caressed her palm. A brief tremor pulsed up her arm. 'Shall we seal our bargain with a proper kiss, my lady?'

'I trust you to honour your word.' She pulled away from him and resisted the irrational urge to cradle her palm to her cheek.

'I will have the target set up over there.' He pointed to a spot on the other side of the yard. 'And then the wager will commence. My late wife often made boasts like that, but alas she exaggerated her ability.'

'Do not judge all women by your late wife.'

'I will bear your words of wisdom in mind.' He inclined his head. 'Do you wish to speak to my father before or after you lose?'

Sibba ignored the slight knotting in her stomach. There were pros and cons both ways, but she knew she could win if she didn't think too hard. 'I'd hardly like for the High King to object to our wager.'

He stroked his chin before laughing. 'Such confidence. I look forward to your service.'

She pressed her lips together. His overconfidence would

be his undoing. 'My bow and arrows are in the boat. I would prefer to use them if possible. May I fetch them?'

He caught her elbow, pinning her in place. 'They can be fetched.'

She twisted her shoulders, but his hand was unmovable. 'Is it all people from the North or just me that you do not trust?'

The dimple flashed in his cheek. 'Merely trying to be helpful. You hit the target three times, and I will say the wager is fulfilled.'

'You don't want to test your shooting ability against mine?'

He shrugged. 'As all you require is to speak with my father's bride and me to proclaim you came in friendship, I see no reason for a direct competition. Had you asked nicely, I might even have granted it without the wager.'

'I will hit any target you set.'

Calwar directed several of his men to set up the target and handed her the bow and quiver.

'Yours, I presume.'

She took them from him. As she took the quiver, their fingers brushed. A warm pulse shot up her arm. A quirked brow and a sudden jerk of his hand showed that Calwar experienced it as well.

Aware of the rising heat in her cheeks, Sibba concentrated on adjusting the bow string. Her spectacularly bad record of being attracted to unsuitable men continued. Her men's safety and well-being must be her first and only priority, not thinking about some man's eyes or that if she lost her wager, she'd be his servant for a year.

The target appeared very simple—a loaf of bread set on a post—but it was very far away. Calwar was correct in his assessment: most archers would struggle to hit the target from that distance.

'Do you want it closer?' Calwar asked. 'Or should we say three out of five?'

'Do you think I can't do it?' she retorted, pretending to fumble with the notch of the arrow. Her stomach was in knots. It was not going to be easy, but if she admitted her nerves she'd be lost. 'Move the target back ten yards. Make it harder.'

'Do you have a death wish?' Cal's mouth drew down. 'I know how hard it is to hit that target at that distance. I practice at that distance several times a week.'

'Even so, move it back ten yards.'

'You are determined to lose this.' He shook his head. 'Why do women always have to exaggerate?'

'Why do men never believe me? Why do they judge me based on some other woman's faults?'

The men behind him laughed and put bets on how many attempts it would take before she hit the target. Or indeed if she'd hit it at all. Most appeared to think she wouldn't. Several declared that if she won, they'd lay gold at her feet.

Calwar glared at them, and they lapsed into an uneasy silence.

'I prefer honest friendship to gold,' she said, concentrating on the target.

'Hurry up and shoot!' someone shouted.

'In your own time,' Calwar said. 'Far be it from anyone here to rush you.'

Sibba's arm shook as she drew back the bowstring, and she tried not to think about how far away that loaf suddenly seemed. She risked three breaths with her bowstring taut and knew she had her eye in.

'Shall we see where this one lands?' She dampened down her nerves and allowed her first arrow to fly.

It hung in the air for an age before hitting the loaf directly in the centre with a solid thud.

Her neck muscles eased. Until the shot hit its mark, she knew she could always fail at that distance. The entire yard went silent.

'Don't applaud all at once.'

'You still have two more to go. A lucky first shot.'

'Skill, not luck, Calwar.'

She rapidly loosed two more arrows. While neither split the first arrow, they landed on either side of the first arrow. Solid but not showy. In terms of shooting, she doubted it would be possible for her to improve upon, but she knew the next time and the time after that she would strive harder.

She looked around at the assembled but now silent crowd. Her entire being seemed to be filled with light and air. She'd done it. She was going to be able to keep her promise to Haakon. 'Did anyone bet for me?'

A very skinny young man with bright ginger hair tentatively raised his hand. 'I did. Do you require the gold, my lady warrior of the North?'

Were Northern warriors that feared? As if any would so dishonour their code as to demand the winnings from lawful bets. She made a low curtsy towards the youth. 'Enjoy your winnings. I would ask instead for your friendship.'

He went nearly as bright as his hair. 'I plan on giving you that.'

'It would appear you will lack a servant,' she said to the glowering man who stood beside her.

Cal's face became inscrutable. 'Would you care for another wager?'

'What is that?'

'I manage to hit the precise centre between your three arrows, and you give me a kiss. If I fail, I will listen to your advice about the proposed marriage after you speak to Rindr.'

Sibba regarded the loaf. Her arrows had made a small circle in the centre. Hitting it would be practically impossible. He simply wanted an excuse for doing the honourable thing. 'Are you wagering this because I am a woman?'

He watched her mouth. 'You are the one who brought the subject up. How badly do you want me listen to your advice?'

The heat rose on her cheeks. She ran her tongue over her suddenly dry lips. The kiss was never going to happen. 'We have a wager.'

He gave a rumbling laugh which caressed her jangled nerves.

He notched an arrow on his bow, pulled back the string, and let it fly. Sibba watched in dismay as the arrow arced its way to the target and landed with a thud, squarely in the middle of her three arrows.

'In my experience, it is best to pay one's debts swiftly.' She brushed her lips against the soft bristles of his cheek. Her entire mouth tingled. But it was over. She'd paid the debt. Nothing more needed to be said. Ever.

He captured her chin and watched her mouth for a long heartbeat. 'I will save the reward for later, much later.'

'Why?'

'I intend to fully sample all the delights of your lips.' He let her chin go and strode away.

Sibba watched him. Her earlier excitement faded to nothing. Calwar was far more formidable than she had considered. And what was worse, he saw her as a woman rather than as a leader.

Chapter Three

Cal forced his feet to march over to the target where the four arrows were solidly embedded in the bread. He glanced over to Sibba. With the wind blowing against her gown, moulding it to her body and revealing her generous curves, she was unlike any North leader he'd ever encountered before and, indeed, unlike any other woman.

A grudging admiration for her filled him. He'd badly underestimated Sibba Norrsdottar's ability and how she could perform under pressure. Her men appeared more than willing to follow her lead. She did fully deserve her position as she had undoubtably won it. A woman leading a band of warriors was something he would have to get used to, now that they were to be allies. Except he did keep noticing the curve of her bottom lip and the way her eyes crinkled at the corners, and the deep-down part of him he'd considered dead had proved to be very much alive. However, he wanted his men to see—and for Sibba to understand—that he respected her position as a leader of warriors.

'Straight through the centre. With the other two widening the hole,' he said, lifting the loaf above his head. 'Impressive, particularly from that distance. But for the slight lifting of the breeze, my arrow would never have penetrated. I will happily attest to your skill.'

The men who had noisily bet against her suddenly discovered they had something else to do and melted away until Sibba was left standing there alone, arms crossed over her bosom, watching him with a puzzled expression.

Cal frowned. She wanted to speak to Rindr before the marriage. What assurance did she want from the woman? And why did she want to halt the marriage? His people's future required this alliance. He agreed with his father that it was the only way to keep the Pirate of Barra from terrorising their people.

'Practice makes for perfection,' she called back, a smile flickering across her face, before she drew her brows together. It was almost as if she needed to be fierce to keep her status.

'We will have to have another contest.' He pulled the arrows out of the loaf and handed them back to her. 'Clearly you weren't exaggerating your prowess. You are a better shot than I am. I say that sincerely.'

Sibba slotted the arrows back in her quiver. He fancied her cheeks went slightly pink at the compliment. She was not entirely indifferent to him, despite her attempt at a scowl. 'You managed to shoot your arrow straight enough. I doubt I could have done that.'

'I know when I'd prefer to have someone as a friend than as an enemy.' He forced a half shrug. 'Part of my charm.'

'Your charm?' She tried to increase her scowl, but the corners of her mouth twitched upwards while the rosy hue of her cheeks became like the fierce dawn over a storm-tossed sea. 'You Gaels have funny ways. It is good we are friends, even if you are cheating over that kiss.'

'Cheating? How so?'

'I brushed your cheek with my lips. Debt fully paid. No one could ask for more.'

He stared directly into her eyes and noticed the shifting colours in her eyes. 'Our deal offered no room for renegotiation. You may speak with the bride before the wedding, but first, you owe me a proper kiss at the time of my choosing.'

She put a hand on her hip. 'Your choosing? Was that in the wager? Are you intending to humiliate me?'

'Why would I need to humiliate you? What sort of man do you take me for? Belittling allies is an excellent way to create enemies.' He tamped down the swift stab of anger. Sibba did not know him, but she judged him. As if he'd ever behave that way towards a woman. He had never tried to humiliate a woman in his life. And he wanted to explore this tug of attraction between them in private. 'And we are allies now.'

Her lips turned up into a sad smile. 'You are different than some men I've known.'

He wondered what those unknown men had done to her and if they still breathed. If she had hunted them down or if he would have the pleasure of doing that. 'Humiliating women is always a sign of weakness in a man. And humiliating your allies means they are unlikely to remain your allies. Two good reasons for me to refrain until the time is right.'

'And how will you know when that time comes?'

He touched the tip of her nose with his forefinger. 'You will have to trust me on that.'

'Shall I meet your father now?' She placed the bow at his feet. 'We have wagered enough.'

He bowed low and tried to ignore the worry which continually gnawed at his insides. Sibba meeting his father would expose his hopefully temporary affliction to the Northmen and could jeopardise the marriage, the alliance, and the fragile peace which enabled his people to farm safely. Somehow a miracle had to happen. Otherwise instead of this blood alliance being the destruction of Thorkell as he'd planned, he could have accidentally caused the destruction of his people as his late wife predicted he would do during the last big quarrel they'd had.

'My father and you will speak, but whatever he decides, I will honour my pledge to ensure you can speak to Rindr before her marriage.'

'I expected no less.'

He pressed his lips together. 'Mark me well, Sibba. I've not said you could spirit her away even if she desires it.'

Her mouth dropped open, but she rapidly recovered. 'Did I ever say anything about Rindr being unwilling? I simply wish to speak to her, woman to woman. Right now, I'm more concerned about where she is.'

His hand caught her elbow. The faint pulse of heat which travelled up his arm shocked him, considering how long his body had been dead towards any woman. When he kissed her, he wanted it to be right. He wanted to wipe away all the pain and the hurt she'd experienced when that unknown had humiliated her. But would leaving the kiss make it worse?

She worried her bottom lip, turning the colour of the sunset after a hard day of a rain.

He gave in to temptation, lowered his mouth, and lightly brushed her lips. They tasted of fresh air combined with a faint tang of sea salt, and he knew he wanted more, but that would have to wait.

'Best to get it over and done with,' he said, stepping back. 'No one around to see. No humiliation. Wager fulfilled.'

Her tongue briefly explored her mouth. In the blink of an eye, he caught a glimpse of the vulnerable woman beneath the mask, the one who some man had hurt.

'I wasn't worried about it,' she said, lying through her teeth, her eyes darting everywhere, and looking at him proved it. 'My point from earlier stands. Debts are best paid quickly. Over, done, and quickly forgotten.'

'Is there any point in wagering if I don't wish to explore the possibilities?'

'There is that.' Her cheeks flamed, and she pointedly cleared her throat. 'Now all we have to do is wait for the other boats to arrive so you can pay your debt.'

'Why did you wish to arrive after the wedding party?' he asked, leading her away from the practice area. 'Confide in me, Sibba. We are allies now.'

'The reason no longer matters.'

He put his hand to her cheek. 'It matters to me. I must insist on honesty if you ever hope to free your men.'

'A stiff breeze could blow that hut down. My men can escape.'

'True, but people would die. Like any good leader, I doubt you enjoy wasting your men's lives for no good gain.'

'I vowed to keep my men safe.' She stood straighter, the vulnerable woman suddenly vanishing as if she had been a figment of his fevered imagination. It was best not to start anything. Best to forget the kiss they had shared. He let his hand fall to his side.

Out of the corner of his eye he saw Father Aidan frantically signalling to him. And he knew his plan of taking Sibba to his father would have to be postponed. He silently prayed that his father still lived. The last thing he wanted was the responsibilities of kingship, including the necessity of marrying again.

'The day draws to a close. You may see my father... tomorrow morning.' Silently he offered up a prayer that his father's affliction would be better.

'But I thought today.'

'I have other matters to attend to.' He signalled to one of his men. 'You may return to your quarters. Tell your men that they are free to roam around if they are unarmed and treat my people with respect. Friendship works both ways, my lady.'

Treat them with respect? What did he think she was? A smooth-faced warrior who had yet to face an enemy in battle?

Sibba tapped her mouth as she walked towards the main hall the next morning. What was Calwar mac Bedwyr playing at? What did that kiss from him mean? A punishment or something more? She was grateful that he had kissed her when no one else was looking, but she disliked her body's reaction to his mouth and his touch.

She'd feel better once she could change into her trousers and tunic, but for now, she kept her gown on as she did not want to give the Gaels any opportunity to take offence.

She had no wish to be made a spectacle of as her former fiancé had done when he'd proclaimed their betrothal in front of everyone. She'd been excited and delighted, thinking that here was a man who understood her and what she wanted from life. But then he'd dismissed her like she was nothing and had vanished for the rest of day. Later she discovered him intimately entwined with a very well-endowed woman. At her surprised shout, he stalked away, leaving his mistress to explain the situation in a loud voice and ensuring the tale spread like wildfire.

The truth that the man simply wanted the power her father's felag would bring him and cared nothing for her had hurt. She confronted him in front of everyone. He had admitted it, laughing at her for thinking otherwise. She had threatened him with a sword, and the betrothal had ended. And she'd vowed never to allow a man to turn her head again. The only way she could succeed was to be tougher than them. Except when it truly mattered, she'd been the one to forget to check the lines, ensuring her father fought one ship down. And by the time they were there, there wasn't anything she could do except take evasive action. She'd turned it over and over in her mind. That kernel of doubt refused to budge, and she knew the best way to make it go was to avenge her father's death.

Sibba made her footstep firm as she strode into the Gaels' hall. She no longer skulked in the shadows; she led from the front.

Several women stilled their spindles and openly goggled at her.

Sibba bit back the temptation to bare her teeth at the gaggle of nosy biddies. Hadn't they ever seen a woman leading a group of warriors before? All she required was to speak to the king and get his permission to take her boat out looking for the wedding party. No boats this morning meant that something had gone seriously wrong.

'I wish to parley with King Bedwyr,' she said in a loud voice. 'Now. I've waited in friendship long enough.'

The women nudged each other, tittered behind their hands, and mumbled something vague.

'Will anyone tell me where he is?' she asked, holding out her hands. 'I mean no harm and wish to speak with him.'

A woman shrugged. 'No one has seen him for days. Ask his son.'

'Ah, Sibba Norrsdottar.' Calwar entered the hall before she could ask any more questions. 'I've been searching for you. The king wishes to speak with you. Immediately if not sooner.'

'I'm here.'

'But never where anyone wants you,' Calwar said with a significant look.

She hated how her stomach appeared to be populated by a cloud of butterflies. 'Shall we go and see your father before some other trifling matter crops up?'

His hand cupped her elbow. 'You are in your battle gown complete with weapons. Afraid people will decide you are not the leader of these Northmen? I gave you my word. You are to be treated with respect.'

Sibba tucked a strand of hair behind her ear and smoothed the folds of her gown. 'Not nervous at all,' she lied. 'Concerned. The king has not been seen for days, according to your servants.'

'My father has many demands on his time.'

She wrinkled her nose. 'The High King is not going to come and greet me in public?'

The tonsured priest with beady eyes came into the hall and impressively cleared his throat before Calwar could answer. 'The woman leader of the heathens may enter the king's chamber only if she has been disarmed.'

'How charming,' she murmured and placed her weapons on the table. The priest's eyes widened. She stopped and retrieved a knife from her boot and a set of knives from her left sleeve. 'Almost forgot. Totally without weapons now.'

Calwar bowed low, hiding his expression. 'If you will come this way, Sibba.'

She followed Calwar in. A thick, choking incense hung in the air, making her eyes water. The king sat on a stool, his white knuckled fingers gripping its side. The right half of his face drooped as if it were made of badly set wax. She'd seen corpses who looked healthier. But a fierce strength shone from his eyes, and she could see that once he'd been a vigorous man.

She silently cursed. Rindr shied away from all illness and would never agree to a marriage with him in this state. Until she saw the man, she'd held a distant hope that somehow Bedwyr would be imposing, vigorous, and commanding great loyalty as all the rumours had it, and Rindr would be eager to cement the alliance. Instead, he was a man measuring his time until he wore his death shroud. Worse, his infirmity made the threat from Thorkell even greater.

'Sibba Norrsdottar,' King Bedwyr said, speaking from the side of his mouth with great deliberation. 'Why are you here? The marriage?'

Sibba curtsied low, seeking to show that she intended to respect him. 'I hope there will be a marriage, but the bride has yet to arrive. I wish to go out today and see if I can spot her or any ship in the fleet.'

'An agreement with her father, the sea king, exists.' Heavy breathing accompanied each word. 'We keep our bargain. Friend or foe, Sibba Norrsdottar?'

Sibba hated the way her stomach knotted. If she answered truthfully, she doubted if the king would allow her to come anywhere near Rindr before the marriage took place. 'We came in peace, and we intend to leave in peace… after the wedding.'

He closed his eyes. 'Good. Son. Hospitality. Knew her father.'

The priest flapped his arms like a great hooded crow and shooed her and Calwar out of the room.

'When did it happen?' she asked after Calwar had silently led her to a secluded nook close to a smouldering fire and away from where her men and Haakon were chatting to the serving women. Haakon, she was pleased to see, appeared in intense conversation with a very curvaceous brunette. Perhaps his heart was not as attached as he wanted to believe. 'When did King Bedwyr become so ill?'

'Several days ago. He started choking on a fish-bone.' Calwar stared intently into the smouldering ash, his shoulders slightly hunched. 'This was the result. He is better this morning. Some say it is a curse, but I stopped believing in such things a long time ago.'

'Is he dying?' she asked, leaning forward. 'Be honest with me. Surely, I've earned that right.'

His scar shone white above his lip. 'It is in God's hands. I pray constantly for his recovery, as do the rest of our people. Father Aidan insists that he will live for many more years.'

'Who are you trying to convince? Me or you?' she asked. She knew of men this sort of thing had happened to. Generally, a curse of some sort. However, Calwar was right: occasionally they did recover, after a fashion.

'Does it make any difference?'

'Rindr had such dreams.' The words hung in the air. She rapidly examined the stones in the yard. If Thorkell discovered the king's affliction, he would strike, and all these people would be put in danger. The Gaels required this union more than ever. Without the safe harbours, Thorkell would be able to close these vital shipping lanes to any who opposed him, and any chance she had of resurrecting her father's fleet or fulfilling her vow to avenge his death would vanish.

His face became intent. 'What are her dreams to you? You only arrived for the wedding and not with the rest of the fleet.'

Sibba pressed her lips together, holding back the damning words about Haakon. 'A friend in whom Rindr confided her dreams for the future. Pretty dreams they were too. Children, a safe home, and looking after those she loved.'

'Does any dream count for much when games of power are played?'

'Are you a cynic, Calwar?' she asked, reaching for a stick to poke the glowing ash.

'A failed optimist.' He inclined his head. 'My father taught me about the duty one owes to the people a king and his family serve. Without that sense of service, one can become a tyrant.'

'Even so...' She shook her head. 'It remains a mess.'

'Life is seldom straightforward,' he said in a low voice. 'A fact brought home to me eighteen months ago when my wife and child died.'

'I'm sorry.' She glanced at him under her lashes. The wife who had been given to reckless wagers, who had tainted his view of all other women, who had made him a cynic. Sibba knew she hated the woman.

His eyes became like winter. 'You never knew her.'

'You obviously cared for them.'

He lifted a brow. 'I did my best to save them, but sometimes one's best is insufficient.'

She shook her shoulders. She should be more charitable. His wife and child had died. And probably his heart as well. Here, she had hoped he might be attracted to her when he'd merely been seeking to hide his father's illness. 'Will you seek to delay the marriage until your father recovers, while holding fast to the promises made at the negotiations?'

He shrugged. 'One solution to an unexpected problem. My people's future security means more to me than any dreams.'

The man was going to be married to Rindr after she refused his father. He'd all but admitted that fact. She could not start any flirtation with him. All her dreams last night had been that—just dreams of a fevered mind. And Haakon's heart would truly be broken. 'I am the leader of a very small fellowship who came in peace and friendship. I have no influence in the matter,' Sibba said much too quickly before her nerve gave way.

'My father may yet recover. His voice is far stronger than earlier. Today is the first day that he has sat up.'

'Do you think that it is possible?'

His face was inscrutable. 'Stranger things have happened. While there is life, there is hope. My grandmother had spells like this and lived for many years. Born under the same star, the priest said.'

She wondered how much he truly believed that and how much he desperately wanted his father to live. But it was not fair to Rindr to be tied to such a man. 'Will you give Rindr a choice?'

'I shall.' He went over to the embers of the fire, stirred it, and watched the sparks fly up. 'Far being from the monster you have decided that I am, I know that the bride must be willing. My father and I are happy to have the alliance without a marriage, but the sea king required blood ties. I have no reason to believe his thinking will alter. And we need the sea skills of the North if we hope to survive as an independent people.'

Sibba's heart sank. Gettir would not give way on this. He required the anchorage if the sea lanes were to remain clear and believed marriage was the best way to bind the High King close. He might even see the king's affliction as an opportunity to gain more power. And where would Haakon fit into this?

'You should have said. The silly second wager was unnecessary.' She wet her lips. 'Totally unnecessary.'

A smile crossed his features, transforming them. 'Admit it. You found our wagering fun. You wanted to show off your skills. I needed to demonstrate mine.'

'My skills match yours.'

His smile grew wide. 'What, in kissing? I remain unconvinced. Are you asking to try again? Is that kiss too distant a memory?'

Heat infused her cheeks. This conversation was spiralling dangerously out of control. He was doing it to unsettle her, not to flirt with her. If he had forgotten the kiss, why mention it? She swallowed hard and regained her composure. 'We need to discuss finding Rindr. I'm worried. No one else has arrived.'

He gave a very masculine laugh. 'A change of subject? I'm easy. The nonappearance of the fiancée does bother me.'

'May I have permission to—'

The frantic blowing of horns drowned out the remainder of her words. Calwar rose and strode towards the door. The serving women all started scurrying about.

Sibba rushed up and caught his arm. 'What is it? What is going on?'

'The horns mean ships are coming in.'

'Rindr's?'

'We both live in hope.' He inclined his head and drew his arm from her hand. 'If you will excuse me, I'm needed elsewhere.'

'We will stand beside you.'

'If you think it necessary...'

Chapter Four

After collecting her men, Sibba raced down to the dune overlooking the shoreline. Four of the other boats from the wedding fleet limped their way onto the beach. The lead boat, the one which had carried Rindr and her family, had its mast half-broken. The once-proud fleet had clearly been through a battle. The remaining three ships from the felag were nowhere to be seen.

'Can we help?' Sibba asked, going up to where Calwar stood, quietly directing his men to assist with the boats. The beady-eyed priest stood next to him, glowering and mumbling as he clinked his rosary beads. 'My men have strong backs and arms.'

Before Calwar could answer, a great creaking filled the air, and she watched with horror as the mast finally collapsed. Several screams rent the air. Her men and Calwar's rushed forward to move the mast.

'What do you think has happened?' Calwar asked. 'My priest says it is a judgement from God. A storm at sea.'

'No sudden squall. These men were attacked. Thorkell is the most likely culprit,' she said, restraining her temper. Divine interventions and omens? Attempts to alter the truth more like. 'Look at how the ships' starboard side bows have been rammed. No sea monster, but a ship.'

Calwar gave a noncommittal grunt, but she noticed his gaze sharpened.

'I warned them that this might happen, and they laughed at me. Gives me no pleasure to be correct,' she said, shaking her head. 'Perhaps we should have been out there searching, but…'

'You can't wonder about might have been. You can only deal with the here and now. Your men will be most welcome to assist.' His hard fingers caught her elbow and pinned her next to him. 'But you remain here beside me until I figure out what precisely is going on.'

The high-handedness of the man! As if she and her men would abuse hospitality in that fashion. But it was not worth arguing over. People's lives were in danger. Sibba ground her teeth and nodded.

He raised his hand and directed his men and hers to secure the ships and tend to the wounded.

'We came in peace to celebrate a wedding,' Sibba said, scanning the horizon for more ships, but the silver sea was empty. 'They saw us as fat sheep fit only for slaughter.'

'How many ships are missing?'

She stared at the sea and willed the remaining ships to show themselves. She knew the men, their wives, and children. Whatever had happened, some had not survived. Women were now widows and children orphans because their leaders had chosen the shorter route. 'Seven ships remained at anchorage when my crew and I left Oban. I know of no quarrels between the captains…'

'Yet you went a different way.'

'The right choice from the state of these ships.' Sibba pressed her hands against her gown. She closed her eyes and remembered the scoffing. She had thought then that they had realised Haakon's indiscretion and, of course, there was no turning Rindr's father once his mind was made up. Both a strength and a weakness for Gettir, her father used to say. 'Although I doubt any of the remaining captains will welcome me telling them that.'

He stroked his chin. 'A pretty tale from a pretty lady.'

'The truth makes no claim to be pretty,' she said, clinging to the remnants of her temper. If her brother or one of the men said the same thing, she doubted he'd have reacted in a similar fashion. 'Would you prefer one of my men discuss the implications of my decision with you?'

'You wish to deny being attractive?'

She stepped away from him. There were many things she was, but pretty was not one of them. Her features were far too strong, her figure was awkward, and she had the habit of looking at men directly. When they'd last encountered each other, Rindr's mother Nefja had made a point of commenting on how she made men nervous.

She gestured towards the shoreline. 'Your father's betrothed travelled on the ship with the broken mast. I suggest we discover where Rindr is and how she fares.'

The priest did a slow blink. His mouth trembled. 'Calwar, I had thought these Northmen were supposed to protect us from the sea wolves from Barra. Could they be feigning? Could we have allowed the wolves in the gate after all this time?'

Calwar raised a brow. 'Feigning? I know you are no warrior, Father Aidan, and have ample cause to hate people from the North, but such a suggestion is preposterous.'

Sibba shielded her eyes. There were no other ships on the horizon. She hated the ache in the pit of her stomach. And that the priest so freely spoke against the alliance. 'They attacked out at sea, not close to the shore. It shows Thorkell feared this union. It shows why it is right and must hold.'

'Sibba Norrsdottar, hear us,' one of the rescued sailors called out. 'We were attacked. It continued until just before we started towards this harbour, and then they vanished.'

'The gods were with us, and we made it here,' another said. 'See! Sibba Norrsdottar has arrived as she promised. We should have followed her advice. She knew the danger from sailing too close to Barra.'

'Who is dead?' Sibba called back. 'Who needs help?'

'Many are injured. Gettir died along with three of his best men.'

'And Rindr? What of her and her mother?'

'Thorkell the Sea Wolf himself seized their hair and dragged them off the ship, laughing as he did it.'

Sibba swore under her breath. The worst of all possible worlds. As an only child, Rindr stood to inherit all her father's possessions. If Thorkell induced her to marry him, he'd control the felag or that part which remained loyal to Rindr's father. She had seen it happen enough times before to know it was a real possibility.

Poor Rindr would not have a say in the matter. Sibba half wished that she'd allowed Haakon and Rindr to flee. But seeing the folly of the past from the present never prevented it.

The priest coughed, bringing her back from might-have-beens. 'It appears the wedding will not happen. Oh, dear. But that is the end of the matter for us.'

Sibba put her hands on her hips. 'Are you always that cold-hearted, priest? A young woman and her mother have been kidnapped, a great war-lord lies dead, and all you can bleat about is the bloody wedding being off.'

Calwar grabbed her arm. 'That bloody wedding, as you call it, is important to my people's welfare. They suffer from the sea wolves as well.'

'They will suffer more. The wolves will surely prey on them should any rescue attempt be made,' the priest said with a faint, triumphant smile. 'We must look to our defences because Thorkell will attack us. Gettir, the great sea king, the supposed answer to all our problems, has fallen. Next time, perhaps your father will take my counsel to heart.'

Sibba rolled her eyes. 'Do you understand women have been kidnapped, priest? Don't they matter to you?'

Calwar blinked rapidly. 'You have no cause to speak to my priest in that fashion.'

He stalked away. Sibba shook her head. Answer given. The man's sole concern revolved around power and not the person. She forgot that at her peril.

'You are partly responsible for this predicament. You wanted this blood alliance. Rindr would have remained in the North except for it,' she shouted at his back. He kept on walking.

'Rindr called for you and your brother as they dragged her off,' one of the men said from where he lay on the sand. 'She wanted the gods to punish you for what you did.'

Sibba's feet skidded into each other, and she turned back to the man. 'What…what did you say?'

'Rindr accused you of betrayal as she was dragged away. I have turned it over in my mind.' His gaze narrowed. 'Someone betrayed this felag, lady, and that someone must have been you. Why are you here? What game are you playing, Sibba?'

Sibba's stomach knotted. Rindr had called for her to be punished because if she had allowed Haakon and Rindr to run away, none of this would have happened. Or not like this. She had done the only thing she could have to save her brother's life and keep the felag safe. Now Rindr was kidnapped.

'Why would I do such a thing? Why would I betray my father's shade like that? Why would I break my solemn vow?'

The man blinked rapidly. 'I'm just saying what she said. It is the only thing which makes sense. Gettir swore some-one had betrayed him.'

'Gettir always blamed someone else when he suffered a defeat. He once accused you of conjuring up a storm,' she said rapidly. If she was not careful, Calwar could side with this man, imprison her, and then Rindr and her mother would never be rescued. She'd never be able to right this wrong.

The man scratched his head. 'Aye, that is true. I'd for-gotten about that.'

'I have vowed before Var to put a knife in the sea wolf Thorkell's throat. If someone betrayed you, it was not me.' Sibba bit out each word, willing the man to remember. 'I'd sooner rot than assist that piece of scum. I argued that the whole fleet should take the northern route. You all laughed at my folly.'

'Who betrayed us, if not you?' one of the men called out.

Sibba was aware that Calwar now stood behind her, arms crossed and seeming to direct his men, but listening to every word.

'I don't know, but I held true to my vow.' She pointed to the sea. 'The tide was right. I was tired of Rindr and her mother's excuses about why we had to delay and delay some more. I was surprised as any that you failed to arrive, and the marriage had not taken place.'

'For three days, we fought the sea wolves but were forced back into the harbour. We regrouped and fought again, but still they kept coming. Late yesterday, the unthinkable hap-pened. Gettir went to Valhall, and Rindr was kidnapped.'

"I would like to see the sea king, if it is permitted?" Sibba glanced at Calwar, who nodded.

Together they walked down to the longship, that great dragon ship. In the centre lay Rindr's father. He had taken several blows to his head and his chest.

'They laughed as they did it,' the man said, catching her arm. 'They knew we were coming. They knew the route we'd take. You were the only other person who knew that. Gettir's last orders were to find Sibba Norrsdottar and her men. Take your revenge.'

Sibba shook off the man's hand, clambered into the boat and closed Gettir's sightless eyes. 'We will ensure a proper Northern burial for him before we avenge this.'

'What is your part in this?' Calwar asked.

'I should have been less impatient. Maybe if we had been there...' Her throat closed. 'I never betrayed anyone. I wouldn't.'

If anything, the warriors appeared even more sceptical, and she knew that for some reason she was losing them.

'My sister lies,' Haakon said, coming up to stand beside her. He nudged her. 'You are dressed like a woman, Sibba. These men won't respect you.'

Sibba rolled her eyes. 'I will find a way,' she muttered.

'She lies? How does she lie?' Calwar asked.

'We left early because Sibba discovered Rindr and me together. She tied me up and forced us to leave.' Haakon's Adam's apple bobbed up and down. 'If I had been there, I might have been able to do something to prevent this happening. Someone betrayed the felag, but not my sister.'

Calwar's eyes seemed to bore down into the hidden place in her soul. 'Is this true, Sibba?'

Sibba ground her teeth. Trust Haakon to make matters worse when he was trying to make things better. And how was she going to get the men to respect her and do what needed to be done, if he went on like she wanted to dishonour the felag's leader? 'Rindr is betrothed to Calwar's father, Haakon. I had no wish to change the way of things. I still don't.'

'But...' Haakon said, screwing up his face.

Sibba held her hand up, and he lapsed into a grumbling silence. 'A youthful folly, a sudden squall of passion which would vanish in the cold clear of day, brother. I thought we would arrive after the marriage, and all would be well. And stop exaggerating. You were never tied down. Men simply sat on you for a little time.'

A great snort of laughter rose from that remark as Haakon's cheeks became stained red.

'Don't muddy the explanation,' Calwar said in a voice which commanded an answer. 'What were you plotting and scheming, Sibba? What are you plotting now?'

'We need to rescue Rindr—and quickly—before the situation worsens.' Sibba pulled her shoulders back. 'I want to be the one to organise that rescue party. My ship can leave at the turn of the next tide.'

'Our shores must be protected first,' the priest proclaimed. 'Sibba Norrsdottar thinks with a woman's heart, not a warrior's brain.'

Sibba forced air in and out of her lungs. A woman's heart? The priest knew little and understood less. 'Rindr stands to inherit her father's wealth and the men who are loyal to him. Neither you nor I wish that sea wolf Thorkell to claim that inheritance through a forced marriage. What I propose is about protecting these islands.'

The priest began squawking like a hen who had just encountered water.

Calwar motioned for the priest to be quiet. 'What are you *suggesting*, Sibba?'

Sibba took a deep breath and attempted to control her temper. 'An alliance between Northmen and Gaels to rescue Rindr and her mother, Nefja. If we do not work together to stop the sea wolf now, then we shall surely fall separately.'

'Why do you think Thorkell will not attack us here given the confusion?'

'Because he is a coward. But he works with spies and betrayers. He certainly knows how strong your defences are and might even know about your father's current affliction.'

His strong fingers curled around her hand, and his eyes appeared to burn into her soul. She silently prayed to any god who might be listening that Calwar understood the danger they all now faced because of the ambush, and she knew in her heart that she could save them if only he'd allow her to lead this expedition.

'I am a reasonable man. I will convene the council, and you may place your case before them,' Calwar said, staring out to sea. 'Then the entire council—including *my father*—will make our decision. I must warn you—my men have little reason to trust a woman from the North, let alone a woman who claims to command men.'

Sibba swallowed hard. She had one last chance to make good her vow and avenge her father's death, if only the Gaels would assist her. If they didn't, everything she'd done up to now would be for nothing. 'It will have to be enough.'

Could he truly trust Sibba Norrsdottar? She had clearly arrived with an agenda, something to do with preventing the marriage. Her brother had as good as admitted it. And now this. Would she help them or was she trying to figure out a way to advance her own goals?

On the way back from ensuring the beacon was lit, Cal turned the problem of Sibba over again in his mind. He was pleased his people did what they were supposed to do and that Thorkell had thus far refrained from attacking this stronghold. What did the pirate sea king want, and how could Cal prevent him from having it? Somehow, he knew Sibba Norrsdottar was the key.

'May we speak plainly, Calwar mac Bedwyr?'

Sibba grabbed hold of his arm and prevented him from entering the hall. She had changed into a pair of leather trousers and a thick wool tunic of a medium green colour. Her hair was now held back in a single braid. Cal suspected she had changed because of the sarcastic laughter from some of the Northern warriors. However, to his mind, her trousers simply highlighted the length of her legs and the slenderness of her waist.

'I always appreciate plain speaking.'

'No one will give me a straight answer. When will the council meet. Tonight? Tomorrow? Three weeks from now? Never?'

'The council will meet, Sibba.'

'Their eyes slide away from me like I have mentioned something untoward. And they all keep muttering about the protocol. Why have a protocol? Every situation is different. I am concerned about the women who are in danger, the women who really matter.'

'The women who really matter?' Cal clung onto the remaining shreds of his temper. 'You mean Gettir's daughter and wife? The ones he and his men failed to protect?'

'Yes, those women.' She banged her fists together, and her face became fierce. 'Or are you going to say it is too difficult? Sorry, but… I want to know, Lord Calwar, and not have the men who served in Gettir's felag harbour false hopes about the Gaels' commitment to the alliance. Everyone seems to be rushing about, but no one wants to answer questions.'

'The situation requires careful consideration which will be discussed at the council.' He pointedly cleared his throat. The alliance was in tatters, but he understood the moral obligation his kingdom bore. Those women wouldn't have been travelling that route except for the proposed marriage. 'I've many demands on my time. The protocols which you airily dismiss with a wave of your delicate hand have kept the people of these islands safe since my grandfather ruled as high king.'

He waited for her to dutifully bow her head and accept the truth in his words.

She put a hand on her hip and continued to block his path. 'We are supposed to be friends and allies. How long must we kick our heels, waiting? I deserve to know that much.'

His jaw tightened. How dare she criticise his response? Didn't she know how hard he was trying? What danger these islands were now in? He glanced over his shoulder and lowered his voice. 'Do you really wish to discuss your plans in the open?'

She scrunched up her nose and rolled her eyes, showing her opinion. 'After careful consideration, what will you decide—to do nothing? Trust me, I'm the person least likely to inform Thorkell of your plans.'

He shrugged and gave what he knew to be a non-answer. Deep down he hated taking the overly cautious approach, but it was the one his father advocated. 'Councils are unpredictable things.'

'Please don't treat me like a fool who knows little about politics, Calwar. I command a longship by right. I've had experience in Constantinople where spies, plots, and counterplots infest the food they eat and the air they breathe.' She tilted her head to one side. 'The sound of the wind and the surf hitting the beach should provide more than adequate cover for our conversation.'

'The decision is not mine alone,' he said, bowing his head. The anger seeped away from him. It was the situation, not her. He didn't blame Sibba for being anxious. Those women were her friends. 'We're not faithless allies, never have been. Can you say the same?'

She lifted her chin and stared directly at him, blue eyes blazing. 'I see. You require time, but time is a luxury we can ill afford.'

'But one we must take.' He wondered if she was simply another of those women like Brigid who lacked the practical experience to understand that it took more than bravado or heart to win and that logistics and equipment played a significant part in any victory. But he knew in that moment that he was being unfair. Sibba obviously had some skill. She commanded a small felag. 'Except for your own ship, the remainder of the Northern fleet lacks even basic seaworthiness.'

She scrunched up her nose. 'The ships can be quickly repaired. The injured men will take longer, but they will heal sooner than you might think when there is a real chance to avenge their fallen leader and rescue his daughter.'

Cal ran a hand through his hair. Today was a disaster for many reasons, including his father's longed-for alliance with Northmen strong enough to ensure the islands' safety had failed. He had not realised how much he had been counting on the security the alliance was supposed to bring, until that cup was dashed from his lips. *Never wail over spilt mead*, his grandmother had whispered when he had failed to serve his father properly at his first high feast, joggling his father's elbow and spilling the bridal goblet all over the rushes.

'Realistically, how long until this council of yours arrives?' Sibba asked in a louder voice, slamming her boot against the hard shingle in front of the hall. 'How long do I have to work miracles with Gettir's men and get them ready to sail again?'

'A few days. Four at most. Men will travel from all parts of the islands. From the North as well the South Island and the lands in between.' He inclined his head. 'I sent runners, and had the beacons lit while you tended the wounded.'

She tapped a finger against her mouth. 'Why are these warriors not here for the wedding? Gettir might have taken offence.'

'Can the dead take offence? Gettir worked the land in the North, he understood the necessity of having the fields ploughed, burning the seaweed to make the ash which we trade, and indeed, keeping the beacons maintained takes men. He would have seen no dishonour.'

'Nothing to do with your father's affliction, then.'

'It was decided. My father decided before he fell ill,' he said between clenched teeth. 'Gettir understood that we wanted few clashes between our forces. I'm surprised he failed to mention it to you or perhaps you and your men were not as important as you might like to think you are.'

Sibba crossed her arms over her breasts which only served to highlight the ample curve. Cal forced his gaze upwards. His growing attraction to her was going nowhere. Other considerations like his duty towards his father and their people took precedence. There would be time enough later. He sent a prayer heavenwards to any saint who might be willing to intercede on his behalf that he would have that time.

'Were you seeking to dishonour the Northmen?' she asked quietly. 'The question will be asked and indeed has been asked by the men who arrived today. I want to know how you would answer it.'

'Avoiding fights was the only consideration, truly.' He smiled down at her. 'Sometimes people make assumptions that they shouldn't.'

'A true enough statement.' She smiled suddenly. 'You didn't believe me about my shooting ability. You assumed I was exaggerating. Right now, you think I've no idea about what is needed in trying to fight someone like Thorkell. Stop underestimating me.'

He pinched the bridge of his nose. 'Trust me a little if you want me to trust you, Sibba.'

She chewed on her bottom lip, turning it the colour of a sunset over the harbour. 'My brother believes we should leave right away, before Thorkell has time to consolidate his gains.' She paused. 'Haakon knows my men can go on the next tide.'

He put his hand on her shoulder. She spoke about what Haakon wanted, not what she intended to do. 'What would that achieve, precisely? A glorious death? Thorkell is expecting a hurried response. His sea wolves will be out patrolling, seeking to feast.'

She flinched slightly, and he let her go. She rubbed her arm. 'I know the odds. I can't do nothing, Calwar. I said I would speak to you about Haakon's proposal, and I have.'

The last sentence sank in. She'd promised her brother. She had guessed what his answer would be. Sibba was nothing like Brigid, a fact that unnerved him.

'Are you conceding that you will lose?' he asked in a

quieter tone and watched her under hooded eyes. 'Before the council has even met?'

Rather than dipping her head and mumbling like a Gaelic woman would have done, she glared back at him. 'My gut tells me the kidnapping was planned. Thorkell wants to make use of the women. We need to prevent that.'

'All the more reason to approach it with cold, clear logic and purpose, instead of rushing in and making an even bigger problem.' Cal forced his lips upwards. 'Explain that to your brother, as he appears to be the one making the decisions.'

She stiffened at the barb. 'You're wrong.'

'Prove it,' he said softly, watching for her reaction. 'Prove to me you are the one making the hard decisions.'

'We must find out where they are being held. Someone needs to see if they can be rescued with minimal fuss before it is too late.' Sibba rested her clenched fists on her hips 'I won't give up, Calwar, even if you have.'

Cal clenched his jaw. He hated that her point about the priest being against any rescue attempt or willing to work behind the scenes to ensure no such attempt was made was more than true. But Sibba was right: they had to do something to rescue the women, and that started with finding out where they were being held.

'The priest is but one voice, Sibba.'

She tilted her head to one side, and he spied the heat-infused rose of her cheeks. He smiled indulgently. If she was anything like his late wife, she would rapidly apologise, most likely in a soft lilting voice.

'One voice among many or one voice above many?' she said in a firm voice.

Cal started. Her words revealed a woman who understood day-to-day political realities. Neither he nor his father could entirely dismiss the priest's concerns without alienating many of their people, but the man did not understand politics.

'The priest must always be listened to.'

'I have always considered that it is up to the leader to decide to act on any advice. Is it different here?'

'Someone has given you that lecture?'

'The emperor himself in Constantinople, as well as when I was growing up.'

A subtle reminder that the woman was far more widely travelled than he was. 'The emperor himself.'

'My father briefly contemplated joining the Varangian Guard.' Her lips curved upwards. 'But you appear surprised that I understand the difference. Or is it that I have spoken with the emperor?'

'Both.'

She bowed low. 'There are more reasons why I won my place at the head of the felag, Calwar mac Bedwyr, than simply being able to shoot straight.'

'You are acquainted with my people's customs,' he said with a deliberate shrug. His insides twisted. Once again, he'd underestimated her. He'd judged her by other women he'd known, and it was clear that Sibba was not at all like them. And yet, a little voice in the back of his mind reminded him that her mouth had tasted like sweet water, and he wanted to sample it again.

'Unusual for someone from the North,' he added at her lifted brow.

Her shrug mirrored his. 'My father used to say that it is useful to know the customs of the people you intend to break bread with.'

'Or go to war with.'

'Breaking bread and making deals is always preferable

to the uncertainties of war.' She held out her hands. 'Trading is our lifeblood. It is why I went to Constantinople as a young woman. Why Gettir wanted to make an alliance with you.'

Calwar reassessed her from under his lashes. He'd made a mistake earlier. Sibba Norrsdottar had a shrewd brain. She was not a token leader, chosen as some bizarre Northern joke but someone who took charge and made decisions. He hated that he had ever doubted her. 'Your brother was right about one thing—you should have told me at the beginning about the liaison.'

'Would you have confided to the prospective bridegroom or a close member of his family if it was your brother who wished to marry another's betrothed?'

He opted for a half-smile. 'It would depend on whether I considered it a sensible idea or not.'

Her lashes swept down over her magnificent eyes, hiding her expression. 'I merely removed him from a perilous situation. What I thought would come to pass has failed to happen. His secret, not mine.'

He held out his hands. 'But now that your brother has told the world? What are your intentions? Do you seek to spirit the woman away? Why should we expend time, treasure and, more than likely, blood if you merely intend on liberating her from our grasp?'

Her small white teeth caught her bottom lip and turned it deep rose. He kept his face blank and waited for her answer. He silently willed her to make it the right one.

'I want Rindr's opinion on the matter,' she said as she looked him directly in the eye. 'Simply because Haakon decrees something, it does not mean the lady in question holds the same view.'

'What makes you think your brother's view will hold sway?'

Her smile reached her eyes, causing them to dance. A half-forgotten feeling, one he thought he'd never encounter again, tugged at his insides, reminding him that he was not as dead as he thought.

'My brother has romantic notions which alter with the phases of the moon. Rindr has other qualities, and she obeys her mother in most things.'

How to say that she expected Rindr to take the politically expedient option without truly saying it? Cal's neck muscle twitched. 'I take it you have some experience with your brother.'

'I have a lifetime of learning to manage my twin. He can be managed, Calwar, if handled properly, but otherwise he is stubborn as a tide which runs against you.' She gave a perfunctory nod, but the blue in her eyes deepened.

In that heartbeat he knew he could spend days looking in her eyes trying to discern the exact shade. He frowned. It had been a long time since a woman had affected him in this physical way. However, he refused to allow his undoubted attraction to her to cloud his judgement or alter his course. Like her brother, he could be as stubborn as any spring tide.

'Will the other north leaders listen to you?'

The light vanished from her eyes. 'Three are missing, two are dead, one is not expected to see tomorrow's dawn, and the other's future depends on the healing skill of your priest. Any dead captain's helmsman would normally take temporary command of his ship until the battle is over.'

'Can you make their subordinates listen?' he asked in a quiet tone. 'Or is this an empty promise?'

'Are you asking to wager on it?'

'Honourable even on wagering,' he said. 'But if you get the warriors to back you, I will see what I can do.'

Her eyes lit up. 'Once I have them, please don't doubt me on this. We need to move as quickly as possible. Two of the remaining boats can be repaired within the week.'

'A small fleet against Thorkell's much larger one.'

'The skill of the commander turns the tide of the battle.'

Cal lifted a brow. Sibba had obviously learned various sayings and trotted them out with the fervency of a true believer. He hated that her passionate words made him want to believe in something more than his duty again.

'You presume to know where they have been taken.'

'Barra.' She gestured towards the harbour. 'You heard what the men said. Thorkell's sea wolves attacked them.'

'And you know the lie of the land in Barra?'

Her cheeks flushed. 'It is an island with beaches and many small harbours. His men will not be able to guard all the entrances. It is why I want to take my boat now and find them.'

'Barra is an island, yes, with a large hill and several harbours, but more important, its large harbour plays host to an island fortress.' He closed his eyes and allowed his mind to picture it as it had once been, back when he was courting his wife. 'An impregnable island fortress.'

Her eyes widened. 'How do you know this?'

'My late wife was from Barra. I've spent time on its shores.' He carefully shrugged and tried to ignore the memory of his late wife, calling him a coward for refusing to start a rebellion which the remaining people of Barra did not want.

'Every fort has its weaknesses.' A frown developed between Sibba's brows. 'Is there a way into this fort?'

His shoulders relaxed slightly. Sibba asked the tactical

question rather than referring to his wife. 'There is always a route in, but it is likely to be difficult. That fortress exacts a very high blood cost.'

'How did Thorkell acquire it, if it is beyond difficult?'

'He took it from my late wife's brother through treachery and deception.'

'The point is he took it.'

'He has no need of alliances. My wife's brother did.' There was little point in explaining his wife's unwitting part in the debacle or how she'd pleaded with him to make things right. His duty lay elsewhere. His father had made that perfectly clear. He winced slightly, hating that he longed to make things right even after all this time.

'There you are wrong,' she said, tapping her fingers together. 'If he was not worried about this alliance, he would not have kidnapped the women. The alliance remains important, and we must demonstrate to him that we are united. What better way to demonstrate unity than to rescue them?' She peeped out from under her lashes and smiled. 'My logic is sound, Calwar.'

'And if they decide against the proposition? How can I go against the council?'

'Then, I will go alone.' She started to walk away but glanced back over her shoulder. 'I will find a way to rescue her.'

'And if she does not want rescuing?'

She went completely still. 'Rindr will want rescuing. I know what Thorkell is like. What he has done to women. Ensuring our side wins gives me a reason to keep breathing. I vowed on my father's pyre to do this.'

A strand of her hair floated free from her braid. He captured it between his fingers. Sibba had far too much life in her, simply to be living for revenge. 'We shall have to consider finding you another reason for breathing.'

'Are you making light of my vow?'

'Sibba,' he said, intending to say something mundane about the drizzle and how they needed to find cover. But the word emerged as a thickened growl, and he knew he wanted to kiss her, needed to taste her mouth again. All he had to do was bend his head and capture her mouth. He wanted to, but the last remaining sensible thought made him release the lock. It fluttered gently in the breeze. 'Do as I ask. I will assist if and where I can.'

He hadn't intended to say those words, but he knew they were true. He would find a way of helping her, if she remained here and didn't go off on a doomed rescue mission with her brother.

'I...I thank you.' She swayed towards him, her breasts brushing his chest. He raised his hand and gripped her upper arms. Her muscles trembled slightly at his touch, and he started to draw her more firmly into his arms.

A shout from one of his men requesting immediate help with the beacons on the south side made them both jump. Sibba retreated three steps, and Cal forced his hands to his side.

'I need to go,' he said. 'The beacons need attending to.'

She tugged on her braid. 'We both should.'

'Our discussion is not finished.'

'Is that what it was—a discussion?'

'Always, with you.' He inclined his head. 'Duty calls. And get Gettir's men on your side. Find a way to become their leader. You must do it.'

'Why?'

'Because the council will only deal with one leader from the North at a time, and you're my preference.'

Her smile was like the sun peeking out from behind dark clouds. 'Thank you for believing in me. Few people do.'

'Prove to me you can do it.'

Cal watched her backside sway as she strode away without a backward glance. If he was thinking with his head, he wanted her to succeed. But there was a growing part of him that wanted to keep her safe, and therefore he hoped someone else would step up to lead. Then he could argue why she should remain on Suthereyjar while others effected the rescue.

'She chose this life,' he muttered. 'On her head but I want to keep her alive.'

Chapter Five

What had she nearly done? Kissed Calwar? In broad daylight? With that nosy priest watching? Or, worse, the remaining warriors from Gettir's felag? If she was seen as Calwar's pawn, she'd lose any hope of commanding a rescue attempt. He was right: she needed to find a way to take charge of Gettir's men.

Sibba curled her fists and strode angrily towards the boats, taking pleasure in being able to take long strides. She'd changed into trousers thinking they'd make her look like a leader instead of some foolish maiden. It had been a mistake to get that close to Calwar and to nearly kiss him where all could see, even if she was wearing her tunic and trousers. She could not afford to do that—not now, not ever. She'd lose everything if she ever gave her heart to a man. Her father's warning made complete sense now.

'Never going to happen,' she muttered, kicking a stone.

'Did you find the king? Will we be able to depart on the next tide, like Haakon insists we will?' her helmsman asked, pausing in his coiling of the ropes which held the mainsail.

Sibba shook her head. 'We wait until the council meets. We need to be prudent.'

He shook his head. 'Your brother will be very unhappy.'

'My brother's unhappiness is something we must endure. The entire felag's safety stands in the balance.'

The man's lips turned up. Sibba was pleased she'd taken the chance and promoted him when several of the more experienced warriors like the tattooed Rekkr had vanished the night before she fought Haakon for the leadership. Rekkr's betrayal rankled because she had considered him someone who would always support her claim. 'True enough.'

'Gettir told me to ignore my gut instinct back on the mainland. Where is Gettir now?'

The man gulped hard. 'Will he be given the correct burial rites? These Gaels are Christians. Gettir proudly followed Odin and Thor.'

'There will be no objection,' Sibba said, taking the decision. The funeral would give her a chance to demonstrate her leadership. 'We will use his flagship. It is in the worst state. His shade will be pleased.'

Her men visibly relaxed at her words. 'Everyone was worried. That priest loathes us. The others have been grumbling about the Gaels and how this alliance is doomed.'

Sibba kept her face carefully blank. 'Gettir entered Valhall earlier. We must ensure his true legacy—the new alliance of Gael and Northman holds firm.' At the sceptical looks, she put her hands on her hips. 'Despite his harsh words, the priest bound up the wounds of the injured and saved lives.'

'What about Lord Calwar?'

'No man will stand in our way. Not if they want to live.'

The cry of her name went up. Sibba noticed several of the men from the other ships were joining in and taking up the cry. She kept her face carefully blank. She was doing what Calwar required. Once she was able to get Gettir's helmsman on her side, the rest would follow like herded geese.

But she must not jeopardise it by kissing Calwar again, a little voice reminded her. Women leaders who indulged in such things lost all respect from their men.

She simply hoped Calwar was with her, rather than standing in her way. She had no wish to kill the man over this pyre.

'Be ready to light the funeral pyre at my command.' She nodded to the man. 'I will get Gettir's men on my side. One way or another.'

Her helmsman nodded back. 'Are you sure you don't want us to go with you?'

'I need to do this myself.'

She strode off towards the makeshift hospital and prayed that none of the Northmen had witnessed her earlier encounter with Calwar.

'You want us to do what?' The burly helmsman towered over her. 'You are far too young and inexperienced to be in charge.'

Sibba struggled to contain the sudden flash of anger. She had never liked Gettir's helmsman. He always seemed far too close with Nefja. 'Appoint me to be the temporary leader, the one to negotiate with the Gaels. You heard about how I won my wager with Lord Calwar. It will stand us in good stead when we face the council.'

'Even if that tale is true, they will turn their backs on us.'

'They won't.'

'Why not?' Gettir's man crossed his arms and spat.

Sibba clenched her teeth, marched up to him, and jabbed her finger towards his chest. 'Because I speak their language fluently. Because I took a safe route here, and more importantly I can put you or any other man on his arse should the occasion demand.'

She whipped her foot around the back of his legs and

sent him tumbling into the straw. She put her boot on his throat and rapidly divested him of his sword. At her gesture, Haakon relieved him of the seven knives hidden about his person.

'Say the words!'

'You are worthy...my leader,' he choked out.

Sibba took the knives from Haakon and placed them in her belt. She slowly removed her boot. 'Would anyone else care to make the same mistake this man did? Would anyone else like to challenge me?'

He lay there stunned and unmoving. Behind her, men half drew their swords, but Sibba held up her hand. She heard the soft swish of the swords returning to their scabbards.

'Why?' the injured captain croaked from where he lay. 'Why have you done this, Sibba Norrsdottar?'

'I don't take kindly to spitting.' She put her hands on her hips. 'Do you require any assistance in rising so that you can tend to the pyre?'

She waited, hoping that the man would not make life more difficult.

The captain shook his head. 'I reckon I can get up myself to swear, but I never thought someone like you could put Gorm on his arse so quickly. Worthy of your father in his prime.'

'I like to think I honour my father. Always.'

'You can certainly tell you are his daughter.' Gorm the helmsman put his hand on his heart and saluted her. 'We need someone who can think. I swear my oath to you.'

'You underestimated me. Make sure you don't do it again,' Sibba said, placing her hands on her hips and making sure her shoulders were back. A warrior to be reckoned with, not a woman to be ignored. 'People will learn to respect me and all who sail with me because I intend on teaching them a lesson, starting with the Gaels of Sutherey-jar and continuing on to Thorkell and his men.'

The helmsman's smile lit up his face. 'That we will. We will avenge all who think us weak.'

'Good to know I can count on you.'

'Next time, though, you won't put me on my arse.'

'Yes, because you know I can.'

The men in the makeshift medical hut burst out laughing. Sibba's shoulders relaxed. Soon Calwar would have to admit that he'd underestimated her when he'd set her this task.

'How do we restore our honour?' someone called out. 'If we do that, I will happily follow Sibba, even though she is a woman.'

'Ensuring Gettir gets a proper send-off is the place to start,' Sibba said. 'We show the Gaels that we honour our fallen Sea King our way.'

'And after that?' the captain asked. 'Our alliance with the Gaels was a good dream.'

The entire hut went silent, waiting.

Sibba kept her shoulders down and her head up. 'We rescue Rindr and her mother just as Gettir bade us to do with his dying breaths.'

'How do you know he did that?' the helmsman asked.

'Because he was a man who loved his family.' Sibba gave the injured captain a hard look and willed him to say differently.

'And Rindr?' Haakon asked. 'What happens with her after we rescue her? Will she be able to choose her husband?'

A ripple of agreement went through the men, and Sibba

wanted to hit something very hard. When would her brother learn to keep his mouth shut?

The helmsman wiped a paw across his mouth. 'One thing at a time, Haakon Norrson.'

'Yes, precisely. First things first.' Sibba raised her arm in the air. 'Are you with me, men of Gettir?'

The hut echoed to the sound of her name.

Haakon came up and caught her elbow. 'Rindr must be allowed to choose. Don't lose sight of that.'

'Don't worry, Haakon. I have everything under control.'

'Do you?' Haakon shook his head. 'It could still go horribly wrong.'

Sibba took a deep breath. Haakon did not know that. And she needed them to stay united, not fall into petty squabbling.

'Support me now, and trust my judgement.' Sibba raised her arm again. 'Let's go and give Gettir a proper funeral.'

The entire hut roared her name again. Sibba basked in the adulation. She refused to think beyond the rescue. 'Everything in its time,' she muttered. Everything in its time.

The longboat blazed on the harbour, sending shooting sparks up into the night sky. Cal stood, watching it blaze. The low murmur of chanting bounced and echoed over the water. In a short space of time, Sibba had managed to arrange quite the send-off.

'Should they be doing this?' the priest asked. 'Who gave them permission?'

'Better than having to find a place to bury them,' he replied, giving the same answer he'd given his father.

The priest nodded slowly. 'I will be glad when these pagans are gone, particularly that bossy woman. It isn't natural the way they are all following her now.'

He gestured with a trembling hand towards where Sibba stood with an intent face watching the conflagration. The fire highlighted her cheekbones and the slender curves of her figure. He noticed she'd remained in her tunic and trousers as if she was making a statement. Whatever happened, that woman was going to war, and she would be taking all the Northmen with her. He didn't know what had happened in that hospital hut, but Sibba had emerged the clear winner. On balance, that had to be good for his people.

'That bossy woman, as you call her, is doing her duty, Father. Nothing more, nothing less.' He gave a curt nod. 'See you do yours.'

He turned on his heel and started back towards the hall, ignoring the priest's bleating while he struggled to keep hold of his temper.

'She's quite something, my sister,' Haakon said, sidling up to Calwar, with a cunning expression. 'Who would have thought she would do that? Magnificent, don't you agree? Her words—"Let me lead until we have rescued Rindr"—turned despair into this.'

Cal stopped and turned back to the youth. He could see Sibba in his cheekbones and in the way he held his body, but he knew Haakon did not possess one ounce of leadership ability or common sense. Otherwise, he'd never have allowed his sister to court danger in that fashion.

'If you care about her, stop putting her in danger instead of making veiled comments to me about what she is doing.' Cal gestured to the rapidly retreating priest. 'You in your way are as bad as the good father. Trust your sister knows what she is doing.'

Haakon widened his eyes, innocence personified. 'You mistake me. I do trust my sister. Sometimes, though, she isn't bold enough. She will regret her action later. I can feel that in my bones.'

'Do I? Good to know that you have your sister's interests uppermost in your mind.'

Haakon pouted and scuffed his feet. 'I wanted to thank you for allowing it to happen. That's all.'

'The dead need to be laid to rest. It did not seem right to force a Christian burial on our priest.' Cal inclined his head. The more he encountered Haakon, the more he knew the men had chosen the correct sibling to lead them. 'Your sister's request was a neat answer to a nagging problem. Even the priest sees the value in it.'

'We should have gone immediately. Sibba says I am a fool, but every fibre of my being requires Rindr to be safe.' He put his hands on top of his head and banged them twice. 'I care about the woman, and I refuse to stop. And I believe she cares for me. There, I've admitted it. You probably hate me for it.'

Cal lifted his brow, wondering what the man saw in Rindr. The woman was pretty enough, but she never seemed to have much personality. A pretty face who echoed the thoughts of those about her. It was the alliance and its potential which truly intrigued him. And Haakon's feelings for the woman did not alter that need.

'We both desire her safety. My father is looking forward to seeing his new bride.'

Haakon's face contorted. 'Your father can barely speak.'

'My father improves and still commands this kingdom. A fact which I consider important to remember.' Cal nodded. 'Now, I have a hall to attend to. People have already begun to arrive for this unexpected council which my father ordered. He will expect hospitality to be offered.'

Haakon's pout increased. He raised his finger to point

but thought better of it and stomped off. Several of the village women sighed in his wake, commenting how handsome he was. He had little doubt that more than a few would be willing to warm Haakon's bed should he desire it.

As he watched, Haakon stopped and answered a saucy woman's comment with one which bordered on the ribald. There was laughter from everyone concerned. Haakon and the woman went off arm-in-arm. A man who women loved and who loved women.

Cal began to understand why Sibba was not so worried about any strong bond between Rindr and Haakon.

He started towards the hall, but Haakon returned without the woman, obviously having forgotten some important point which Sibba had sent him to ask. Cal schooled his features. He could think of several things Sibba might wish to know—starting with whether she could have more men and ending with a better idea of the layout of Thorkell's lair. 'Something else you wish to add?'

'My sister adores danger. I meant to warn you earlier.' He stuck his chest out like some proud cockerel. 'And no one can make her do anything, a lesson I learned a long time ago. If her mind is made up to go, she will go. She has vowed to destroy Thorkell, and she won't stop until she does. She blames herself for our father's defeat. Not her fault, of course—that line snapped, and we were too late—any more than this is.'

'I will not have my people's alliance with the North jeopardised,' he said instead of remarking on Sibba's misplaced blame. 'Will you give me your word on that? Your sister has.'

The insolent youth pulled at his beard. 'Such a suspicious mind.'

'I asked about your intentions, but Sibba appears to be

taking charge of all the Northern warriors. I gather that includes you.'

'What do you mean?'

Cal thrust a finger towards the puffed-out chest. 'I've seen what Northmen can be like. What say you? Do you intend on destroying your sister's command before it has begun?'

Haakon's shoulders crumpled slightly. 'I love my sister. I will keep her word. We do it her way.'

'Good. I am pleased to hear that.'

Haakon tucked his head into his neck. 'My sister explained to me she won her wager and will speak to Rindr before any marriage. I agree to be guided by what Rindr wants, in case Sibba failed to explain.'

'I've every intention of allowing Sibba the opportunity to speak with Rindr. Your sister appears to have a sensible head on her shoulders, unlike some I could mention.'

Haakon's gaze narrowed. 'I should tell you that Sibba makes it a point to always win, in case you're tempted to wager with her again, I mean. You wouldn't want to undermine her either.'

Cal schooled his features. The brother seemed to be trying to warn him off. Was his desire for Sibba that evident? Impossible. And with Sibba's new position, it would have to be a marriage, which he had little desire for. He had made a big enough mess of the last one.

'I make it a point to always win the important wagers.' Cal nodded to him. 'If you will excuse me, I need to ensure my father is fully aware of all developments.'

Sibba rubbed the back of her neck and tried to concentrate on the remains of Gettir's funeral pyre which the ocean now slowly consumed. She had done the decent thing. Gettir would be feasting in Valhall. And his men appeared to accept her as their current leader. They wanted what she promised: to get Rindr and her mother back unharmed. She fully intended to achieve her stated aim, provided the women were alive, but she knew she required a practical and workable plan to do it. She could not simply sail off immediately, hoping for divine intervention, like Haakon suggested. In short, she had to deliver a minor miracle and prove their faith in her was not misplaced.

Cal had been right about one thing: the other ships would need several days before they were seaworthy. She just didn't know if they had enough time or whether a full-frontal assault would work. Thorkell had to be expecting something unless he considered them vanquished and was about to turn on the islands.

'As soon as we can,' she muttered. 'As soon as we can.'

'Sister, I've spoken with Calwar mac Bedwyr.' Haakon kicked a pebble, sending it skittering out over the harbour and nearly hitting the smouldering pyre.

Sibba frowned at him, but he repeated the gesture several times.

'Haakon, show some respect.'

'You are the only one who watches, sister. Gettir's power has drained away. You lead the felag.'

'The other captains wait to see if we can rescue Rindr. They may very well pledge their allegiance to the man she marries if they consider him a better warrior.'

She willed him to understand what had happened and how the currents of power had shifted, instead of being caught in one of his sulky moods where he was liable to lash out at anyone and everyone.

He nodded towards the hall. 'Calwar is a slippery creature, Sibba.'

'Cal did not immediately agree to whatever your outlandish request was.'

'It is *Cal*, now?' Haakon put a hand on her shoulder. 'Promise me you won't wager with him again. He plays to win and uses any means necessary. Be careful with wearing your heart on your sleeve. You know how that was abused the last time.'

She hated how her mood sank. Haakon was not saying anything that she wasn't already aware of. She had little intention of wagering with the man for anything, let alone something personal. 'He has promised I may speak at the council now that I control the felag.'

'Some like that priest will speak against anything you propose.'

When had her brother become this down in the mouth? Of course people would speak against her. She relished the challenge of it.

'Some always speak against things, brother, before they happen. And sometimes afterward, when the success happens, they pretend that they were always for a thing. It's how the world works.'

Her brother crossed his arms. 'Why should they lift a finger for two women who will have lost everything?' He paused and looked up to the sky. 'No one assisted us.'

His voice held a distinct tremble.

Sibba shook her head. Trust Haakon to overdramatise. 'We didn't lose everything, Haakon. We retained control of the felag and the best ship. Right now, people look to us to take a lead.'

'But our lands are gone!'

'Our father lost those before the sea wolf attacked,' she reminded him quietly. She refused to have Haakon coat the past in a veneer of honey and indulgence. Their father had had no patience, a sharp tongue, and an even quicker temper. It was why he had set off before she'd finished her checks. Her mind shied away from the memory of her father's final words to her. 'He was trying to regain them when he had the misfortune to meet Thorkell's wolves.'

Haakon sighed. 'You know what I meant.'

'Gettir had great wealth in the North and on the Isle of Man. As his only living child, Rindr stands to inherit everything. Thorkell should treat her well enough.'

'Has Thorkell ever treated a woman well?' Haakon held up his hand. 'You've heard the rumours, same as me.'

'Rindr is more use to Thorkell alive and under his sphere of influence,' Sibba explained, hoping her words held more than a ring of truth. 'She can be a rallying cry for him. He may try for the Isle of Man or at least attempt to wring concessions based on Gettir's holdings.'

'You think he means to marry her.' Haakon's face crumpled. 'Why does everyone want to marry her for what she can bring them rather than who she is?'

'Pull yourself together.' She slammed her fists together, making her brother jump. If he kept on like this, he would be in floods of tears and useless. 'I won't stand for soppy sentimentality, Haakon.'

He rubbed his eyes on the sleeve of his tunic. 'Do you think they will help us?'

'If they don't, their problems will multiply.' She clapped Haakon on the back. 'Cheer up. We will win in the end. Thorkell must be defeated.'

'All you care about is your vow to avenge Father's death. You care nothing for my plight.'

Sibba pressed her lips together to keep the words from slipping out. Haakon was being unkind. She cared deeply about things besides her vow—things like the welfare of her men, where the next meal was coming from and ensuring her boots had new soles before winter. Practical things. She simply did not believe Haakon's attachment was wise or long-lasting. 'We need to put food in our bellies. My brain is too hungry to think.'

'My father would like to see you, Sibba,' Cal said, coming up to them as they finished their meal of hard bread and cheese. 'As soon as possible.'

Sibba hated how her heart leapt at his intent face. She wished Haakon had not put ideas about wagering into her head. The first thing she'd noticed about the man was the shape of his mouth. She concentrated on dusting the crumbs from her fingertips, aware the Northern warriors watched her. 'Why me?'

Cal gave a half-smile. 'Because I told him that you are most competent of the Northmen's leaders.'

'You have no idea if that is true.'

'You foresaw the problem and took the longer way. Your boat was the only one to arrive unscathed. You arranged for Gettir to be laid to rest. You were the only person to stay watching the pyre, giving him honour until the last spark flickered.'

Sibba pushed the remains of her meal around on her trencher. Calwar made it seem like she had done something important. 'Someone had to ensure he had the correct send-off. Gettir was many things, but no Christian. I saved your priest a job.'

'If you wish someone else to speak, tell me who that someone is. Why must we fight?' He made a steeple with his fingers. 'Or are you frightened my father won't hear you out? He will.'

She lifted her head and met his gaze full on. Her stomach knotted. If she could get the king on her side, the council would be that much easier. 'Then, I accept.'

'The men and I will go with you,' Haakon declared.

At Cal's warning glance, Sibba put a hand on her brother's arm. She nodded towards where the other Northmen sat, gloomily eating. She doubted if the full extent of their loss had sunk in. 'Remain here. See if you can learn anything, anything at all. There will have been a traitor in Gettir's company. He could have survived. We don't want Thorkell warned before we can mount a rescue attempt.'

'You're sure the traitor is not amongst our men?' Haakon said in an undertone, looking over both his shoulders.

'That is the one thing I'm positive of,' she said and pushed him towards the men. 'Don't tell me you are frightened of them.'

Haakon tilted his head to one side. 'Why are you certain?'

'Because we were left with the ability to fight, and Thorkell knows how much I despise him. No, if a traitor exists, he will be amongst the other crews.' Sibba looked at the hall. 'Or even amongst the Gaels. Look for him. Find him for me.'

'You are clutching at straws in the wind, sister.'

'Are you coming, Sibba?' Cal said with a frown appearing between his brows. 'Or are you going to confer with your brother all evening?'

'Off to play dice, me,' Haakon called and sauntered away.

'I'm ready to plead my case now.' She rubbed her hands together, trying to get feeling back into them. It was always the same. Whenever she was frightened, her fingers went cold and numb. 'But I've given my oath. We will rescue Rindr and restore honour to Gettir's felag with or without Gaelic assistance.'

A fug of incense hung in King Bedwyr's chambers, making Sibba's eyes and throat sting. A fire blazed in the centre of the room. The king was seated on a chair with a fur wrapped around his shoulders, but his colour appeared more human than aged parchment.

'I understand you wished to seize my bride before she could become my wife,' he said, taking a breath between each word. 'You wanted to destroy the alliance.'

'I wished to speak with my friend and be certain that she was willing to marry.' Sibba concentrated on trying to make her voice sound reasonable. The last thing she wanted to do was to endanger the alliance. 'Gettir's men agree that his last words were to save Rindr and his mother, and that is what I think we should be concentrating on, not trying to dictate what happens afterwards.'

She waited, wishing she could warm her hands by the fire. King Bedwyr had to see that the alliance was more than one person.

His right eye twitched. 'A willing bride,' he murmured. 'Must have.'

'My father would never take an unwilling bride,' Cal said in a firm tone. 'We're not monsters, unlike some I could name.'

'But Thorkell would.' She pressed her hands together and ignored the sick feeling in the pit of her stomach. She had made so many promises lately that her head spun. 'I have been turning it over in my mind. Can we be sure that those three ships were sunk? Might they have been captured, instead?'

Cal's brows drew together. 'Gettir's men suggested they were lost, but in the noise and confusion of battle, I suppose anything is possible.'

'The missing captains were loyal to Gettir, some of his most loyal men.' Sibba hesitated but then knew he had to hear the worst. 'They may remain loyal to his daughter and swear allegiance to whichever man she makes her husband.'

She pressed her hands together and hoped that Cal and his father would now understand why they had to act as soon as possible before the balance swung firmly in the sea wolf's favour.

'Are you saying we shouldn't attempt to rescue the women?' the king asked with great care. 'I'm confused. I thought you wanted them rescued. My son said that you did.'

Sibba held on to her temper. She needed them to understand the danger and why they had to act sooner rather than later, even before they had all the equipment required. She couldn't risk Gettir's warriors being turned if any of them had been captured. The missing captains were not the most able, but they were reasonably competent and utterly loyal to Gettir.

'We must be prepared for all eventualities,' she said when she felt she could trust her voice. 'Time is of the essence because once Rindr marries, then her inheritance will surely pass into her new husband's care, whoever that husband may be. Unlike the Gaels who believe in only one wife, Thorkell is a Dane and may take as many wives as he pleases.'

'How many wives does he currently have?'

'Formal or informal?' Sibba asked. 'I believe he married a Danish princess several years ago, but I have no idea if she still lives. He certainly married a Gaelic woman from the Black Bay, and I believe he keeps a stable of concubines.'

'Having met the woman in question, I cannot imagine that she will be fond of the idea.'

'Depends if the choice is offered to her. Should Rindr perish, her mother would inherit, and Nefja is unlikely to be very picky.' Sibba balled her fists and willed the pair to understand that she spoke of real dangers, not hypothetical ones. 'Caution can save lives, but sometimes calculated risks must be taken to spare greater harm. A question of balance.'

Cal crossed his arms and sighed. 'There is that.'

'A woman who can think beyond her needlework,' the king said, slightly slurring his words. 'You best keep an eye on this one, son.'

'Why do you think I brought her to you?'

The king gave a hiccupping grunt which could have been a laugh and waved his hand, indicating the audience was over.

Calwar led her out of the chamber. 'I hope you see that my father wants to be on your side.'

'But I should not count on him.'

'He will do what the council suggests. However, if you speak as well tomorrow as you did today, you should prevail.'

A small glow of warmth filled Sibba. Calwar approved of her ideas. 'I have managed to convince one person. Good.'

'We will speak in depth soon, Sibba.'

'I look forward to it.' Sibba turned away and, when she was out of sight, hugged her arms about her middle. Calwar was on her side, or if not totally, she was convinced that he would fall in with her plans. She could do this, and in the doing she would be able to fulfil her vow to her fathér. A little voice in the back of her brain asked if she also enjoyed the shape of his mouth and the way his hand had felt against her back. She ignored it.

'I'd sooner trust a Byzantine prince with my gambling winnings than Calwar. With a prince, you know he is going to try and take your money,' her brother said after they had finished their meal.

'He is our only hope of getting the council to agree to my scheme.'

'He is flirting with you, Sibba. I won't have my sister hurt. I've been asking around. His wife died, running away from him, one of the women said, and…their baby died as well.'

Sibba stiffened. She thought she'd carefully concealed her growing attraction to him. And Cal had never explained about his wife or his relationship with her. Only that she had been reckless when wagering.

'What do you mean *hurt*?' she asked, keeping her voice neutral and trying to avoid the pitfall of gossip.

'It is plain as the nose on my face—he expects Rindr to refuse the king's suit, and he will offer himself as the replacement bridegroom to save the alliance and gain control of the felag.'

Haakon said it with a superior smile as if he was explaining something obvious to a simpleton. Sibba hated the way the butterflies started dancing in her stomach. What had Haakon seen that she forgot to conceal?

'What does Calwar's future have to do with me?' She shook her head and laid a heavy hand on her brother's shoulder. 'You will have to give a better argument, Haakon. The best argument is that Rindr needs to be able to make a choice about her life's partner. Or do you now think the love of your life might choose another?'

Haakon screwed up his face as if he'd bitten into a particularly sour plum. 'I saw the way you looked at him earlier, as if he was a particularly tempting sweetmeat. I've never seen you look at any man like that, not even the rat-faced fiancé.'

'You see shadows of romance everywhere—an infection of the brain, I swear it. He and I?' She opted for a laugh which came out strangled. 'Absurd. Why would I want to give up something I've longed for all my life—the chance to properly lead a felag?'

Haakon covered her hand. 'Don't make a spectacle of yourself over him. Rat-Face made you look foolish.'

Sibba forced her shoulders to relax. Haakon hadn't witnessed anything. This was manipulation through a fishing expedition. 'You'll have to do better if you think I would agree to kidnapping Rindr to prevent her marrying Calwar.'

Haakon screwed his face up and protested his innocence.

She rolled her eyes. 'You needn't trouble yourself on that account, Haakon. I know where my duty lies. And it is in making sure I know our strengths and weaknesses. If you will excuse me, gentlemen, I'm going to investigate the boats again and see what needs to be done to make them seaworthy.'

Without stopping to look behind her, she rose and swiftly exited from the hall. Once she was out in the open air, she sank down and buried her face in her hands. She felt like she was a skald juggling too many brightly coloured balls. How long until she missed and dropped one?

Chapter Six

The boat's hull was smooth, without any chinks. It would serve, as would the two other longships she'd inspected. They could divide the Northmen up between the boats and leave once the council was finished.

Sibba listened to the sound of the surf hitting the shore. Far easier to be out here, seeing to the boats, than to be lying awake on her pallet, going over and over in her mind what mistakes she'd made and whether, if she had been there, she could have prevented it. Or, worse, thinking about Calwar's shoulders or the high planes of his cheekbones and hoping his easy words of assurance were more than that.

A true commander would be focussed on the task ahead, not dreaming about some man, particularly as she knew he'd never rescue her because she wouldn't give him the opportunity to do so. She hated how the thought made her breath twist in her throat.

'I wondered if I'd find you here,' Calwar said, looming out of the darkness as if she had conjured him.

In the faint starlight, his hair gleamed as if touched with silver moonbeams. Maybe she could rescue him, a little voice argued.

She rapidly rose and wiped her hands on her leather trousers. Idle thoughts belonged to women who had time to spin fine cloth. 'I wanted to inspect the ships myself. Alone and unhurried.'

'Alone and unhurried.'

'I want to give an accurate report to the council. It might help them to reach the correct decision.'

'This early or this late?'

'The rain has ceased. It seemed like an ideal time as I suspect we might get a shower or three later.' Sibba waved her hand. Little point in explaining that she'd briefly slept in her longboat rather than returning to the hut which was now packed with slumbering men—or worse, taking a place with the women. She'd noticed how they stopped and stared at her as they couldn't quite believe a creature like her existed.

His smile lit up like the sun peeking through the clouds, and it warmed her straight down to her toes. 'Suthereyjar prides itself on changeable weather. Part of its charm. People have been known to grow to love it.'

'Luckily I'm adept at adapting.'

'Good to know. Hopefully once the women are rescued, we will be able to convince you to remain.'

She turned back towards the hull and made a show of running her hands along its ribs. Anything to stop her mind from trying to find a hidden meaning in his words. But he believed they could rescue the women. A start. 'I can learn more through touch than sight. This is the last of our boats. When the council give their decision, I want to know my options. I will be leaving for Barra.'

'Is that why you are wearing diamonds in your hair?'

She put a hand up and realised how wet her hair was. 'Forgot my couvre-chef, and I became so absorbed in my task that I didn't even notice the drizzle.'

'Soon you will be acting like you were born and bred on these islands.'

'Drizzle happens in the North as well.' She cleared her throat and tried to redirect the conversation. The last thing she needed was false hope. 'Amazing how easy it is to discover the chinks once you know what you are doing. There's nothing major to fix here, but some potentially problematic damage.'

'Will the boats be repaired in time?'

'The men know what to do, but I want to ensure we don't miss anything.'

She risked a breath. She had returned the conversation to safer waters. Talking about her hair was bound to lead to criticism. She knew she'd have to dry it before she strode into the council chamber. She had decided on wearing her trousers rather than a gown as it should force the council not to view her as a helpless female but someone who could lead her men and keep her promises.

He captured one of her hands. 'Are you claiming that your fingers are sensitive?'

She knew she should pull away from him and his seductive voice, but somehow her hand felt right in his. Her heart pounded so loud that she thought he must hear it.

'A skill I have developed and something I try to do every time the boat is pulled up on shore.' She arranged her face into a smile. 'If there is a fault, it is best dealt with quickly. It has proved useful in the past. My life is dedicated to ensuring my men are kept as safe as possible. My men now include the men of Gettir's felag.'

She waited for him to drop her hand. His fingers curled tighter, and he gave a little tug. She took a step closer to him, and their chests nearly touched. His mouth was a whisper away from hers.

'I, too, can tell important things by touch.' His other

hand reached out and cupped the back of her head. 'How soft your hair is and the smoothness of your skin.'

'Why are you saying this? What do you want?' she whispered. 'You should look on me as an equal, not some maiden to be sweet-talked.'

His hand stilled on her head. 'Because it is the truth?'

Every fibre of her being wanted to lean into him and rest her head against his chest. Against all reason she wanted his words to be something more than a joke. 'That is not what I meant, and you know that.'

'Are you going to be angry with me for bringing these matters up?' His hand smoothed her hair back from her forehead. 'I keep thinking about them at the oddest times. And when I saw you, I thought to speak with you alone. You and I. Cal and Sibba, not the king's heir and the presumptive Northern commander.'

'The smoothness of my skin or indeed the softness of my hair has no bearing on what we are going to do—namely rescue Rindr and her mother.' She was glad of the dim light as she knew her cheeks glowed with heat. Men played flirtatious words with other women, never her. She wasn't decorative like Rindr or her mother, she reminded her body, she was useful. A difference existed. The thought was like cold water coursing through her veins. 'We need to think about that. Everything else is secondary.'

Her voice was far too breathless for her liking.

He tilted her chin upwards. 'That is merely your opinion. There is time enough for this. For you and me. Nobody could object unless you do.'

'My opinion matters to me,' she whispered but did not move away from him. A very large and unruly part of her hoped that it wasn't a joke and he did intend on kissing her again. She ran the tip of her tongue over her suddenly tingling lips. 'What do you want to do? What is so important?'

'This. Thought about it all night.' He lowered his mouth and moved it against hers.

Heat jolted through her body. At the gentle pressure, her lips parted, allowing him to drink from her.

His hand roamed down her back, pulling her against the hard muscle of his body. Her entire being thrilled to the touch, and she arched forward, seeking his heat. The kiss deepened and their tongues tangled, twisted, and tangled again. She heard a moan and didn't know if it came from him or herself.

Grasping on to her last ounce of sanity, she pulled her face from his. His hands instantly fell away. Cool air rushed between them. Her chest heaved as she struggled to get her emotions under control.

'What was that about?' she asked between gasps. 'What am I supposed to do, Calwar, now that we have swapped spit?'

'*Swapped spit* is not how I'd put it.'

'It is how I have.' She balled her fists and put them firm on her hips. 'How I must.'

His lips curved upwards. 'The gloaming and you. Should I apologise?'

She explored her lips and refused to lie. 'No need. Do you intend on doing it again?'

'I dislike predicting the future.' He traced a line about her lips. 'It seemed to be the most natural thing to do.'

'Was it?' She hated how her body tingled. He meant nothing by it and could not possibly know that it was the most thoroughly she'd ever been kissed. If she kept her head on straight, all should be well. She wasn't some maiden to fall for stars and pretty poetry. It was something pleasant to do and had no meaning. Liar, her mind screamed. Wicked, wicked liar.

'Yes. My opinion counts for something in this land.'

He was either the most accomplished liar in the world or his words held some modicum of truth. She knew every fibre of her being wanted to believe that he was telling the truth and that he was attracted to her in the same way she was to him.

'Nothing to do with our earlier wager?' she asked, unable to rid herself of the habit of a lifetime.

His soft laugh bathed her in its warmth. 'I did tell you that I intended to kiss you again. I like to keep those sorts of promises. Hopefully you found it as pleasant as I did.'

'I doubted that you were serious, but yes, it was pleasant and ultimately meaningless. We both have our duties, and they lie elsewhere, Calwar. I tell you this now before either of us says something we will regret.'

His eyes turned serious in the grey light. He caught her hand and wouldn't allow her to pull away. 'Who made you wary? Why would you think I'd joke about something like this?'

'Men do, sometimes.' Sibba ignored her pounding heart and gave a careful shrug. She gathered her pride about her like a shield. 'I know what it is like. I've spent most of my life in the company of men. Most stop noticing me and fail to guard their language because I've ceased to be a woman in their eyes. I'm simply another warrior when I'm dressed like this. Quite the education. I've heard their jokes and inwardly cringed for the women and for them.'

He hovered a thumb above the outline of her mouth, making her lips ache anew. 'Sometimes people take the wrong lesson from their education. Men are people in the same way that women are. Unique. Stop judging me against other men as I've never judged you against other women.'

She turned her face away and tried to concentrate on the ship's hull and breathing steadily. 'All this talking will not get me closer to discovering the weaknesses of where Rindr is held.'

'Should I apologise, or should I seek the man who has made you afraid?'

Her tongue explored her swollen lips. 'No apology is necessary. And my former fiancé died, ingloriously. I've no wish for futile gestures. I'm very self-reliant, you see.'

He remained silent for several heartbeats. Sibba wondered if she should turn and go, mumble an excuse, or simply walk away. She suspected it made a difference that the only man to kiss her previously had been her late fiancé. She didn't want to speak about the jeers and laughter, or how Haakon told her to be more attractive and to try harder to be softer and more fragile when they were in Constantinople. The trouble was that every time she tried, she ended up bringing unwanted attention to herself and always felt clumsy and awkward. Somewhere, somehow, she'd missed the correct lessons.

'He was wrong about you,' Cal said into the silence just as she'd worked up her nerve.

'You didn't know him. And you really don't know me. Most people—'

He put a finger on her lips, silencing her. 'Maybe not, but I know enough about you to understand that he made mistakes. Unforgivable mistakes, and you are still paying for them. Clothes don't make people respect you. Your actions are what count.'

'Don't think so.'

'We can wager on it, if you like.' His husky laugh did much to soothe her nerves.

'Never wager what you can't afford to lose,' she said.

'True enough.'

He reached for her and firmly drew her into the circle of his arms. She gave in to temptation and laid her head against his strong chest and listened to the steady sound of his heartbeat. This was dawn-lit madness. Later when she faced the council, she would once again be the sensible person she always was. She had to be. Too much depended on her. And they both had different duties.

She stepped out of the embrace and threw back her shoulders.

'This is not going to lead anywhere. You and I. It can't do.'

He tilted his head and made no move to gather her back into his arms. She wrapped her arms tightly about her middle. 'You sound very definite about that.'

'I simply wanted you to know that I am not looking for marriage. I am happy as I am, leading my felag. I have plans.'

'What sort of plans?'

'There isn't room in my life for a man,' she said, aware that she was explaining it badly. And he had not asked to be part of her life. She knew if it continued, though, she ended up giving him a piece of her heart, and she couldn't do that. It had been too hard when she'd discovered the truth about her fiancé and how he'd betrayed everyone. How in believing in him, she had betrayed everyone. She pushed the thought away. 'My vow to avenge my father is paramount.'

'I see.'

She suspected he did see all too well. And she noticed

that he did not say he had no intention of remarriage. It could be that Haakon's supposition about Cal being offered instead of his father was right. Better nothing was started. Her heart panged.

'I wanted you to understand…' She lifted her chin. 'I need to go now. The council will be today.'

He put a hand on her shoulder. 'You think far too much of the future, Sibba. But yes, the council will be today. We will have enough for a quorum.'

'I suspect I think too much of revenge. It is why I am out here, making sure the boats are ready. I will listen to your precious council, Calwar. Then I will set to rescuing Rindr and her mother. The Northmen are free to do as we please.'

'Whatever the council wills?'

'I never agreed to be bound by their decisions. I will simply take any help offered.' She swallowed hard and tried to think steadying thoughts. 'May I speak? May I formally ask for assistance at the council?'

'You and the other Northern captains may attend.'

'Attendance is not the same thing. You wish me to keep silent.'

'Best I can offer. It is up to my father's liegeman to decide who speaks at council.'

'And you are…?'

'His son.'

She suspected he was both. He held a lot of power in this kingdom. If he wanted her to speak, it would happen.

'I'm trying to honour Gettir's wishes. I did swear an oath to him, Calwar. One of the reasons I did not hesitate was that I knew of his loathing for Thorkell and his wishes to rid the waters of the man's piracy.'

'I told you. I prefer *Cal* from my friends. And I would

like to consider you a friend, Sibba. I already consider you one.'

It would be easy to like him if he wasn't so exasperating. 'A new alliance, Cal. Both our peoples would benefit from it. Gettir's death didn't change that.'

'Do you expect to return alive?'

She looked deep into his eyes and knew she had to tell him the truth. 'I expect to fulfil my oath. Nothing more, nothing less.'

He nodded briefly, but his face became grim. 'I understand, Sibba.'

'Good. It makes it easier that way.'

She turned abruptly and started to walk away. Before his arms became too tempting and before she blurted out the truth—that she wanted to live.

'Even though you wear trousers, Sibba, everyone can tell you are a woman.'

She turned around. 'What do you mean by that?'

'It is up to you what you wear, but the reason your men follow you has nothing to do with your clothes and everything to do with the confidence you give them.'

'I never forget that.'

Cal regarded the rapidly filling chamber and tried to concentrate on the matter at hand, rather than thinking about his early-morning encounter with Sibba. It had been only her good sense which had stopped the kiss from escalating. And he should not have mentioned her trousers, except they highlighted her femininity rather than detracting from it. He knew she was more than capable. She did not have to wear trousers to prove it, especially as it might antagonise some of his men. Like her, he did recognise the necessity of rescuing Rindr and her mother.

Men had travelled from all the islands, more than he'd anticipated. Many brought their wives and children, a sure sign that they expected to go to war. The king's estates normally provided for the women and children when the men did his bidding. Why fight for a king if he failed to keep the warrior's loved ones safe?

He bowed his head, honoured that his father remained so revered, but also keenly aware that everyone could now see the old man's infirmity. The succession should be clear, but ancient custom allowed for all male members of the king's family to try. His cousin, for instance. Cal knew that when the time came, he would have to prove himself as worthy as his father. He silently prayed that the test of worthiness would be a long time coming. Thus far, his father appeared to grow a little stronger each day.

'Are you ready?' the king asked. His words were more distinct than yesterday, but he still spoke from the side of his mouth.

'We should have dealt with the sea wolf years ago,' one of the men standing near Cal's father said. Several others stamped their feet in agreement.

'Good to see the support,' Cal said, greeting each man in turn.

His father stretched out his clawed hand when Cal reached him. 'I had visions of the Northmen destroying each other.'

'And now?'

'We cannot be insulted in that fashion and expect to retain control of these lands.' A violent coughing fit rendered him gasping for breath.

Cal waited until his father had regained control. 'It was a grievous insult, Father. We are both agreed on that.'

'We must take a stand, my boy.' His father closed his eyes. 'And I require your help.'

Cal tried not to think how many years he'd waited in vain to hear those words from his father. And now, he knew he only said them because he had little choice.

'We have had these lands since time began,' Cal said. 'I will not see them fall. Any help you wish from me is there for the asking.'

'The priest,' his father mumbled out of the side of his mouth.

'The priest will speak, and the council will hear him out, but I refuse to allow our honour to be compromised.'

The doors creaked, and Sibba strode in, flanked by her brother and the other Northern captains. With her trousers, dark blue tunic, and fur cloak swinging from her shoulders, she appeared to be the essence of a warrior. Father Aidan went white and then red at the sight, muttering about the unnaturalness of it all. However, he noticed several men quietly appreciating her slender curves and the length of her legs. Cal gritted his teeth and tried to contain the sudden surge of jealousy.

Early this morning, things had very nearly exploded between them. She did not want or require any commitment. And he forgot those words at his peril.

Instead of giving in to the urge to demand certain people keep their eyes on the floor and any ribald remarks to themselves, he returned her brief nod and indicated she and the other Northmen should sit towards the front and to one side. She gave the barest of curtsies.

Sibba and the men quietly filed to their places, taking up two rows.

'Why have all these Northerners invaded our council?' the priest demanded in an undertone.

'I requested their presence,' Cal's father said, his voice holding echoes of his old authority. 'Our allies deserve our respect.'

The priest bowed his head and clacked his rosaries, mumbling how the king always knew best.

Sibba forced her back to stay as straight as a newly forged sword. She wished she could hear what the priest mumbled to Cal and his father.

'Will they accept our petition?' Gettir's old helmsman muttered. 'I doubt it. You tried, young Sibba, but they are not minded to assist the likes of us. We should throw our lot in with someone who will assist us in getting Gettir's women back.'

'Smile and give them some time to come around to the idea,' Sibba said between clenched teeth. The men had not wanted to come, saying that they did not see the point in being humiliated. She worried that they would stand up and walk out at the slightest provocation. Perhaps that was what Thorkell wanted—to drive a wedge between the former would-be allies.

The king cleared his throat, and all fell silent. 'My son will preside over this council.'

Having said that, he sat back and closed his eyes.

Cal stepped up and welcomed everyone. He quickly related the situation with Rindr and her mother's kidnapping.

'Why are the Northmen here?' someone called.

'I am coming to that,' Cal said.

'We want answers now. It is far from customary for Northmen to attend our councils,' another shouted.

Sibba kept her eyes forward and ignored her men, but she gestured to them to remain seated. Clearly the priest had been spreading his poison.

Beside her, the captains shifted in their seats, muttering under their breath about the treacherous Gaels. She signalled to Cal who raised a brow but indicated that she should step forward.

'We come to petition the council,' Sibba said, stepping forward before any more voiced their objections. 'It is my understanding that such a thing is permitted.'

'But…but…but you are a woman,' the priest squeaked. The rumbling of agreement from the council members made Sibba's heart falter. Surely, they couldn't refuse her request on the basis of her sex? That would be short-sighted in the extreme. 'Why do men allow a mere slip of a woman to put words in their mouths?'

Sibba clenched her fists and forced a breath. The initial anger passed, leaving a sense of clear, calm purpose. She'd encountered that tactic before. The priest wanted her angry so that she'd sound hysterical. 'My fellow captains have decided that I should be the one to speak. Hopefully the Gaels of Suthereyjar will not seek to dictate which of us is given such an honour.'

Her voice wavered slightly at the words *speak* and *honour*. She pressed her lips together and forced herself to wait for the king's reaction.

He waved his hand, indicating that she should continue.

'We remain your allies and as such would not dream of dictating who you chose to lead.' Cal inclined his head, but his eyes blazed a fierce blue at the priest who muttered about the world going to ruin and crossed himself several times.

She nodded and forced her fingers to relax. She had won the point. And having accepted her once, they were likely to continue to do so. 'We travelled here to celebrate a wedding and the creation of an alliance, but that joy turned to sorrow with the news of the kidnapping of the bride and her mother.'

She was pleased at how steady her voice remained while she spoke. She noticed that the hall grew progressively quieter until the end when she asked for the council to provide support, it was utter silence.

She stood in that silence waiting, trying not to look at Cal and wonder if she had made the situation worse. Maybe she should have let one of the other captains speak. Maybe she should have let her brother.

Then like the rush of a spring tide, the sound of applause and stamping feet roared in her ears. Several warriors slapped her on the back, making her eyes water, and told her that Gettir could not have done better and that they were bound to get the assistance they required now. Sibba gave a tight smile. She wished she felt that positive.

Cal knocked his staff on the ground three times, and the chamber fell silent. Sibba studied her hands.

'The North have asked for our help,' he said. 'Will we give it, or are we cowards?'

'Never cowards!' someone shouted, and again the chamber erupted into applause. The priest appeared to have swallowed a very bitter plum.

'Shall we help?' Cal asked, cupping a hand to his ear. 'I can't hear you.'

Sibba heard one or two *no*s, but they were overwhelmed in the resounding chorus of *yes*es. Calwar had known what he was doing. For the first time in a long time, Sibba believed that she had someone else on her side who was willing to get things done.

Cal struck his staff against the floor again, and the room fell silent. 'The council has spoken. Now the king shall make his decree on the subject.'

'The mood of the council is that we should support the North in their quest to free the kidnapped woman Rindr Gettirsdottar and her mother, Nefja,' the king said before rising. He swayed slightly, but Sibba could see the strength and determination of his character etched on his face. Despite his current affliction, she could see his fierce intelligence.

She made a deep bowy. 'Thank you, Your Majesty. We gratefully accept your offer. Together we will succeed. We will rescue Rindr and show Thorkell that his evil ways can no longer continue.'

'Very prettily said, Sibba Norrsdottar. It is good we are allies.' He took a step forward. 'Now I shall go.'

Cal instantly handed him a cane, and the priest hurried over, murmuring something. The king waved him away with an impatient gesture.

Sibba frowned. Something needed to be done about the priest's influence if Cal was going to be away, rescuing Rindr. She had to hope he would be.

'Go? Where are you going? There is a rescue to be planned.'

'My son will figure out the finer details.'

The crowd parted, and he walked very slowly out of the room.

'What sort of support?' the priest asked once the door had closed behind the king. 'Are you asking us to shed blood?'

'We hope to avoid a battle,' Sibba said.

'I don't understand. How do you expect Thorkell to give up these women?' The priest gave a pitying smile. 'Are you simply going to ask him for them?'

'We want to rescue the women, unharmed and alive. If we can do this, without disturbing anyone or causing anyone injury, so much the better.' Sibba raised her chin and concentrated on breathing steadily. If she reacted to the baiting, she'd lose everything. 'Why seek trouble if there is a possibility of avoiding it?'

The priest's mouth dropped open. 'Are you truly that naive?'

Sibba dug her fingernails into her fists. It was as Cal had predicted. The priest wanted to bait her. 'I've a thing called hope. I'm not afraid of fighting should it come to that, Father, but I'm merely saying that the only thing which is certain is if we do nothing, harm will come—either for the people of these islands or for the felag which I currently lead.'

The priest's face scrunched up. 'It is up to Calwar to decide the finer details,' he said finally. 'I stand by the king's decree and look to the eternal souls of my people.'

'Now you begin to see why Sibba leads her men,' Cal said with a smile. The muscles in Sibba's neck relaxed. Cal believed in her. 'I wish to thank you, Sibba, for the confidence you place in my men and me. We will not fail you. We will ensure this insult to both our people does not go unpunished.'

The hall erupted in the stamping of feet and clapping of hands.

She sat down, and several of the Northmen patted her on the shoulder and told her well done. She closed her eyes tightly and savoured the praise. She wished her father was here to see his daughter being accorded this respect.

She took a deep breath and struggled to get her emotions under control. She had done one thing, but the harder task of rescuing Rindr and her mother remained.

'All well and good,' the priest said when the noise had calmed down. 'But what happens next?'

'I believe I shall discuss everything with Sibba in private,' Cal said.

'In private—why?' Haakon called out.

A great urge to shake him hard swept over Sibba. Why did he need to bait Cal? Did he have no common sense? They'd won, and he wanted to throw it away.

'One must be aware of the possibility of spies and other traitors.' He slammed his fists together. He rose and motioned to the door. 'Unless anyone has any objections.'

Sibba followed him to the small alcove, hung with tapestries depicting biblical scenes. 'What is going on?'

'I want to put a proposition to you. We—you and I—and several of my men make a reconnaissance mission while we wait for the ships to be repaired.'

Sibba stood up straighter. A reconnaissance mission could work. It would give her something to do while her men made the necessary repairs. 'What purpose would that serve?'

'To see if there is any way in which we can get into the fort. Or if Thorkell will need to be defeated in a large sea battle.'

Sibba's tiny bubble of hope dissipated. He wanted to show her that it was impossible and that her scheme for rescuing Rindr was doomed to failure. She knew there had to be a way of getting into that fort undetected, but exactly how eluded her.

'You, me, and how many others?' she said around the lump in her throat.

'Three, so a total of five.' He gave her a stern look. 'Your brother must remain here as surety.'

'My brother is a competent warrior. He always has a place in my felag.'

'Good, then he can act as my father's bodyguard.' He ran

his hands through his hair, making it stand on end. 'Ease my mind, Sibba. Let your brother watch over my father for the day or two that this mission will take.'

A stab of remorse hit Sibba. His worry about his father must be gnawing at his insides. Perhaps she judged him overly harshly. Perhaps he, too, searched for a way to get Rindr and Nefja out without bloodshed before any showdown with Thorkell.

'Are you willing to trust him with that task?'

Cal gave a self-deprecating smile, and she knew it would be easy to really like the man. 'I trust you not to lie to me about his competency. My sole condition, Sibba is that we go on this mission first so that you can see the situation with your own eyes.'

'What happens if I want something more than a reconnaissance mission? What if I require my brother's assistance?'

'If you decline, Suthereyjar can serve as a base to attack Thorkell from, but we will offer no other assistance.'

Sibba put her hands on top of her head. Haakon would be furious about being left behind, but if she emphasised the honour of being made the king's bodyguard, he might be placated. Haakon always did enjoy being held in honour. She understood Cal's unspoken reason was to keep Haakon and Rindr apart, but she appreciated the excuse.

'My brother will do his duty. I give you my word on that.' She grasped his hand. His fingers, strong, warm, and capable, curled about hers. She left them there for a few heartbeats longer than she should have done. 'When we return, we can discuss the next steps and whether they include Haakon. He is a good man in a fight.'

He gave her hand a squeeze and stepped back. 'I will

give you command but will serve as the navigator. I know the waters and the sort of vessel to use.'

Her heart thumped. 'Me?'

'Your scheme. You alone know what you need to see. I simply know how to get you there.'

'With a few refinements from you.' She bit her lip and resisted the urge to throw her arms about his neck, trying to puzzle out what Cal wanted from this. 'We should be co-leaders. Gael and North working together.'

His eyes crinkled at the corners. 'We will make a good team, but I'm content to navigate.'

Her heart skipped a beat, and she wanted to believe that he truly meant it about cooperating. 'If we get the chance to rescue them, I'll take it.'

His expression became inscrutable. 'You are the person leading the team.'

She knew then that he deemed any small rescue attempt doomed to failure, but she also knew somehow she had to find a way to make it not only possible but probable and in-evitable. She refused to allow Rindr and her mother to rot.

Chapter Seven

The wind whipped the waves into white-crested monsters, sending them crashing over the bow of the small fishing vessel. The boat, little more than a coracle with a slender mast and sail and none of the stability of a Northern long-ship, rocked violently to one side and then the other. The storm had come out of nowhere. When they left the harbour this morning, the sun had twinkled the sea to a vibrant blue. A light breeze had ruffled the sail as they pulled away from the harbour. Cal had said that he was merely going to show Sibba the fishing grounds and the northern islands and that they would be back at some point in the next few days, but nothing would happen until the Northern ships were fixed in a week's time.

Before leaving, Sibba informed her captains that they were to attack Thorkell's fleet in a week's time—whether she was there or not. Her helmsman touched his finger to his nose and agreed to captain the longship in her absence. 'We will give you that opportunity if you haven't returned,' her helmsman pledged.

Haakon had thankfully seen the sense in his remaining with the king as his bodyguard. Apparently, the older man was a keen tafl player and gambler. Haakon wanted to try his luck.

Sibba put her hands on the side of the boat to keep herself from falling into the several inches of water which had accumulated at the bottom of the vessel. Cal's choice of boat appeared to be far less steady than she'd like. She had seen far too many ships swamped in her travels, particularly on the Bosporus and the Black Sea. But neither Cal nor the three men he'd brought seemed concerned about the water constantly sloshing around them. They kept up a cheerful banter, almost exulting in the bad weather, swapping tales about how many times they had made this passage.

Sibba hunched down and adjusted her leather cape to make it cover her hair better and keep most of the rain out. Her leather trousers were dipped in pitch and largely waterproof as well. She enjoyed travelling on the sea most of the time, but not in the teeth of a gale. However, they were too far out to risk returning to Suthereyjar.

Cal swore it would take longer to do that than to continue to the inlet on Barra where he wanted to make landfall. She chose to believe him. Now in the gloom she could make out a line of white sand with a dark green hill rising behind it. Land and, more importantly, safety.

She pinched the bridge of her nose and tried to focus on taking deep breaths. The last thing she needed was for Cal or his men to tease her about being nervous on the sea. If they were unconcerned about the boat's seaworthiness, she would pretend to be as well.

'Is that Barra I see?' she asked, protecting her eyes with her hand and trying not to worry if this mission was going to fail to accomplish what she desired—a key to getting into that island fortress. There had to be a way of getting in before Thorkell realised what they were up to. If they could take him by surprise, they could release the captives with the minimum amount of bloodshed.

Cal cupped a hand around his ear. 'You will have to speak louder.'

'The ship will not take much more.' The water sloshed over her ankles. 'How far to Barra? And are there any hidden dangers in our approach?'

'Not much farther.' Cal pointed towards a barely visible white line on the horizon. 'We make for that beach. We will be there before you know it. It gets slightly tricky with the shoals and the shifting sands, but I know the water very well. I have put boats in here many times.'

His late wife. She held back the query about her extended family and whether any remained on the island. Would they assist them if they were there? Or would they prefer to keep their heads down, fearing reprisals? Worse, could she stand to hear stories about the woman who still held Cal in her thrall? 'Where is Thorkell's lair?'

'Other side of the island. We will travel by night and rest during the day. Day and a half across the island, by my reckoning.'

Sibba hated how her heart knocked. Suddenly it felt all too real. 'Is this beach away from his eyes and ears?'

'I know the lands, and I know that harbour,' he said shortly, turning his face so all she saw was his profile which appeared carved out of stone. 'My wife's mother's old lands. Thorkell cleared them of people long ago.'

Sibba wished Cal's easy words filled her with more confidence. She had to trust his instincts even if her stomach was a mass of ever-tightening knots. 'Thorkell must know that.'

'He only cares for his fortress and nothing else,' one of Cal's men said, reaching over to tighten the flapping sail. 'Barra was prosperous until he came. Now it is a barren wasteland. Most of the people have left. Those who remain barely scratch out a living. Thorkell demands tribute upon tribute.'

'It will be prosperous again,' Sibba said, putting her hand on her knife. 'Once we remove Thorkell and his minions, people will be free to farm how they have done for generations. It is not just for Northern trade that we do this but also for the people under his yoke. I wish your priest had understood this, instead of speaking against my plea for help.'

The man concentrated on tightening the sail. 'I pray that you are right, my lady. That yoke is heavy and getting heavier.'

'They still need to eat, even Thorkell knows that. He may have set men to work it. It is easier to plough a worked field than one which has never been sown before.'

Cal gave a snort of laughter. 'Trust you to be practical. But there are other fields closer which he will use. Our landing will go unnoticed.'

'You have used this route before. I mean since Thorkell took over the island.'

His jaw clenched. 'When the occasion demanded it, I have and returned to tell the tale.'

The words were clipped and seemed designed to stifle any further questioning.

Sibba clenched her fists and then slowly relaxed them. She was worrying over nothing, and Cal was right: they had to land somewhere their presence would go unnoticed. And he had used this landing before. 'Men with empty bellies are often unpredictable, or so my father used to say. Thorkell is no fool. He will want to ensure a steady supply of food for his growing band of warriors.'

Another huge wave washed over the boat, soaking everyone with bone-chilling cold before Cal could respond.

'We need to start bailing. This boat appears to be less

than seaworthy.' She reached for the bucket which had rolled a little way from her.

A third huge wave lifted the boat up and set it down, cracking the mast and tossing Sibba in the air. Caught unawares, she was thrown to one side and made a wild grab at the side of the boat. Missed and tumbled repeatedly as the boat thrashed wildly about, first lurching one way and then the other on the storm-tossed sea. With a crack, the mast tumbled into the sea, and the boat went up again, rising higher. She caught a glimpse of the deep abyss over the side. This was it. She knew in her gut that the boat was about to turtle and that she had no wish to be trapped under it.

She pushed off from the side and landed in the ice-cold sea. The grey waters closed over her, dragging her down.

It would be easy to stop struggling and let the sea take her. She had always known that there was a possibility of drowning. She had seen enough men drown to know that she had very little hope of surviving. A brief time in the sea as cold as this one and people died. Except, she wasn't ready. People were counting on her. She had to find a way. She had to take the chance to live.

She kicked her feet hard and struggled to get her head above water, looking for the boat or any flotsam so that she'd have something to cling to do.

'Anyone? Did anyone else survive?' she called out. All she could hear was the roar of the sea and the storm.

In the time she had been underwater, the upright boat, now missing its mast, had drifted away from her. She tried to shout, but it came out as a feeble cry. It could not end like this—her in the sea. She wished she'd learned to swim better, but now she had to do something to save herself. All she could think was how far away the shoreline appeared and how quickly the boat was advancing towards it with its oars dipping in the water.

'Grab hold.' A voice rumbled near her ear. 'Do as I say and grab hold. I am not going to allow you to die. The men will get the boat to shore.'

'Cal?' she whispered, wondering if she had started to imagine things.

He had to be on that boat, rowing with all his might for the shore, not in the water beside her.

'Grab hold of the mast, Sibba. Stop being awkward. Being rescued is not a sign of weakness.' Cal shoved the wooden spar towards her.

'What?' She blinked hard to clear her eyes. She tried to concentrate on moving her arms and legs to keep afloat, the few skills she'd learned back in Constantinople where the waters were far warmer.

Cal had loosened the sail from the mast, and it was now a floating T-shaped spar.

'It will give us some ballast and keep us afloat while I kick our way to shore. I take it you can't swim?'

'What about the boat?'

'The men will land her where they can. They should be fine, but they can't return for us, not in this weather. All were clinging on from what I could see before I jumped in the water to save you.'

'And the weapons?'

'Can't use a sword if you are dead.'

'Some truth to that.'

'You can appreciate a joke. A good sign.'

She paddled over to the mast and levered her body up. The little bit of flotsam helped far more than she thought it might. And the shore did appear closer. She closed her eyes and opened them again. She might survive this ordeal.

'Am I glad to see you!?'

'A minor miracle but a pleasing one.' He lifted her up slightly by her trousers' waistband so that her body was more on top on the mast. 'Now, can you kick? Or will I have to do this for the both of us?'

'Give me a chance to catch my breath.'

'In your own time, then.' He started to kick, and the makeshift ballast began to move steadily towards the shore.

The stiff, cold wind blew through her, making her teeth chatter. The formerly ice-cold water now seemed warmed like the waters in a bath house in Constantinople. She knew the potential for it being a deadly trap, but she sank back into its welcoming embrace. She could give up and let go.

'What are you doing? Hang on to the spar, Sibba. Don't give up. I won't let you.'

She gritted her teeth and forced her legs to move. 'I can kick better from here. And I do know how to kick, Cal.'

'Thank God and all the saints for that. Some people can't.'

'I'm a practical person, remember?'

He gave her a look. 'If we stay in the water for too long, we will die.'

Sibba focussed on the shoreline. It was doable. She simply had to forget the siren call of the sea to stop. 'Tell me something that I don't know.'

'A hut with dried peat stacked beside it sits in a hollow just beyond the dunes. We get there and I will build a warm fire to dry us both out.'

'You know how to give hope.'

'Sometimes it is the only thing you have.'

Sibba didn't like to dwell on how long it was taking them to cover the distance to the shoreline. She simply concentrated on moving her legs and was grateful for an incoming tide which helped to push them closer to the shore. About halfway there, the rain stopped. A feeble sun emerged. Every so often, Sibba conjured up the image of a roaring fire, and it gave her the strength to keep kicking.

Finally, Cal stood up. 'Shallow enough to walk. No point in hanging on any longer.'

Sibba forced her hands from the mast. Every particle of her ached. She stood in the swirling surf and attempted to move forward. Her legs were like jelly. All she wanted to do was sink back into the welcoming water and allow it to push her up on the beach, but she knew she couldn't do that. Forward, always forward.

'Sibba? Did you hear me? You can stand up.'

She gritted her teeth and stood. One step and then she forced another. She glanced at the shore. The white sand appeared to stretch for miles before it met the green-topped dunes. And her legs wobbled. Cal appeared to be moving much faster and more purposefully than her. Soon, he'd be on shore, and she'd be... She gritted her teeth and re-doubled her efforts.

'Where is this fire you promised? My bones ache.' She tried for a laugh, but it came out strangled. Sometime soon she was going to have to get out her wet things. She had seen men survive the sea and succumb sometime later to the cold which had seeped into their bones. She had survived, and she was determined to remain alive.

'Let's get you on dry land first. Properly. Lie in the surf and you may yet drown.'

She shaded her eyes. The beach was devoid of all life or indeed human habitation. Just brilliant white sand against a steel grey sky. 'And the boat?'

'They will have landed in the next cove.'

'You seem pretty certain about that.'

'It is what I ordered them to do after you fell off. Less chance of hitting the hidden rocks. They will meet us at the hut.' He gave a half-smile. 'Despite your unreasonable fears, boats like mine do not tend to capsize in rough water. They spin and bounce around, but they normally glide over the waves. Perfect for these waters and weather conditions. I told you to trust my navigation.'

Sibba gritted her teeth. He made it sound like she had overreacted. But he was right: she'd failed to trust him. She silently resolved to do better.

'The mast started to move and I tried to avoid it.' Sibba paused and wiped the salt water from her eyes. It suddenly seemed important for him to know why she'd acted the way she had. 'I was reaching for the bucket before that.'

'Reaching for a bucket? Not launching yourself over the side?'

Sibba regarded the horizon. 'I didn't expect you to risk your life for me.'

'I would have done the same for anyone else in that crew.' He held out his hand. 'A simple *thank you* might be in order.'

'Thank you,' Sibba said, tucking her head into her neck. If her mind was working straight, she'd have said it straight-away. And she hated that she'd hoped he'd jumped in because it was her. 'I should have said that before. I've no wish to seem ungrateful. Unexpected bravery but, oh-so welcome.'

His hand closed about hers. 'You were concentrating on other things.'

'Everything aches,' she whispered and withdrew her hand. 'I am not sure how much farther I can go. You might be better leaving me.'

She fell to her knees in the few remaining inches of surf. Tears pricked at her eyelids. So close but her body refused to cooperate. She knew intellectually if she did not move, she'd die. Already a deep bone-chilling cold penetrated to her very centre. But her legs refused to obey her.

'Why would I leave you when we have come this far?'

She peeped up at him. He was standing there strong and sure. And he wouldn't leave her. Her heart was certain of that.

It would be easy to love a man like that. She swallowed hard. Whatever happened, love had nothing to do with whatever bond was between Cal and her. She couldn't afford finer feelings, not when there was her vow to fulfil. She had failed her father and watched helplessly as his boat was swamped, but this time she would succeed.

She closed her eyes, and the image of her with a child on her hip rose. She banished it. It was no good even thinking about a future like that. She had to concentrate on the important things like rescuing Rindr, ensuring Thorkell's reign of terror ended, and leading her men to a place of safety where they could raise families and prosper. Until that happened, she had no right to consider happiness in her future.

'Give me a little time, and I will regain my strength. Maybe I can even help gather the wood for this promised fire, provided you have a flint that works…'

'We need to get you warmed up before you start spouting any more nonsense. And dry peat will do the job. It is what we use on these islands. Wood is far too precious to use for a simple fire.'

Exhaustion rolled over her in waves. She frowned, trying to concentrate on standing up, but the warm water tugged at her feet.

'Dried peat. Not wood. I will remember that.' She moved her legs forward, or attempted to. 'Always willing to learn, me.'

'Stop being stubborn, Sibba. Accept help.' Cal scooped her up. His strong arms closed about her. The steady thump of his heart resounded against her ear.

He covered the distance to the high-water mark quickly. After a few more steps in the white sand, his foot caught, and he half stumbled. 'We will get there, Sibba,' he murmured.

She lay within his arms for a few heartbeats. It was pleasant to be carried, but she also knew he had to be cold and exhausted as well.

She pushed against his chest and tried to keep her teeth from chattering. 'I will be fine. Out of the water now. Above the tideline. No danger of drowning, even if I lie here for a night and a day.'

'People can drown on dry land if their lungs have filled with salt water.'

'I haven't had too much.' She pushed once more against his chest. 'And you did do most of the work to get us on-shore. I owe you a life debt which I will struggle to repay, Calwar.'

He sighed and put her down gently onto the white sand. She immediately rested her head against her knees. The all-pervading cold had seeped into her bones, but she was on dry land. She was going to survive. She could fulfil her oath and kill Thorkell.

He sat down next to her. Their shoulders touched. Like her he was absolutely drenched. 'When you are ready, we will go together.'

'Don't you trust me to follow?'

'I'd rather not have to do a return trip. The way to the

hut can be complicated, and I've seen what the cold can do to a man.'

'I should point out that I am a woman.'

He rolled his eyes. 'Are you always this awkward after someone saves your life?'

'I was trying to make a joke. I do that occasionally.'

He raised a brow. 'I will try to remember that for the next time.'

'A joke?'

A twinkle shone in his eyes and warmed her. 'If you like…'

They sat there with their shoulders barely touching, not speaking. Sibba rested her head against her knees. The uncontrolled chattering of her teeth ceased, and a tiny particle of warmth crept back into her bones, but she knew the danger of not getting properly warm. She would find the strength from somewhere to get to that hut and the promised fire.

'I'm ready to go farther,' she said and forced her tired muscles to stand. 'Dry driftwood appears to be lacking on the beach.'

'Are you always this independent?'

'I pride myself on it.' She squeezed the seawater out of her hair before flipping the braid back over her shoulder. Time enough to worry about getting clean later. One thing at a time. Each step forwards would take her a little closer to her goal. 'Why build a fire where it can serve as a beacon? You must know of somewhere safer.'

He gave a crooked smile, but she could see the weariness in his blue eyes.

'How do you know this hut exists?'

'It belonged to my wife's family. It will be there. It was there a few months ago when I had cause to visit it.'

His face took on a remote quality. Sibba held back the question about why he'd returned to such a dangerous place. When he was ready, he'd tell her.

'Then, we go there. As long as I don't have to run, I am certain I can walk.'

'You are far stronger than you first appeared, Sibba.'

'I also pride myself on being self-reliant.' She smiled up at him. 'You do know how to give a compliment.'

'The secret is understanding what the lady wants to hear.'

Chapter Eight

The thatched-roof hut was nestled in a hollow just behind the sand dunes. The thatch was clearly in need of urgent repair, but it would suffice for one night. A clear spring ran in full spate slightly to the back and right of the hut. The stack of dried peat remained just inside the door where Cal had left it shortly after his wife died.

To Cal's disappointment, his men had failed to arrive, even though he'd left strict instructions that they were to make their way there as quickly as possible. All he could do was hope that they had not run into any further difficulties.

He busied himself with sorting out the dried peat and bits of kindling.

To his relief, no one appeared to have used the place since he was last there. Even the old trunk of his in-laws' belongings was there, half-covered by old bracken. He had thought himself a fool when he'd left the trunk eighteen months ago, naively believing the matter would be settled and marital harmony would be restored. At the time, he'd wanted her to recover from the difficult labour she'd endured. Giving in to her demands and travelling to Barra had seemed the best way forward. He had quietly taken soundings and quickly realised there was no appetite for a return to his wife's family's rule. When he'd returned, she and the babe seemed stronger, and she'd seemed to take the news in good spirits. But less than a day later, she appeared with her quiver of arrows in the middle of a council meeting, announcing her intention to lead an expedition. When he rebuked her, she grabbed their child and headed for the cliff. He liked to believe she didn't know the cliff was unstable and had merely been trying to goad him into action.

Afterwards, he'd never found the time to make the hazardous journey to retrieve the items from the hut; something else always commanded his attention.

He pushed aside all thoughts of the tragedy and hunkered down to concentrate on practical things like starting the fire. Thankfully, his flint was dry enough, and the fire rapidly grew. When it seemed strong, he put on several pieces of dried peat.

In his experience, the peat provided a searing heat over a longer period than wood. And all the blessed saints knew Sibba and he needed the warmth. They'd spent far too long in the cold water. Sibba kept failing to answer questions coherently.

He tried to keep a steady stream of chatter, but increasingly Sibba answered absently or not at all.

'You see how the peat works,' he said, forcing his voice to be cheerful.

No real answer. Her head had dropped down on her chest.

'Sibba, you can't sleep. Get warm first.'

She made a cat's paw with her hand. 'I'm tired.'

'You sleep, you die. You need to warm up.'

Her lips turned up into a little smile, but her eyes held a distinct glaze like she had drunk far too much mead. She ineffectually stabbed a forefinger towards him. 'Not just me. You. We were both in the water.'

'Let me worry about me.'

She rolled her eyes. 'Typical man. Did you know that, Calwar? You're a typical man.'

He gave a light laugh in response to her overly tinkling one. 'I've never tried to be anything else.'

'Maybe you should. Maybe you should allow people to worry about you. You don't have to be strong all the time.'

The warmth from the fire started to seep into his bones. He belatedly realised Sibba's slurred words were right. He had not appreciated how cold and wet he was and how parched his throat from swallowing seawater. His limbs began to shake, but out of the corner of his eye he saw her teeth chattering and noticed how blue she was about her mouth.

'Get your wet things off.' The words came out harsher than he intended.

Sibba sat up straighter and with a great effort, stopped her body shaking. 'My things? No need. I'll dry out. I'm already warmer than I was.'

'They're dripping wet. You've created puddles on the floor.'

She shrugged and turned her back on him. 'Want to try making me?'

He frowned at the suggestive tone in her voice. He hated that something within him leapt at the prospect. 'You stay in those clothes, Sibba, and you will die. I've seen it happen before. Must I come over there and strip you?'

'You are making puddles as well, Cal.' She gestured with her arms. 'This felag needs both of us to succeed. Isn't that what you said earlier?'

Rather than answering, he opened the trunk, searching for something, anything that could help. Luckily there were two old furs resting on the top. The banner proclaiming his wife's old house remained firmly in the trunk. The time hadn't been right to raise it eighteen months ago, and he had to wonder if it ever would be.

He shoved the furs towards Sibba and slammed the trunk shut.

'Why are these here?' she asked, putting her hand to her throat and swaying slightly.

'Your clothes should be dry before morning.' The words explaining about his late wife's scheme stuck in his throat. 'Wrap these around you. I am going to get some water to wash our mouths out with. I feel like I have swallowed half the sea. Once the necessary chores are done, I will take your advice.'

She gave a brief nod but ignored the furs. 'I'll be warm before morning. Honest. I'll not slow you down. Hate doing that. Was too late with my father...'

He had no doubt that she would try, but sometimes things were beyond people. Just as he could not figure out how to do what his wife had wanted without incurring too much bloodshed. Even now, the stench of his own cowardice and awkward words still clung to his throat. Pragmatism, he'd told himself at the time, but now he was uncertain. Maybe there was a way. He dismissed the thought as a cold-water fancy rather than something solid.

'Get undressed, Sibba. It will give you the best chance. You need to see the fortress with your own eyes. Then you can decide what the next step is.'

Without waiting for an answer, he grabbed a jug, went out to the peat-soaked stream, and gave the snowy-owl double hoot as a signal to his men. Anything to avoid thinking about what could be done to stop Thorkell. If he could find a way which would not endanger either his father's kingdom or the Gaels who remained on Barra, would he rescue those women?

He heard no answer to that question or to the call to his men.

A steady mist started to fall again, closing the skyline down. He hoped the men had made it safely to the shore and were waiting somewhere dry until the morning before travelling to the hut.

A mixed flock of ravens and rooks settled into a tree near him—as if he required another bad omen about this journey. He knew in his heart that he should have told Sibba the truth that the fortress would be impossible to penetrate and that they would have to devise a way to ensure Thorkell was defeated in sea battle.

He shook his head. The soaking in the cold sea had clouded his judgement. When he started seeking omens and supernatural signs, he knew he needed to stop thinking and start doing something productive.

By the time he turned, the fire glowed in the hearth throwing shadows onto the walls but, more importantly, providing welcome heat.

In the time he'd been gone, Sibba had undressed, carefully placed her sodden clothes near the fire, and unbound her braid. Her drying hair formed little ringlets at her temples. Her mouth had returned to its more normal rose-dawn colour, but the cold still pinched it.

Cal placed the jug down heavily and averted his eyes. He'd no business thinking about her in that way. Or indeed worrying about her. It was no good telling his brain that he always worried about his men. There was something different about Sibba. When the wave had washed her overboard earlier, he had followed her in, intent on saving her. Normally he'd have thought about his safety or that of the others on-board, but this time, he knew that he needed to save her whatever the cost. That bothered him.

'What is this?' she asked in a low voice.

'A drink to take the salty taste away.'

She took the jug and drained it. She wiped the back of her hand across her mouth rather than daintily blotting it. 'I will need a wash. Is the stream far?'

He put his hand on her shoulder, and her flesh quivered under his fingertips. 'Tomorrow, when you are warmer. In the daylight. You might slip.'

Her cheeks coloured prettily, or maybe it was the heat from the fire. 'Before we go to find your men. I will be able to think better once I've washed.'

'An interesting excuse, but let's get through tonight first.'

'The truth.' She lifted her chin, and the fur slipped slightly, revealing the long column of her slender neck and the curve of her shoulder.

He threw another few pieces of dried peat on the fire. They blazed dramatically. He tried to keep his mind occupied, but it kept circling back to Sibba and the way her lips had moved under his. He tried to keep up the banter, but he gradually noticed her words were becoming more and more monosyllabic.

Her head had collapsed onto her chest.

'Sibba?' He gently shook her shoulder.

A violent shiver convulsed her. Her deeply pooled eyes sought his. 'Cold, Cal, so cold.'

He gathered her hands in his. They were frozen. He silently cursed. He'd been overoptimistic about the furs. Overoptimistic about everything. 'Try moving about.'

'Moving about? I'm too tired.'

'To get warmer. Use your brain. Squats or running in place. And keep talking to me.' He struggled not to notice the way her lashes made a forest about each eye. To think he'd overlooked her when they first met. 'You mustn't sleep until you are warm. Honest truth. You sleep, you die.'

'Is it? Is that why you remain in your sodden clothes?' She pressed her fingers against her temples. 'I don't require rescuing, Calwar. I require you to ensure your own safety.'

Cal frowned. 'Move closer to the fire.'

'You say the silliest things, Cal. I'm wrapped in two furs, and you have none. We should be equal.'

He tried to concentrate on the shadows flickering against the rough walls of the hut and the sound of the rain hitting the roof. 'Equal?'

'I've no intention of throwing away your life after you saved mine. Get out of your wet things. We need to find a way to warm up. Properly.'

His mouth went dry. He knew the traditional way of warming up involved being skin-to-skin, but if that happened with Sibba, he would have difficulty controlling his body. He didn't want to jeopardise their partnership. Far too much depended on it. 'We do?'

'Yes, we do.' She took a step forward, tilted her mouth upwards, and he found it impossible to resist the temptation. He brushed his lips against hers, a feather-light touch. Nothing more. Just one single sample.

Sibba's body tingled as she brushed her mouth against Cal's one more time. The effect of his mouth touching hers was like a spark touching tinder. A slight glow of warmth infused her, driving out the insidious cold and making her feel alive.

She instinctively knew that they both had to get warm. And the best way was to use body heat, or so she'd heard from old warriors. She'd never volunteered to find out if the theory worked.

She'd worry about the consequences later. At Northern feasts, other women often coupled with men without a second thought or expectation of anything beyond the morning.

Even though she had never indulged, it did not mean that she was unaware of what was happening—the fumbling, the sighs, and the self-satisfied expressions. She knew what could happen to women and why a morning gift was the accepted custom as any child rightfully belonged to the father.

She wrinkled her nose. Bearing a child? Proof of how addled her brain was. Before anything like that could be a consideration, she had to rescue Rindr and avenge her father's death. And she was more than capable of looking after any child. What mattered was getting warm and letting Cal know that she had no expectations beyond that.

A violent shiver convulsed him, and she knew he was as ice-cold as she was, simply hiding it. They both needed to get warm as quickly as possible.

'Just for tonight,' she said.

'Are you sure?' he murmured against her lips.

She pushed aside all thoughts about the future and curled her arm about Cal's neck. 'Kiss me. Kiss me proper.'

He groaned, and his arms went about her, holding her body against his. 'If I start, I may not be able to stop.'

She glanced up at him. His face was a study in planes and shadows. 'I wasn't thinking about stopping. Quickest way to warm up. When the rose dawn of the sun creeps into the doorway, that will be the time to think.'

She cupped her hands about his jaw and allowed the fur to slip off her shoulders. It tumbled to the ground unheeded. She pressed her lips against his cool ones and drew a small circle with her tongue.

He instantly deepened the kiss. His mouth opened, and their tongues touched, retreated, and then tangled.

The small curl of heat skittered inside her, grew quickly. The ice cold which had invaded her bones retreated. Every part of her came alive, burning with heat, even that hardened bit which she had thought had died after her father's murder. Life was no longer interesting shades of grey but full colour and bright.

She rested her head against his chest and listened to the thumping of his heart. 'Better?'

He gave a husky laugh. 'I will have to think on it. Maybe try again?'

As he bent his head, a violent shudder went through him again.

She tugged at his tunic. 'We must get you out of this before we go any further.'

'You are impatient to see me naked?'

'I've no wish to deal with you turning into a frost giant. What a tale that would make for some skald—the warrior woman who turns men into blocks of ice.'

He captured her hand and placed it on his chest. 'No longer a block of ice.'

She tilted her head to one side. 'I'm not playing games. You remain far too cold.'

'Never let it be said that I didn't obey the lady.' He tossed the tunic on the floor. And his skin glowed golden in the firelight.

She ran a hand down his chest, feeling the indents from his various scars, her fingers brushing his nipples, which instantly hardened. Unable to resist, she lowered her mouth and drew circles with her tongue on his chest. He groaned in the back of his throat. She stroked his chest, except it felt more like stroking one of the marble statues she'd encountered in Constantinople rather than touching a living person.

She settled back on her haunches. 'That is better.'

'Sibba...we should discuss—'

She placed a finger against his mouth. 'Tonight is not for thinking. Nothing that happens tonight has any bearing on the future.'

She hoped he'd understand what she was saying. She wasn't naive. She was aware of the possibilities of a child but trusted in her ability to look after it. In any case, she wasn't thinking beyond rescuing Rindr and her mother and fulfilling her vow. Somehow, she needed to find a way. Some minor flaw which could be exploited and used against Thorkell. But tonight wasn't about that. Tonight was about them banishing the cold.

'Do you know what you are asking? Truly, or is this a game for you?'

She allowed her hand to trail down his chest. 'I know what the cold can do to a man.'

'The last thing I need is a fuss.' He turned away from her, rapidly undid his trousers, and pushed them off, laying them out near the fire.

Sibba tried to look anywhere but at his well-muscled bottom and singularly failed. She hated how her heart pounded and wondered if she should confess to her ignorance at the actual mechanics of coupling between a man and a woman. Or, worse, had he guessed her inexperience?

To cover her embarrassment, she bent down and retrieved the fur. 'Wrap this around you if you desire. But I am not playing a game. Why would I?'

He took it from her, and their fingers brushed. Warm sparks travelled up her arm. She gasped and nearly dropped the fur, but he caught it and wrapped it about his middle.

She adjusted her remaining fur so that it was tight about her body. 'You should get warmer now that your clothes are off. It is amazing how warm these furs are.'

Her voice sounded high and tight to her ears. She tried to concentrate on the fire, rather than feasting her eyes on his well-turned-out form.

The dried peat crackled and spit while the shadows danced on the walls.

Trust her to completely misread everything. She sighed and went over to the pile of dried peat. She picked several up and tossed them on the fire.

'Is this what you want?' he asked, coming to stand beside her.

He did not touch her at all, and when she risked a peek at his profile, his eyes appeared intent on the growing embers.

'I want us both to get warm.' She strove to make her words come out slowly and steadily as she ignored her pounding heart. 'This mission must succeed, and this is the best way to cure the ice cold one gets from the sea—or so I've heard.'

'And that is the only reason why—'

'I don't make a habit of jumping into the freezing sea. We are doing this your way.' She put her hand up, suddenly tired. She hated that she had made another mistake and thought he desired her. 'Forget it. Forget I suggested anything. We will get warm enough sitting in front of the fire.'

He caught her hand and raised it to his lips. 'Shall we try again? I thought your idea most pleasant, but a man likes to think you want him, not just another warm body.'

Her heart skittered against her chest. 'Merely *pleasant*?'

His eyes sparkled like sunlight on the ocean. 'Definitely intriguing. And mostly likely to succeed.'

She licked her suddenly dry lips. 'Success is an important factor in my suggesting the option.'

'There we agree.'

He lowered his head to hers, and his lips moved persuasively over hers. Softly he nibbled at the corners of her mouth before tracing the line of her jaw. When he reached her earlobe, he took it in his mouth and suckled. The heat within her bubbled up, burning away the cold.

She raised her arms about his neck. The fur she'd wrapped around herself fell with a swoosh to the floor. She dimly heard his fall as well.

He slid his hands down her back and pulled her close so that they were practically melded together.

'You begin to understand what I desire,' he said against her mouth. 'But was afraid to ask for.'

'Skin-to-skin. Best way to warm up.' She arched her back, pushing herself against the hardness of his erection.

His mouth travelled down her neck. His tongue lingered in the hollow between her neck and shoulder, making ever-growing circles.

One of his hands captured her breast. The back of his thumb drew circles around her nipple, mimicking the circles his tongue made. Her nipple hardened to a tight bud.

She groaned in the back of her throat.

He bent his head and took the nipple in his mouth, suckled until the world seemed to explode in heat and light.

The deep cold which she had been sure would never completely fade retreated in front of the searing heat from his mouth.

He eased her back onto the discarded furs. She reached out and touched his chest. His flesh had become molten, instead of marble-cold.

His hand slowly travelled down her flank until it reached

the apex of her thighs. There it stopped to explore her curls. First hovering above and then delving deep into her inner-most folds.

Her hips jutted upwards, seeking relief, wanting him to fill her completely. She had never thought coupling would be this exciting.

'I want you,' he rasped against her ear.

She ran a hand down his back, revelled in its silky smooth-ness. 'Then, have me.'

He returned to her mouth, thrust his tongue in, and deeply penetrated her. Her hips lifted, and he drove into her, mirroring the movements of his tongue. Her body opened and welcomed him in.

For a few heartbeats they lay there, connected and con-joined. Then acting on instinct, she moved her hips up-wards again, giving in to a natural rhythm. He joined her until their bodies were both slick with sweat.

Finally, she thrusted upwards, her body clenching about him and holding him firmly within her. The waves of de-sire crashed all around her. Nothing in her life had pre-pared her for that sense of total fulfilment combined with total abandonment.

A long while later, Sibba floated gently back to earth. Her body thrummed with energy, and she basked in the heat they had generated. The all-pervading cold had van-ished like it had never been.

'Thank you,' she said touching his cheek with her hand. 'An excellent remedy. Far better than holding my hands over the fire.'

His body shook with barely supressed laughter. 'You have such a way with words. I'm pleased it was more effective than sitting beside a fire. Good to know I'm useful for something.'

Sibba frowned. Men, particularly Gaels, had odd notions. 'You saved my life. I wasn't about to allow you to toss yours away. Why do you doubt me?'

He traced a line down her face, and the banked heat within her began burgeoning again. 'I'm learning that doubting you is a very bad idea.'

She put her hands behind her head and stared up at the roof, trying to make sense of it. 'Sometimes I have good ideas. And it is good to know what it feels like.'

His hand halted in its downward quest. He put a hand on her shoulder. 'Sibba, answer me true. Was this your first time?'

She raised herself up on one elbow and silently cursed. The words had slipped out. 'Did it show that badly? I can only apologise if I wasn't very good.'

'That isn't what I asked.'

Somehow the words seemed inadequate, explaining. She had wanted him to have the same sort of wonderful, life-altering experience she had had. And it was probably nothing of the sort. 'Poor Sibba, always getting things wrong about men' had been something she'd overheard Nefja saying to Rindr the afternoon before she found Rindr and Haakon. 'It was bound to happen sooner or later,' she said to Cal.

He smoothed the hair from her temple. 'Unexpected, that is all.'

She wrapped her hands about her knees and rested her head. *Unexpected*. 'We come from different worlds, Calwar.'

He pressed a kiss against her back. 'Not so different, and I am honoured that you chose me.'

'I hardly wanted to freeze to death. Quickest way to warm up,' she said with a strangled-cat laugh. 'Tonight. We never mention it again. Time out of mind.'

He removed his mouth from her skin. 'One night only.'

His voice, suddenly remote and devoid of life, confirmed her suspicion: she'd managed to get everything wrong.

Rather than pursuing it, she turned onto her side. 'We should try to sleep. Morning will come soon enough. The grey light of the gloaming already flickers. Soon we will be about our business and put this night behind us.'

The words were awkward and the opposite of what she really wanted, but they sounded appropriate. He withdrew his hand from her side. She wished she could unsay the words. She wished she was brave enough to say what she wanted, which was for the night to last for ever. Most of all, she wished she could find a way of rescuing the women which would not endanger everyone else.

He absently twisted a lock of her hair about his finger. 'You must be one of the most practical people I've met.'

'Practicality keeps me alive. I shall take that as a compliment.' And she had to hope that practicality would keep her heart safe and stop her from dreaming about halls, children, and a handsome Gaelic warrior, but she greatly feared that might be impossible.

'It was meant as one.' He pulled her back into his arms so that her bottom touched his middle. 'I have little time for women as decorative objects who flutter about accomplishing little of substance.'

'Best not to dream, but to be content with what you have,' she muttered under her breath. 'Only because we must survive the night.'

'Did you say something?'

'Does that marvellous trunk of yours run to boots?' she

said and hoped Cal would accept a change of subject. 'I kicked mine off when I first went into the sea.'

He pulled her more firmly into his embrace. 'I'll check in the morning. But sleep now.'

Her bottom nestled against his groin. And she knew she was sliding inexorably into love with him, a situation which would make their current mission dangerous. She couldn't afford finer feelings or dreams.

She screwed up her eyes. Tonight might have been a bigger mistake than she'd dreamt possible. And yet she knew she didn't want it to end.

'This arrangement lasts only for tonight,' he murmured in her ear. 'But—'

'I know,' she whispered before he could say anything more. 'Come the daylight, we speak no more of it. We go forward because the past is closed to us.'

He buried his face in her hair and mumbled something indistinct, and she knew in her heart how it had to be. Wanting it to be any other way was asking for humiliation. She knew that she'd hold this night close to her heart for the rest of her life.

Chapter Nine

The bright sunlight filtering through the roof woke Cal with a start. It took him several heartbeats to realise where he was. All the cold and fogginess in his head from last night had vanished.

Sibba's warm bottom was curled into his centre, and his body began to harden to the point of pleasurable pain. He wriggled to create space between them and concentrated on breathing steadily.

Her words before she drifted off to sleep echoed in his mind—*only because we must survive the night.* And it was no longer night.

He could well imagine what Sibba might say if he tried to kiss her senseless and demonstrate what had passed between them did not have to be confined to last night. He needed to play by her rules if his scheme was to stand any chance. First, he would demonstrate how hopeless any rescue attempt would be, and then he would convince her to help him increase the fleet so that no one would consider attacking the Gaels and their new allies. He had to put duty above his own feelings. Duty meant keeping the greatest number of people safe.

He put his hands behind his head and stared up at the blackened rafters, remembering how his late wife had warned him about waking her unexpectedly and that love-making was supposed to be confined to the night. It had seemed to him that the carefree girl he'd married vanished on their wedding night to be replaced by a woman obsessed with priest-dictated rules to the point of stifling all finer feeling. Cal pushed away thoughts about Brigid and his failure to understand her in the way she'd required.

After he'd dressed, he put his hand on Sibba's shoulder and gently shook her. 'Good morning. I found those boots for you. On foot from here on out.'

She sat up suddenly, her eyes wide and her hair delight-fully mussed. Her hand instinctively reached for a knife and then relaxed. 'Calwar?'

'You do remember what happened yesterday,' he said, keeping his voice low.

'Yes, yes.' She scrambled to pull on her shift, covering her magnificent body. 'My clothes are dry now. All is well. Fear not. I've no intention of saying anything more about what passed between us.'

Cal forced his hand to remain at his side, even though he wanted to draw her into his arms and kiss her thoroughly.

'About yesterday… We did what we had to to survive. But if anything…' he said, trying again, painfully aware Sibba appeared to have misinterpreted his first statement.

She shook her head and backed away from him like a scalded cat. 'No regrets or recriminations. No gossip or confidences.'

'I merely wanted to say that I enjoyed the experience.' The words sound far too weak, but he had a warrior's tongue, not a skald's, something Brigid used to complain bitterly about. 'Warmed me up brilliantly.'

She tucked a strand of hair behind her ear and lifted her head. For a moment he saw a very vulnerable woman, but then she pulled her shoulders back and gave them a swagger. 'Did it? Good to know that the old sailor told an important truth.'

He caught her hands. They quivered in his palms. He silently cursed the misbegotten dead fiancé and any other man who might have hurt her. She expected to be hurt, which was the last thing he wanted. 'I hope to do it again sometime soon. But it is up to you. Always.'

He let her hands go and waited. She watched him like a wild animal caught in a trap.

'What—fall into the water? Nearly drown? No, thank you very much.' She kicked the old straw, sending a pile skittering across the hard-packed floor. 'I always knew Gaels were crazy.'

He tilted her chin, forcing her to look up into his eyes. 'Stop trying to alter the meaning. You know well what I meant. Properly, in a bed mounded high with furs.'

Her tongue flicked out and wet her lips. 'Do I?'

He gave in to temptation and tasted them to see if they were as luscious as he remembered.

'Yes, you do,' he murmured against her mouth. 'You and I were excellent together. Soft words seldom trip off my tongue, Sibba.'

She retreated three steps and looked wildly about her. 'Did you hit your head? Your men will be showing up soon.'

He let her remain out of reach. 'When we have more time, then.'

She screwed up her face. 'My view remains unaltered.'

Cal inwardly sighed. He wanted to believe it meant more. She'd willingly given him her virginity. He would have taken his time if he'd known, rather than behaving like an animal in rut. He wanted to make it good for her. He wanted her to experience what he had and to know that it was excellent.

'Should the chance arise, the offer is there. I want to show you how good it can be.' He angled a kiss, but she turned her head. He brushed her cheek instead. A single tear tracked its way down. 'Sibba? What is wrong? I never wanted to hurt you.'

'Night-time has ended. Don't make me want something I can't have.'

'The night might have passed, but we can enjoy each other. There is something between us. Lie to yourself if you want, but don't lie to me. I felt your body move against mine.'

She tucked her head into her neck so all he could see was the top of her head. 'We need to focus on freeing Rindr and her mother, instead of talking about such things.'

'We will free them.' He caught her hand and raised it to his lips. 'The two things are not mutually exclusive.'

Rather than answering, she pulled on the soft leather boots he'd discovered at the bottom of the trunk. 'Where is this stream? I need to freshen up, preferably before your men arrive.'

He tilted his head to one side. 'Shall I go with you?'

She reached for her knife. 'Daylight holds few terrors for me. I am perfectly capable of looking after myself. My aim rarely falters.'

He tried one last time. 'Don't you want someone to wash your back? I can be an excellent body servant.'

Her cheeks coloured, a deep rose. And he was struck how new she was to this. It was almost as if she refused to believe that a man might be interested in her in that way.

'Someone should stay here in case your men appear. If

they are not here by the time I return, we can discuss our next move.'

There was very little he could do to argue with her obstinancy. He had thought that making love would bring them closer, but a barrier had grown between them because of his ill-chosen words.

'Shout if you require anything.'

She briefly nodded. 'I will remember that.'

'If you are not back in a reasonable time, I will come and haul you out.'

She gave one of her smiles, the sort which lit up her being from within. Its existence gave him hope that he could find a way back to her. 'I never took you for an old woman.'

'And I never took you for being reckless beyond belief,' he said, smiling back at her. 'This island belongs to Thorkell and not to me.'

She sobered. 'I can look after myself.'

'I have already saved your life once in the last day. I don't want you to throw it away cheaply. Your men need you.'

'I've little intention of throwing my life away.' Her chin jutted forward. 'I've every intention of fulfilling my vow and avenging my father. Just because what happened between us happened, it doesn't give you the right to start worrying about me.'

He put his hands on his head. He would have worried about her if they had not become intimate, but he doubted she wanted to hear that. 'That came out wrong. I know you can look after yourself.'

'Apology accepted. And I do owe you a life debt.'

'Do you want to know where the stream is?'

She gave a half-smile. 'Yes. Best if you tell me the way, and then I won't get lost.'

'We wouldn't want that.'

She smiled and quickly kissed his cheek. The tiniest brush of lips, and he forced his hands to stay at his sides. He would take that kiss as a win. 'I can look after myself, Cal. I've no expectations that anyone else will. It is hard to change a habit of a lifetime.'

Rather than telling her how unbearably sad he found that statement, Cal explained how to find the small fishpond and watched her stride away. She moved with an awkward gait, favouring her right side.

'Are you sure you will be fine? Are you sure you remain uninjured?'

She made an annoyed noise in the back of her throat. 'Do you always worry so? I turned my ankle when we were walking to the hut.'

'You've hurt your leg. How bad is it? Is it something which will jeopardise our plan?'

Her eyes spit blue fire. 'You won't leave me behind that easily. I will be ready for anything Thorkell throws at us. My shooting arm remains fine.'

He blinked twice. Leave her behind? 'I wasn't intending on it. I was merely concerned when I saw your limp.'

'Your concern is misplaced.' She clomped away, sighing loudly about men and people who tried to cosset other people.

Cal pressed his lips together. *Stubborn* did not even begin to describe Sibba. And he wanted to put things right between them. He should never have let her out of his arms without kissing her awake.

Too late for regrets. Brigid had often accused him of having far too many. Somehow, he would find a way to show Sibba that they could be good together for however long that lasted. The way his growing feeling for her made him feel alive instead sleepwalking through his existence scared him. He refused to become that vulnerable ever again.

'Men!'

Sibba took great pleasure in stomping down to the stream, while carefully avoiding putting much weight on her left ankle. The pain would wear off before the day was out, she was certain of it. Besides, the mission was far too important for Cal to worry that she would struggle to scamper any distance.

They had slept together. And suddenly he was concerned about her health or rather her fitness to be a warrior. As if, because he'd kissed her thoroughly, she could no longer nock an arrow or swing a sword.

It reminded her so much of her fiancé and how he thought he'd control her actions, telling her what to do and how to dress after kissing her twice. What was worse, some part of her had accepted that he had the right to. She'd gone out of her way to please him, only to discover that all he required was her father's felag.

'Never again,' she muttered, splashing into the cold stream, and starting to wash the salt from her body, ignoring that little voice which proclaimed Cal was different. He genuinely liked her.

After her fiancé's betrayal, she'd vowed that she'd never allow anyone to control her in that way again. And she hadn't. She had to remain true to her ideals and goals, which meant avenging her father's death, rather than being concerned about Cal's opinion.

Except she'd spent the night in Cal's arms, and all her dreams of being loved, cared for, and kept safe came rushing back. She wanted to stop making the hard decisions which made her head pound and her stomach twist in knots.

She wanted to dissolve into his kiss and see if the way her body felt was down to her need to get warm or because she had wanted to be with him. But he had not been there when she'd turned over.

She scrunched up her face and smiled. Dreams of a young woman, not a war leader. Her father had warned her that she could be one but not the other. 'Distractions diminish concentration, Sibba-girl.'

Maybe if she survived her vow...

She ducked her head in the water and washed the salt from it. Simple practical tasks which forced her to concentrate on something other than the way Cal's skin had tasted.

After washing, she sat beside the stream on a flat rock, carefully putting her hair into a tight braid. She flexed her left leg several times and decided she could put more weight on it than she had first believed.

She practiced walking slowly but steadily as she picked her way back to the hut.

'Here you are, my lord,' a voice she didn't recognise called out, right before she made it through the final screen of bushes. 'Did the woman from the North survive?'

'Where are my men?' Cal asked back. 'Do not deny that you have met them, Father, or how else will you have heard of Sibba Norrsdottar?'

'Is that her name? I had wondered. The Northmen who visit my village have spoken of little else in the last few weeks.'

Sibba forgot to breathe. Had Haakon's bribing of the soothsayer accomplished something? Haakon would be insufferable when he found out.

'My men?'

'Safe. Eating their breakfast, if I know Annis. She's the one who sent me to find you.'

'Did she, indeed? My late wife's third cousin can be a formidable force.'

Sibba's hand went to her knife. She crept as close as she dared.

A priest with his tonsured head and robes was clearly visible in the doorway. Two other men stood beside him with a third outside. They were clearly Gaels, but Sibba decided not to take any risks until she knew why they were searching for her.

'It is good of you to express concern for the woman. Sibba mistakenly believes that you, along with all other priests in the world, wish her harm,' Cal said.

'I am a man of peace.'

'Even peaceful men can become angry.'

'My Christian duty drew me here.' The priest raised his right hand. 'Your men begged me. "The Northern monsters are on patrol." So my three friends joined me to ensure my safety.'

'I appreciate it.' Cal came out of the hut. Sibba noticed that he was wearing a large sword. 'I've no quarrel with the people of Barra. My father and I offered sanctuary to any who wish it. The offer remains. The farming land is not as good as here, but there is peace.'

'We know,' one of the men answered. 'We are here to see the priest comes to no harm from any Northerner.'

Cal tilted his head to one side. 'When have I ever harmed a priest?'

The men shuffled their feet and mumbled something about his late wife which did not quite reach Sibba's ears.

'Brigid and our son are not the reason I'm here.'

'You travel with a woman warrior,' one said in a loud whisper. 'We wanted to see her. That is all.'

'And you wanted to see if it was true that a woman could

be a warrior and that my men were not pulling your leg.' Cal gave a short laugh. 'I can assure you it is true. She is every bit as skilled and accomplished as they say. She beat me in an archery match.'

Sibba straightened her back. Cal had mentioned her winning when most men would have remained silent. She silently blessed him for that.

The men muttered about the impossibility of anyone beating Cal.

'I ask again. Did the woman survive?' The priest folded his arms. 'It is all very well and good learning about her exploits. But if she is dead, she is no good to us.'

'Why do you need her?'

The priest went red to the top of his bald pate while the other three shuffled their feet. The boy's eyes went wide. Sibba reckoned he'd spotted her. She put a finger to his lips and winked. The boy's face lit up.

'It will be a real shame if she died, particularly as she might be coming to save us,' the boy said in a lisping voice.

The priest told the boy to stop speaking out of turn.

'He should speak more often,' Cal said with a faint smile. 'He speaks more sense than the rest of you. Sibba Norrsdottar might be able to save you in time, provided you decide to trust her.'

'You mean she will save us from all the Northmen? A mere woman?'

'Another rumour, son, that's all,' the burly farmer said. 'I should have known better than to let the priest fill your ears with old wives' tales.'

Cal inclined his head. 'I would not consider it beyond Sibba's capabilities, but these things take time. She can't plant her sword in the ground, causing Thorkell to vanish in a clap of thunder and a puff of smoke. That only works in stories told around the campfire.'

Sibba's mouth dropped open. She had travelled here to save Rindr and Nefja and any of Gettir's felag who might be alive and loyal to Gettir. Beyond that she had no interest in the people of this island. She was not planning on staying. A saviour was the last thing in the world she was. 'Cal, we mustn't get their hopes up.'

'Have you forgotten your skills at fighting?' Cal gave a soft laugh. 'Or are you too frightened of Thorkell's band to attempt an assault, even if you have the proper force behind you?'

'I'm not frightened of Thorkell,' she answered, standing up. 'Not in a fair contest or battle.'

The priest jumped and practically tripped on his cassock. The boy's face lit up like a thousand bright lamps, and he clapped his hands.

'A rumour arrived with Thorkell's request for the sheep and cow, nothing more,' the priest said, glaring at the boy who gave an impudent grin back. 'Thorkell is anxious to discover her, considers her dangerous.'

She tilted her head to one side. On the one hand, Haakon's soothsayer had come through, but Thorkell sensed danger. The exhilaration vanished from her body as quickly as it had arrived, leaving her with an overall sense of disappointment and missed chances. All Haakon had done was ensure every person on Barra knew she had a price on her head.

'If she is dangerous to him, she must be good for us, Pa,' the boy said. 'We should keep her safe, not deliver her to Thorkell. If this woman is indeed the person.'

'I can't fault your logic.' Cal inclined his head. 'Sibba can shoot arrows better than any man I have ever seen.

Her throwing arm is pretty good as well. And I can see the knife glinting in her hand. From this distance, I doubt she will miss.'

The priest gulped hard. 'I…I have come in peace.'

Cal tilted his head to one side. 'Seeking the warrior woman to do whatever dirty work you have in mind—is that the sort of peace you mean?'

'Just so, seeking her because I believe she comes to kill Thorkell,' the priest said, giving an unctuous smile. 'To give her help, like the boy says.'

Sibba exchanged glances with Cal. At his nod, she went over to the farmers and relieved them of their weapons. To her relief, they rapidly handed them over.

'Why are you doing this?' the boy asked.

'To be on the safe side,' she said hunkering down so her face was level with his. 'It can take some time to ensure a plan will work. No point in continuing with one that will fail.'

The boy nodded solemnly. He put his eating knife on the top of the pile.

'My men should be with you. Why did you come with these farmers and not them?' Cal said, after the boy returned to his father.

The priest tucked his hands into his robe. 'Your men are resting. Eating a hot meal. One of them confessed that he should have been here but thought the woman must have drowned.'

'And you decided to check.'

'I thought it best to travel here, rather than their taking the risk in broad daylight. Thorkell… Well, he sent a group of men to this man's farm this morning, and they were barely able to get the men hidden in time,' the priest said, rocking back on his heels. 'We didn't want to take any chances.'

'The priest tells the truth,' the boy said. 'You are kin on account of your late wife.'

'Because he is worried about the warrior woman succeeding?' Cal asked in a quiet voice, going over to the boy who shrank back against his father.

'Because he thinks Northern warriors will be coming soon. As my father said, if they are his enemies, we must consider them friends.'

Cal regarded him for a long moment. The sun was at his back, preventing her from being able to fully discern his mood. What did he want her to do? Vow to free this island? She had only come for Rindr and her mother. Her gut instinct told her to save lives, not take them. These people could prove useful.

Sibba slid her knife back into its sheath. 'Sometimes you have to trust priests to tell the truth rather than to mumble nonsense.'

'You seem certain about this, Sibba, and I will trust your instinct.'

'He came with two men and a boy who appear to be Gaels, not Northern. They offered up their weapons,' Sibba said in measured tones, silently offering prayers to any celestial being that she was right. 'I doubt any priest would make common cause with Thorkell. He has been known to shoot them full of arrows simply for sport, even if they deliver something he greatly desires.'

The priest ducked his head. 'He allows me to administer to my flock as long as I don't interfere.'

Sibba exchanged a glance with Cal. The priest was naive if he didn't think feeding the other men in the party was interference.

Cal nodded to her, went into the hut, and collected a few things. 'We should go. Every breath we take here, we risk discovery. But listen to what these men have to say about the fort and its defences.'

'I want to see it with my own eyes.' Sibba gritted her teeth. She had to find something she could use. There had to be a way of rescuing the women without simply attacking.

'We should go first to my house,' the burly farmer said. 'Reunite you with your men.'

Sibba frowned. 'I came to see the fort.'

Cal gave a half shrug. 'I want to see my men as soon as possible.'

'It could be a trap,' Sibba murmured in a low voice.

'If a trap is set, then we are in as much danger here as we are going with them.'

'You mentioned patrols have increased,' Sibba said, hooking her thumbs in her trousers' waistband to keep her hands from shaking as they picked their way along the winding track through some undergrowth. 'I wondered why.'

'On account of the wedding two days hence,' the boy called out. 'They want to make sure everything goes smoothly.'

His father nudged him in the side. 'And the warrior woman, don't forget. They are worried about her and her longship.'

'Do you really have a longship, my lady?' the boy asked, his face showing his wonderment. 'A really real one?'

'Thorkell said she had, and Calwar says as well,' his father said. 'Don't go disrespecting her none.'

Sibba climbed over a fallen log. What Haakon had done with bribing the soothsayer was a double-edged sword. There had to be a way of turning it to her advantage, but thus far she couldn't see how. 'I'm pleased to know my fame has preceded me. My ship remains in Suthereyjar for now.'

'Why?'

'This was supposed to be a quick reconnaissance mission, but I fear it will become something else if Thorkell thinks I am here. I've no wish to put you in danger.'

'How much gold has Thorkell offered, or has he merely put it out that he requires Sibba Norrsdottar?' Cal said abruptly, silencing the men. 'Whatever the price he has offered, we will meet it.'

'Don't you understand the immediacy of Thorkell's marriage changes everything?' Sibba broke in before the priest answered. 'What do people know about the wedding?'

'His latest bride and her mother arrived a few days ago,' the oldest farmer said. 'The gossip is that the bride's father died tragically at sea. He offered to provide them and the men who travelled with them safe harbour while they searched for whoever attacked them.'

Sibba noticed that Cal struggled to keep a straight face. There could be little need to search, given what Thorkell's men had done to Gettir's ships. But it confirmed that the other ships had survived in some fashion.

'Thorkell has two living wives already—one from the Black Pool in Eire and the other from the North. Interesting that he is adding a third,' Sibba said.

'When Thorkell met the woman, he fell instantly in love with her and knew that only a marriage would suffice,' another said. 'My wife thought it very romantic.'

Very romantic or very convenient? However, she couldn't judge Rindr too harshly. The alternative would have been death.

'Because only a marriage would satisfy the mother,' Cal said before Sibba could make a cynical remark.

The farmer scuffed his feet. 'You have already heard this

tale. Is that why you are here? Nothing to do with freeing us from the tyrant's yoke?'

Sibba swallowed hard. The way he said it made her ashamed not to have thought about the people inhabiting the island before now. All they were trying to do was scratch out a living, and they had to contend with this tyrant.

'There are a number of reasons we are here,' Cal said, shifting the swords to his other shoulder. 'These lands did belong to my wife's family. I would like to see them protected, if I can.'

'Is a large wedding planned?' Sibba asked, making her voice go all breathless.

'Large enough.' One of the farmers gestured with his hand. 'All the villages around here have been asked to supply at least one sheep and one cow for the festivities.'

'Quite the burden.'

'He will not look kindly on those who don't,' the farmer mumbled, shuffling his feet. 'We have all seen what happens to those who go against the great Thorkell.'

'Maybe…' the third farmer said and stopped. 'No, forget it.'

'If Thorkell discovers you even spoke to us, he will punish you,' Cal said. 'Is that what you are trying say? Thorkell will punish you because he can.'

'You had best throw your lot in with us,' Sibba said. 'We can protect you.'

The priest stopped. 'We'd like to believe that, my lady, truly.'

Sibba's heart sank. These were frightened people. And she also knew that they wanted to protect their families rather than help strangers or indeed rise against the sea wolves. And yet here they were, risking their lives to take them to Cal's men.

Cal put his hand on the boy's shoulder. 'And you stumbled across my men while out searching for this cow you intend to sacrifice to Thorkell? Decided to help them out of the goodness of your hearts?'

The farmer swore as he stubbed his toe against a tree-root. Everyone halted. Sibba picked up a fallen branch and handed it to him. 'Easier to have something to lean on.'

Cal put up his hand, and everyone fell silent. In the near distance were hoof-beats.

'In the brush, quickly.'

Sibba followed Cal. 'What is going on?'

'Visitors.'

'I will go back and watch,' the boy volunteered and ran off.

'Headstrong, that lad. But he hates the Northmen.' The farmer gave a wry smile. 'Present company excepted, my lady. He has taken a shine to you.'

'I will try to be worthy of his regard,' Sibba whispered back.

'I do believe you will be.'

She noticed Cal was smiling at her. 'What?'

'Sometimes you are a kind person, Sibba.'

She put a finger to her lips. 'Don't tell the other captains or they will stop listening to me.'

'I'll remember that.'

They lay there, shoulders barely touching and breathing as quietly as possible. Sibba prayed that they might have a modicum of luck.

Finally, the boy returned and said that the patrol had gone another way, off towards the farm by the hanging rock. They started off again.

The priest rubbed the back of his neck as he walked alongside Sibba and Cal. 'You summed it up quite accurately earlier, particularly after we heard of this warrior woman.'

'You're leading us to them,' Cal said with a grim smile. 'I want to see they are unharmed.'

The oldest farmer shuffled his feet. 'Not so sure it would be wise, Lord Calwar. Thorkell really wants his livestock. Maybe we should take the cow and sheep and then take you to your men. You can see the fortress and know it would be impossible to attack.'

'Did you just disrespect me or my father?'

The men blanched and shook their heads. The young boy kept muttering about the time and that the cow and sheep needed to be there.

Sibba cleared her throat, and they all turned to look at her. She made her smile as sweet as possible. 'We need to stop the wedding. Everything hinges on us preventing that wedding. When do the livestock need to be there? A few days' time?'

The oldest farmer gave an indulgent smile. 'It would appear the woman in question is intent on it. If it puts Thorkell in a good mood for a little while, where is the harm in it?'

'What is it to us if it happens?' the boy asked, cocking his head to one side.

'Thorkell may be harsh, but as long as you obey his commands, we are allowed to live in peace,' the priest said. 'We have spoken of this in the past.'

Sibba rolled her eyes. Living in peace? Barely living, and she knew what would be happening to the islanders and how Thorkell and his men would be using them as a living larder when they required slaves for the eastern and northern slave markets. Human beings were one thing her father had always refused to traffic in.

'Rindr and her mother will do what they must to stay

alive, including arranging some sort of advantageous marriage to Thorkell. They are born survivors,' she said rather than commenting on the naivety of the priest and farmers. The rapacious Thorkell was never going to be satisfied with merely the odd cow or sheep.

'We don't even know if it is Rindr and her mother,' Cal reminded her in an undertone.

'Priest, does anyone know what the bride looks like?' Sibba asked.

'Blonde and pretty. Violet eyes. I forget her name.' The priest smiled. 'If I ever heard it. But everyone has spoken of her wondrous beauty.'

Sibba schooled her features and concentrated on the farmstead on the horizon where the boy said they were headed. Once the marriage was consummated, Rindr could require all the remaining captains and ships to swear an oath to her new husband. It would mean Thorkell's power in the region would be practically unstoppable. She jogged ahead until she reached where Cal walked with the oldest farmer.

'We must find a way to get into the fort before the wedding,' she said quietly. 'It is our only hope for rescuing Rindr and ensuring peace in these waters.'

'How are we going to let your small fleet know about the alterations?' Cal began ticking off his points on his fingers and she knew he had not understood what was about to happen.

She gestured to the others and waited until they all had arrived.

'We simply don't have time. The Gaels have certain customs, but Northmen have different ones.' She rapidly explained the situation in stark terms and why the marriage should matter to the priest and the farmers.

Cal's jaw's clenched, and she knew he had realised the enormity of the problem. The other men watched her with wide eyes and open mouths.

'We can't have that,' the priest whispered. 'They'll never leave this island.'

'What do you suggest?' Cal asked quietly.

'We use these farmers and their gifts of cows and sheep to get us into the fort.' Sibba paused. 'If they would be willing...'

'All of us? You have a look of the North about you, even if we put you in Gaelic clothing. They are looking for a woman warrior,' Cal reminded her.

'Your men need to make the boat ready as well as sabotage the other boats. We can get Rindr and her mother away without too much bloodshed. They'll trust me.'

Cal's brow lowered. Sibba's heart sank. 'You're intending on storming the stronghold. You promised me that this was a reconnaissance mission only. We lack the men.'

She forced her neck to relax. 'I need to be there, inside the fort. I can get those remaining warriors who are loyal to Gettir's memory on our side. In and out.'

He raised a brow. 'In and out is impossible. I was going to show you this. How are you planning to get in?'

'The priest and his men will offer me up. They discovered me and thought to bring me to his lair.' She balanced on her toes, waiting for him to understand what she was saying. In her opinion the risk was worth the reward.

'Offer you up?'

'I'll be their prisoner,' Sibba said, thinking quickly. The plan she longed for started to form in her head. Simple but effective. 'Saves having to find me clothes.'

'What will I be doing?'

Sibba smiled. 'You will be taking in the cow and sheep. No one will notice until too late.'

'But if you are a prisoner, how are you going to free the others?'

Sibba lifted her chin. 'With a little help from the priest.'

Cal watched her with narrowed eyes. 'I see. You have already decided how it will go. No consultation, no asking someone else's opinion.'

Sibba was aware that the priest and the others watched them with interested expressions. The last thing she wanted was a fight with Cal, but if he thought she would become a delicate flower after lying in his arms, he was sorely mistaken.

'It is our best chance, Cal. Thorkell likes to think he is the big man. Once they have me, their guard will be down. You can slip in and create a diversion while I get Rindr and her mother out.'

A muscle jumped in his jaw. 'Before you start developing this foolhardy scheme further, we need to get my men. They must have a say in this.'

'They are at the farmhouse. We can go there if we must.' Sibba crossed her arms. She hoped Cal wasn't going to be difficult about this. He had to see sense, and she refused to have a blazing row in front of bystanders about what she could and could not do. They might have slept together, but it did not give him the right to dictate her movements or the risks she was prepared to take.

He reached out and grabbed her elbow. 'You will do as I say.'

She pointedly looked at his fingers. He released her. She rapidly created space between them. 'I will do what is best for the felag. I trust you understand the difference.'

Cal watched her from under knitted brows. 'Agreed. What is best for our fellowship.'

'Was that so difficult?'

Chapter Ten

Sibba concentrated on keeping light conversation with the boy and his uncle instead of nursing her anger at Cal's obstinancy and his insistence that he knew the best way forward. Simply looking at the fort would achieve less than nothing. Thorkell had to be confronted, even if it was the last thing she desired.

She should have known that Cal was only paying lip service to her ability to lead. Yes, it would be a risk to go into Thorkell's lair as herself, but it had to be done. That marriage had to be prevented, or Thorkell's power would increase to the point that he could attack Suthereyjar. They had to act while they still had the time.

The lad's steady stream of questions about where she'd been and the battles she had taken part in provided some respite for her busy mind. Sibba answered as truthfully as she could, trying not to embellish what she had done, but the boy became more and more awestruck, asking her repeatedly about the emperor's court, what it was like to see the great church of Hagia Sophia, and what it felt like to liberate captive women. She made certain her voice carried when she explained how she'd rescued various women in Constantinople.

Cal's only response to her words was to kick a stone hard and send it skittering down a slope.

'Are you planning on rescuing anyone on this island?'

Cal's shoulders tightened, and Sibba knew he was listening intently. She put a hand on the lad's shoulder. 'It depends on the circumstances, but I am resolved to do what is necessary to avenge my former leader.'

'We will speak of this later, Sibba,' Cal said. 'We are nearly at the farmhouse.'

Sibba fluttered her lashes. 'I've no wish to give secrets away.'

The instant they set foot in the yard, the buxom farmer's wife rushed from the house. She threw her arms about the boy and hugged him. 'I've been so worried.'

He scrunched up his face and complained about being nearly a grown man and off on an important mission. Sibba exchanged a look with Cal which made her feel as if they could work together. A tiny bubble of hope grew in her breast.

'Were they here?' Cal asked, banging his fists together. 'Quickly now, Annis. Are my men safe?'

The woman's eyes widened when she spotted Cal, and she made a low curtsy. 'Thorkell's bullies left a little while ago, Lord Calwar.'

'Empty-handed, I presume.'

'Your men are in the hayloft.' Annis gestured to the far barn. 'You can trust me, lord. You know that. We're distant kin through Brigid.'

Cal inclined his head. 'I'm grateful. I hold your trust in high esteem. And I've no wish to visit trouble on you.'

Annis put a hand on her ample chest. 'Is this the warrior woman they spoke of? The one who must not reach the fort?'

The boy broke in, chattering about how Sibba had travelled the oceans and had been to Constantinople.

'You appear to have made a conquest, Sibba,' Cal said under his breath.

'Merely tried to make the journey go more quickly.' Sibba pasted a smile on her face. Her stomach gave a loud rumble.

'You must be famished,' Annis said. 'Come in and have some pottage.'

'I should go with Cal and see how the men are doing,' Sibba protested. 'Cal is as hungry as I am.'

'Lord Calwar is perfectly capable of doing that on his own.' Annis made a clicking noise in the back of her throat. 'Besides, I dare say he is used to going without a meal or three whereas you look in need of one. The men were certain you wouldn't survive your time in the sea.'

She looked starved and half-drowned. Was that what Annis meant? Was it any wonder Cal had not tried to kiss her this morning? Sibba gritted her teeth. She'd set the rules, knowing it might happen, but he could have ignored them. She had to stop her heart from building dreams, but it failed to listen.

'I can wait until Cal is ready,' she said, pasting another smile on her face. 'I would hardly want you to go to more trouble than necessary.'

Annis's smile trembled, turning wary. Sibba winced. Without meaning to, she had abused some unwritten law of hospitality.

'He may take a long time. The food is ready now,' Annis said with a frown.

Cal inclined his head. 'I will be in shortly. You'd hardly want to give offence by not accepting hospitality, now, would you, Sibba?'

Sibba regarded a stray pebble. Cal had very neatly ensured that she occupied a lesser role. She needed to discover a way to reassert her authority. Her stomach gave a loud grumble before she'd figured out the correct words. 'Forgive me. I would be happy to accept your kind offer. I find I have started to salivate at the scent of delicious food on the breeze.'

The full force of Annis's smile returned. 'Excellent.'

Turning her back on Cal, Sibba followed Annis into the neat farmhouse. A loom stood in one corner, and a pot of pottage steamed over the embers of the fire. Two little girls were involved in carding wool and looked up with big eyes when Sibba entered.

'We must get you into more comfortable clothes,' Annis said after ladling out a portion of the delicious-smelling pottage. 'Wearing trousers must be cumbersome.'

'I'm used to my clothes. Besides, I doubt anyone would take me for Gael.'

Annis tilted her head to one side. 'You do have the look of the North about you, what with those fine bones and deep blue eyes. And your hair. Can you really lead men?'

Sibba concentrated on a knot-hole in the table. 'I shall take that as a compliment. Yes, I can and do lead men.'

'It was meant as one.' Annis pushed the trencher of pottage towards Sibba before sitting down heavily on the bench. 'It is good to see Lord Calwar looking happy.'

Sibba pushed the pottage around with her spoon. 'He appeared distinctly put out, to my mind.'

'You don't know him as well as I do.' Annis patted Sibba's arm. 'He has had a lot of sorrow in his life.'

'I doubt I have anything to do with his improvement. Time has a way of healing grief.'

'True, but his wife led him a merry dance.' Annis sighed.

'Brigid was a hard woman to like, even if we were kin. Always boasting and blowing her own horn, but my goodness, she was beautiful. As if all the saints and angels had combined to create the most perfect-looking woman.'

Sibba tried to quell the sudden butterflies in her stomach. It followed that Cal's wife had been a beauty and more than likely a paragon of womanly virtue. Everything Sibba was not. And what had passed between them last night belonged in the past. It had been the meeting of two bodies, nothing more, nothing less, even though her heart kept whispering *Maybe*. 'He does not speak of her.'

Annis ladled another spoonful of pottage into Sibba's bowl. 'I have eyes in my head. I saw the looks which passed between the pair of you just then.'

'More like looks of exasperation and frustration combined with hunger than a burgeoning romance.' Sibba dipped her spoon in and rapidly ate up the pottage. 'Delicious and nourishing.'

She hoped it would suffice to alter the subject away from the potentially tricky shoals of Cal and their unusual relationship. What had passed between them last night had been only to keep them both alive. She hated how her mind screamed *Liar*.

Annis covered Sibba's hand with hers. 'I never liked her, you see, not since she played a horrible trick getting some wool tangled and blaming my sister. She might have been all beauty on the outside, but something which delighted in cruelty lurked on the inside. I suspect Lord Calwar knows about it and all.'

'She used to play tricks?'

'Not all the time. Sometimes. Like the waxing and waning of the moon. She would get this fiery look in her eye and do the oddest things. And then sometimes she'd sit in a corner glowering and hardly speak. Touched by fairies, some called it.'

Sibba had known several people like that when she was growing up. 'Never easy for anyone.'

'I thought it must be hard to be married to a woman like that. Some whispered that it was all her fault Thorkell came, that the rumours of her beauty first alerted Thorkell to the island fortress.'

'I understood it was the brother who was more interested in gold than his people,' Sibba said firmly. 'It is not always the women at fault, even though they suffer the most.'

'True enough, but she was safe in Suthereyjar, guarding that banner of hers, the one all the men around here pledged to follow.'

Sibba remembered the banner she'd seen hidden in the trunk. 'But what good would it have done?'

'Thorkell would have had them all killed before they reached the fortress. That banner possessed no magical properties, I'm sure of it. I bless the fact that cooler heads prevailed.' Annis shrugged. 'Lord Calwar seems more relaxed now. The wariness has gone from his eyes. That's all I wanted to say, not blathering on about silly pieces of cloth.'

Sibba pushed the now-empty bowl away. 'If that is Cal being relaxed, I would hate to see him tense. And he does care about the people under him. Deeply.'

Annis cocked her head and fluffed out her skirts. 'The menfolk are returning. We can speak later...after they've gone, if you wish to know more about her.'

'I'm going with them. I want to see the fortress in the harbour for myself.'

'You don't want to go there, my lady. No Gaelic woman does. They only go if they are forced to...and they rarely return.'

Sibba balled her fists and forced a calming breath. 'As the leader of this expedition, I must go wherever is necessary, regardless of the danger.'

'You must go where?' Cal said, striding into the room. His eyes did hold a bit more warmth, and the planes of his face did seem harsh.

Sibba shook her head. Thoughts like that would lead to moonstruck madness, a state she wanted to avoid but one which she feared that she'd already tumbled into.

'To Thorkell's fort.'

'If you do, you will be captured.' Annis sat down with a large thump. 'They desperately seek a woman warrior.'

Sibba lifted a brow. 'I know.'

'Sibba will not be doing anything foolhardy,' Cal said.

'Tell her, Lord Calwar. She will die if she goes there unprotected.'

'Cal is not from the North. None of the surviving Northmen will follow him. Nor will the bride believe him.'

Annis crossed her arms over her ample bosom. 'Why will she believe you?'

'I like to think she trusts me. Gettir's men know the favourable position I once held. I have the brooches of the other captains to prove I speak for them.' She put a hand on her hip. Her mind raced with possibilities as her plan started to crystallise. Risky, but it was their best and only option if she could convince Cal.

'Can we speak alone, Sibba?' Cal asked. His tone showed it was not a polite request, and he stalked out.

Sibba waited several breaths before nodding towards Annis. 'Thank you for the meal and the hospitality. You changed my outlook completely.'

Annis touched her elbow and bent her head towards

Sibba's ear. 'I always find my husband gets gruff when he is worried about me.'

'I'll bear that in mind, should I ever have a husband.'

Cal clung onto the few remaining shards of his temper until they reached the solitude of the haying barn. He'd hoped the walk to the farmhouse and then conversation with the farmer's wife would have put all notions of Sibba travelling to Thorkell's fort out of her head. It was beyond dangerous for her, now that Thorkell's men were actively searching for a woman warrior. The tyrant didn't want to sit down and have a cup of ale with her; he wanted her dead.

He breathed in, taking in the warm, dry new hay and the dust of the old. The normally calming scent just increased his annoyance. He wanted Sibba alive, and to do that he had to take charge of the operation.

'What are you playing at, Sibba? Why is it important for those people to think you are some sort of hero?'

She fluttered her lashes at him. 'Am I responsible for other people's thoughts?'

'All you are going to do is get yourself killed and everyone else along with you. Dead heroes serve little purpose.'

'What happened to your wife's banner?'

Cold sweat broke out on the back of his neck. 'What do you know about that?'

'That it exists and that the time has not yet come to unfurl it. One day maybe, but not yet, according to Annis.' She paused. 'It is why you returned to Barra with that trunk.'

'I reached the shoreline and knew asking my men to sacrifice their lives for Brigid's dreams of glory was impossible. But I did as I promised. I took it to Barra.' His mouth twisted. 'My wife failed to see things that way. She failed to understand how the islanders blamed her family for the misery.'

'What did she do?'

'She snatched our son from his cradle and ran to cliff, shouting that I didn't deserve a child. Shouting that her son had a coward for a father.'

Sibba hated the way her heart pounded. She knew Cal's reputation and how he'd fought off the Northmen and ensured Suthereyjar remained independent. 'The last thing you are is a coward.'

'I thought the fairies finally had her—first the quiver full of arrows to make Thorkell a pincushion, and then this. Brigid didn't mean to put our son in danger. She adored him. It was all for show.'

'Except…' she prompted him.

Cal closed his eyes, and the scene which regularly haunted his dreams rose in front of him: his wife balanced on the rock, their son held over her head, crying as he attempted to speak slowly and gently to her. The waves roaring. The sudden crack as the great boulder shifted. She took a step to steady herself, but her foot missed, and the boulder tumbled down.

'I clambered down, hoping for a miracle,' he finished. 'But all she could say was that she had loved me once.'

He kept silent about how she took a large part of him with her and how he'd felt like he was a dead man, watching the waves lap at her and their son. He'd carried them both up on his own, knowing he'd failed her, but he also knew the impossibility of her demands.

Rather than recoiling in horror, Sibba gathered his cold hands in hers. 'I'm not asking you to be anyone, Cal. I want you to be there to support me if I require it, that's all.'

He stared up at the rafters and choked the relief down.

She understood that he had tried. It meant more than he thought it would. 'And the banner?'

'Let's keep to the task at hand.'

He breathed easier. 'I want to keep these people alive, not sacrifice them to make a point.'

She held out her hands. 'I'm trying to get us in to see Thorkell, and more importantly to rescue Rindr and Nefja before either of them is forced to marry. If that happens, Thorkell will be able to command the felag's complete loyalty.'

He stopped breathing. 'Even yours?'

She drew in her breath. 'I would be given leave to go, but I doubt I would last long. Thorkell would have me declared a wolf's head to be killed on sight. Trust me when I say I'll act to keep people safe, but the best way to do that is ensure Thorkell no longer leads that felag.'

Cal clenched his fists. Sibba was being overly reckless. She seemed to have no comprehension about the danger and, worse, no fear. 'Thorkell tricked my wife's family.'

She rocked back on her heels and studied him under her lashes. 'Even Thorkell will be wary of breaking these particular rules.'

'He will kill you before he allows you near those women.'

She rolled her eyes. 'He won't. He needs me to ensure obedience from the other captains. They will take it amiss if I fail to return or if I am harmed.'

Cal sighed and ran a hand through his hair. He hated that he had started to care for the woman when she seemed intent on throwing her life away. He had just started to feel alive again. The mere fact that he cared about what happened to her frightened him. He tried to tell himself that it was same sense of responsibility that he'd feel for any of his men, but he knew he felt more for her.

'What makes you think so?' he choked out rather than admitting anything.

'After the ceremony, Thorkell will request all the surviving captains swear an oath of loyalty to Rindr and then to himself. I'm one of them. I hold three other badges and speak for those men too.' She put her hands on her hips and stood with her legs slightly apart as if she was on-board ship. 'Why do I have to keep on proving my worth to you?'

'Is that what you are trying to do? Prove your worth?'

'I want to ensure the safety of the men under my command. Lagging behind or, worse, not going would mean me shirking. I've never shirked anything, and I don't intend to start simply because of what we shared last night.'

'You have it all wrong.'

'No, you do.' She put out her hand. Her bow-shaped mouth trembled slightly. 'Annis told me about your wife. That she used to take crazy chances and demand the impossible. I am not Brigid. Help me or step out of my way. That is all I ask as your commander. You gave me command.'

All the anger and frustration drained out of Cal. He put his hands on her shoulders. 'No one, least of all me, doubts your bravery, Sibba. But what is to stop Thorkell from murdering you after the oath, if it gets that far?'

She gave a smile which made his heart go tight. 'You.'

'I don't follow.'

'These men, these farmers will fight if they think someone will lead them. I want you to be that someone. You need to get into the fort while I make the diversion.'

Sibba rapidly explained her plan and how she'd altered it after speaking to the lad and his mother. Cal listened and had to admit that if viewed objectively it did have merit, but the person in the greatest jeopardy was Sibba. His heart kept screaming that he should be keeping her safe, rather than letting her take unnecessary risks.

'Are you saying that I saved your life only to allow you to throw it away?'

'Would you be saying that if I was a man?' She banged her fists together. 'Think of me as one. I…I order you to.'

'Would I be doing this if you were a man?' he asked softly.

He lowered his mouth to hers and deliberately drank. Their tongues tangled. He laced his hands into her braid and worked it free. Her hair tumbled like liquid red-gold all about her shoulders.

He backed her up against the wall, but she put her hands against his chest. Her eyes were luminous. 'Why are you doing this?'

'I want you, Sibba, because you are a woman. I think you want me as well.'

She looked at him with her eyes wide, and he saw how innocent she was in the ways of men. 'Why did you kiss me?'

'Because you refuse to listen, I must show you.'

He trailed his lips down her throat and palmed her breast and teased the nipple until it became a hardened point.

He lifted his head and deliberately took a step backwards. Her chest heaved, and her hand tentatively explored her mouth. With her hair tumbling about her shoulders, free from its braid, and her mouth a delectable rose, she looked incredibly desirable. The fire deep within him became a raging inferno which he could barely contain.

'Would I have done that if you were a man, Sibba?' he asked, struggling to regain control of his body. 'I know you are a woman, and I want to be inside you. I don't want to be looking at your corpse, because I like you alive. Allow me to be the one who challenges Thorkell. I am the stronger swordsman.'

She watched him with wide eyes and a passion-kissed mouth. 'Unfair. What is between us has nothing to do with the duty in front of us.'

A bubble of pleasure burst inside him. She wasn't immune to him. She wanted whatever existed between them to be more than that one night. The knowledge made him far happier than he'd been in months, but he also understood what she was saying: she refused to allow that desire to distract her. 'It nearly worked.'

She scrunched up her nose. '*Nearly* doesn't count.'

He laughed and pushed a strand of hair from her forehead. 'I want to keep you safe. You want to run towards danger. What am I to do?'

'Run towards it as well,' she said in a low voice.

'You leave me with no other choice,' he said, hoping it was the truth.

She assessed him for a long time under her lashes, and he wondered if he had revealed more than he had intended. 'You would have unfurled that banner if you thought you had any chance. It wasn't your fault. None of it was.'

'I know that now,' he whispered. The final bit of that cold, hard place in his heart melted. Sibba understood.

'You see? Not a coward.'

He frowned. Had she guessed how much he cared for her because she was Sibba? Or was it simply that she thought he cared because they were on this mission together? He didn't know, and that bothered him. 'What are you saying?'

'Do not ask me to stop protecting vulnerable people when you would do the same.'

'I do what is expected of me.'

'You must do more.' She hunkered down in the dirt

and drew a diagram with her finger. 'I'm trusting you to be there, ready to follow my lead. If I can get you and our men in, we can get Rindr and the others out. You can take them safely back to Suthereyjar while I keep Thorkell completely occupied. I have cursed loud and long that Haakon hired that soothsayer.'

'What did Haakon have to do with that?'

Sibba rapidly explained about the soothsayer and how she had decided to use it as their way in. 'Haakon will be insufferable, but his luck is just like that.'

He noticed that she did not mention getting back alive herself. He knew in that heartbeat that he wanted her to. He refused to allow her to throw her life away, not when he had just found her, but he couldn't stop her. He wanted her to be Sibba, not some other woman. A lump developed in his throat, and he swallowed hard.

'How do you know he will let you see them?' he asked quietly.

She sat back on her haunches, and her eyes danced. 'My father told me a long time ago that Thorkell fears being humiliated in front of his men. He fears being shown to be the little man. He can't afford to put me to death without speaking to me.'

'Your plan is…' he started and then stopped, watching her face start to fall. He knew he couldn't do that to her. And she was right: her scheme did make some sense. 'Your plan has some merits.'

'It is our best chance of stopping this marriage.' She bit her bottom lip. 'Our only chance to get everyone in that compound.'

'And if something happens to you?' he asked quietly.

'I can look after myself. I simply need you in the crowd and ready to act when I ask it of you. Can you do that?'

'I would fight Thorkell for you.'

She ducked her head, and he knew the part of her plan she'd kept hidden from him: challenging Thorkell for the leadership of the felag. A fight to the death. Thorkell possessed a formidable reputation as a dirty fighter. Sibba did not stand a chance, but he knew he wanted to give her one. 'I can do my own fighting, but thank you for the thought.'

'I am serious. If you or Thorkell requires it, I would be honoured to be your champion.' He tilted her chin upwards so that she had to look him in the eyes. 'You must be the bravest woman I know, but don't be too proud to accept help.'

She put a hand on his cheek. 'I will take that as a compliment.'

He turned his face into her palm. 'I can't stop you, Sibba, even if I think it might be a mistake. You made that clear. Therefore, I want to be there for you.'

She twined her arms about his neck. 'When you have to cross that bridge, I will inform you. Now, kiss me like you mean it.'

He lowered his head and obliged, drinking deeply and silently promising he'd do everything in his power to keep her safe. She was starting to become beyond necessary to him, and that frightened him half to death. 'Sibba, if it wasn't my fault that my wife died, then it wasn't your fault your father perished.'

'Kiss me one more time, Cal. That's all I ask.'

Chapter Eleven

'This is it?'

'Aye, my lady, the stronghold.'

The sheer rock cliffs with an imposing wooden palisade loomed above Sibba sitting at one end of the rowboat. The steel grey sky with its heavy rain clouds reflected her sombre mood. Cal had been right: this fortress could withstand most attacks. However, her approach was different, and thus far, she and the farmer along with his lad had not been stopped or questioned, merely waved through.

It took all of her willpower not to turn and look back at the other boat, the one which contained Cal, his men, and the cow to check on their progress. Her plan depended on Thorkell's men failing to connect the passengers in the two boats.

With any luck her distraction would mean they should be able to get into the stronghold with their weapons and free the captives. She had made Cal promise that he would see to the captives before he attempted to do anything about protecting her.

She didn't want to tell Cal, but she was pretty sure they would have to fight their way out, and she doubted she would survive. Instead, she had enjoyed his kisses and the feeling of his hands against her skin last night. Memories to last a lifetime, however short that was.

'Are you all right, my lady?' the farmer's boy asked. 'We can still turn back. Abandon this before anyone gets hurt.'

'Absolutely fine. No need to turn back.'

She pressed her hands against her eyes and forced the depressing thoughts of failure out of her brain. She would succeed because she had to. Too many people depended on her getting this right. She was the only one who could take a stand of this nature. Thorkell would have to listen and respond or be branded a coward for ever.

She concentrated on breathing steadily and going over the plan in her mind. The first part was to get in the fort while providing enough of a distraction while Cal and the others disembarked. Then she could consider how she was going to convince Rindr to stop the wedding. And if she couldn't do that, or the wedding had already taken place, she had the final option: challenging Thorkell to a fight to the death.

'Last few strokes, my lady,' the farmer said. Sweat poured from his face, and he kept tugging at his collar. Sibba gave him an encouraging smile. His lad gave one last tug of the oars, and the boat bumped the dock.

Several of Thorkell's minions were on the dock, searching each of the boats thoroughly.

'Should we make our presence known?' the farmer asked in a hoarse whisper. 'I've never been in a situation like this before.'

'Leave it to me. You can row away if you'd like. If anyone asks, I paid you good coin to row me out here. That is all you know.'

'All I know. Right. Hear that, lad? All we know.'

'Plenty good will come if I'm allowed to follow my scheme. Stick to the plan. Always.' Without waiting for an answer, she jumped onto the dock, removed her all-enveloping cloak, and cleared her throat.

No one paid her any mind; instead they appeared to be taking bets about the cow in Cal's boat.

'Take me to Rindr Gettirsdottar. I wish to speak with her and her mother. Be quick about it,' she said in a loud voice.

The men stopped what they were doing and nudged each other. Sibba forced her shoulders to remain steady. No worse than when she had blagged her way into the emperor's quarters in Constantinople. Except the stakes were higher than a dare from Haakon.

A burly warrior looked her up and down as if she was a piece of meat. 'Who are you?'

Sibba rolled her eyes. The man's belligerent attitude was precisely what she required to create a massive distraction and allow Cal and his men to get ashore unchallenged. 'Does it matter? I've asked to see Rindr Gettirsdottar.'

The man scratched his head. 'Are you allowed to?'

'Why else would I be here?'

More and more people started paying attention to their confrontation and ignoring Cal's difficulties with the cow. Her scheme was working better than she had hoped. Sometimes, one had to use bravado and walk in through the front door.

'Rindr Gettirsdottar is Thorkell's bride, isn't she?' she said in an even louder voice. 'I was given to understand she survived the attack which killed Gettir.'

The man scratched behind his ear. 'Yeah, you have that right. But who are you, and why are you dressed like that?'

'Sibba Norrsdottar. One of the last surviving members of Gettir's felag. I wish to speak to Rindr. I need to get my latest orders.'

The man frowned and quietly conferred with several

other warriors. Sibba crossed her arms and tapped her foot, hoping that she seemed annoyed and impatient while her entire being felt alive.

'You wish to see Thorkell?' the man finally asked. 'Because if you are the warrior woman who the soothsayer said would be responsible for his death when she read the last runes, it might not end well for you.'

'My guess is she is some sort of joke Thorkell has sent to test us,' another said.

'Yes, what warrior would be that bold simply to come here like that?' a third man said and beckoned to other warriors, asking them if they wanted to bet on what this was.

'Unless she believes the soothsayer?'

The first man scratched his head. 'Soothsayers have a way of saying things so they turn out to be correct whatever happens. Very slippery characters. Might be Thorkell's idea of a little joke.'

'I can assure you I'm no joke,' Sibba said. 'And I believe Thorkell is expecting me.'

'You can never tell with soothsayers. I've heard tales about skulls hiding snakes which years later cause difficulties.'

'Will you allow me to see Rindr? She'll want to see me. It is vital that she has someone from her father's felag supporting her at the ceremony, particularly someone who holds pledges from the surviving captains.' Sibba patted her pouch and allowed the brooches the other captains had gifted her to jangle. 'Thorkell will want the swearing of oaths done properly when the time comes during the ceremony.'

The man shook his head. 'Never heard of you. Take my advice. Go away from here, and stop wasting my time. Tell Four Fingers to stop testing us. A woman like you could not be a great warrior in any case. You're far too pretty.'

'A back-handed compliment. Shall I show what I am capable of?'

He scratched his head again. 'Would a true warrior be so reckless as to walk in here knowing there is a price on his head?'

'Her head.'

'I don't follow.'

'I'm the only person on this island aside from Thorkell who commands a felag. Allow me to speak with Rindr, and we can sort this confusion out.'

As she hoped, the other warriors had started to gather around, wanting to know what the hold-up was. Two boats scraped on the dock behind her, and the cow started moo-ing plaintively.

Sibba positioned herself between Thorkell's warrior and Cal. 'Are you going to escort me there or not? That man in the rowing boat told me that Thorkell wished to speak to me. I came. Ready to speak with him—if he is not a coward.'

'Thorkell is no coward.'

'Glad to hear it. I understand he has a habit of avoiding challenges and hanging back when his ships go into battle.'

'Thorkell has proved his worth.' One of the men gestured to the fort. 'All this belongs to him now.'

'All I know are the rumours I've heard.'

The first speaker scrunched up his face. 'How do I know you are who you say you are?'

'Take me to Rindr Gettirsdottar. She will vouch for me.'

'Rindr is in seclusion before the next part of the marriage ceremony,' a warrior said, pushing forward and elbowing the others out of the way. His eyes widened. He made a faint noise in the back of his throat. 'You should not be here, Sibba. Not after what happened to your father. Let it go.'

Sibba stared up at the newly arrived warrior with the heavily tattooed face. Rekkr the Homeless had been in her father's felag. It was intriguing that he had washed up here, as she had always thought him loyal to her father. 'Why not?'

Even Rekkr's tattoos showed his concern for her safety. Sweet but unnecessary. He placed a heavy hand on her shoulder.

'You've no hope of altering things, little one. Your brother should not have sent you here. I'll figure out a way to get you out. Like I used to when you were a child.'

She clenched her teeth and held back the cry that she was a woman grown. Rekkr had departed in the night along with six other men before she won her place, back when everyone had thought it would be Haakon. Back when men were vanishing in the night. She had warned Haakon that warriors had gone because of their instinctive distrust of his ability, and he'd refused to see the problem. The overnight loss of seven warriors had led to her challenge.

'But you'll vouch for me being who I say I am,' she said rather than launching into an explanation.

'Aye, if I must.'

'You must, Rekkr. For my father's sake. He commanded your loyalty once, and you served him well.'

Rekkr placed a heavy hand on her shoulder. 'This woman is no trick of Thorkell's. She can fight. Gettir would have been pleased to have her in his felag. Anyone would.' He lowered his voice. 'Is that what you wanted me to say, lass?'

'It will do.'

Several of the men crowded about, clapping Rekkr on the back and asking if this was the warrior woman he had held in such regard back in Constantinople. Rekkr confirmed it was and that she had managed to shoot several of the roughnecks employed by the Byzantium merchant who'd been intent on robbing them. And how he owed her a life debt.

Sibba batted her lashes and pretended modesty at the exploits. Out of the corner of her eye she spotted Cal and his men moving the very reluctant cow up the ramp unimpeded. Stage one and a bit completed. They'd managed to offload their weapons without being searched. The muscles in her neck relaxed. On to the next and potentially more difficult part: getting Thorkell to accept her challenge.

The first man came forward and roughly grabbed her arm. 'Right you are. Off to Thorkell. That golden reward is mine.'

Rekkr pulled an axe from his belt. 'You were about to let her go. Let her go now and back away slowly, or face the consequences.'

'What are you saying?'

'I claim the honour of taking her to Thorkell,' Rekkr said. 'I'm the one who recognised her.'

'I spoke to her first,' the first man said.

Rekkr's knife came up swiftly and caught the man under the chin. 'Do you really want to try?'

The colour drained from the man's face. 'I know your reputation, Rekkr. I know about the men you command. I know about your skill at throwing knives.'

'And I know Sibba's worth. I'll be the one to take her, for her father's sake.'

The man took two steps backward. 'If it is that important to you...'

'It is. And I claim it in lieu of the gold you owe me from our last game of dice.'

'I merely want to know that Rindr is alive and keen for this marriage to happen, Rekkr,' she said when she judged that Cal and his men had disappeared into the throng. She shuffled her feet to make it appear that she was uncomfortable under the lavish praise. 'Haakon and I now belong to Gettir's old felag. I heard a rumour that she is here. I want to know what she wants.'

'You do? I hadn't realised.' Rekkr ran a hand through his hair, making it stand on end. 'Thorkell said that there was a woman warrior, and that a soothsayer had travelled a great distance and warned him about her. He took the warning to heart, particularly after he defeated Gettir like she predicted. But I hadn't considered it would be you. No good can come of this, Sibba. You were foolish to come here—and in this manner. I'd have got you out, but everyone saw the manner of your arrival. Why did you and Haakon always have to be showy?'

Sibba clung on to her temper. 'I came in peace and without weapons. I came because I care about Rindr and want to show she is supported.'

'Do you think Thorkell will care about that? He'll only see that you are a warrior, perhaps the one who is destined to kill him in battle. You'll be dead before nightfall or a wolf's head.'

The back of her neck crept. Rekkr had confirmed what the priest's rumour implied: Thorkell had ordered her death. Perhaps she should have taken the coward's way and hightailed it back to Constantinople and safety when her father died. It was too late for regrets. She'd set her course. Cal and his men depended on her getting this right and creating a diversion in the main hall, which would leave the men loyal to Gettir unattended. She had to enable the rescue to happen. 'I oversee the last of my father's boats. I won my place, Rekkr—fair and square. Currently I pledge my loyalty and that of the felag to Gettir, and that means to his daughter Rindr, who can be every bit as formidable.'

A slight exaggeration, as she doubted Rindr could fight her way out of a cloth sack, but it would serve.

'You are in charge? Not Haakon?'

'Won fairly and properly. Currently I speak for the other boats, the ones which remain free.'

The man gulped and examined the dock for a long time.

'If I'd known, I might have stayed. We all might have,' he said slowly. 'You had a better understanding of the men than your brother. Your brother could never even remember the names of the women he'd bedded two weeks ago.'

She inclined her head. Unexpected, and maybe something she could build on. Any ally right now was bound to assist. 'Thank you for that.'

'Will you be taking her to Thorkell, Rekkr?' one of the men asked. 'Or are you going to stand there, talking to her?'

'The woman wants to see Thorkell. She has a right.'

'You must be sure to reward this farmer for bringing me here,' Sibba said, waving vaguely at the lingering man who had delivered Cal and his men. 'Several pieces of gold, wasn't it?'

The farmer went red and agreed it was.

Rekkr snapped his fingers at one of the guards. 'Pay the man. Then get him out of here. Thorkell does not want Gaels here. Thieves, vagabonds, and spies, the lot of them.' In an undertone, he said, 'I know I owe you a life debt, Sibba, me and the other men, but don't ask too much.'

She watched him under hooded eyes. How much was too much? And how far could she nudge him?

'How many of my former comrades-in-arms now follow Thorkell?' she asked striving for a lighter tone.

'Six plus me, but even I don't think we can get you out of here alive should Thorkell strike. You should have left it, Sibba. Trusted the gods to put things right.'

'You're a god now?'

His smile split his face in two. 'We both know it weren't right how Norr died.'

She smiled back at him. That nervous ache in the pit of her stomach had gone.

'Did I ask you to get me out alive?' she said. 'All I want you to do is get me in front of Thorkell. I can do the rest.'

'Sounds like something your father would have said.'

'Do you ever speak of him to the other men you brought here?' she asked quietly, keeping her gaze resolutely from where Cal stood glowering, watching her. The entire plan depended on him not revealing himself unless he had to. She hoped that he would understand she was safe and that he should concentrate on freeing the others. 'He thought very highly of you, Rekkr. It was why he made you Haakon's bodyguard.'

She hoped Cal heard the words and realised that she did not require protection from this man.

'He was a far better Sea King than the sea wolf, but we all make mistakes in this life.' Rekkr put a heavy hand on her shoulder. 'I hope you haven't made a serious one, Sibba. You have no idea what you are walking into here.'

'All I am asking for is a fair fight if it comes to it, Rekkr, without my wings being clipped.' She held out her hands. 'But I remain hopeful that Thorkell will see reason. Like me, he wants trade to prosper. He will want to see his new wife happy and contented with all her men accounted for before he enters the battlefield which is marriage.'

Rekkr's tattooed face turned grave. 'That is something to ponder, young Sibba. Something to ponder indeed.'

Cal tried not to think about Sibba on the dock in the crowd of men. To his astonishment and amazement, she appeared to have matters under control. Her plans thus far had been flawless. But his heart kept telling him she was also alone and hugely vulnerable with that giant of a man placing a huge paw on her shoulder.

'Should we stay with her?' one of his men asked.

He fought against the primitive urge to rescue her. But he'd given his promise that he'd wait until she asked for help, that he would respect her skill as a negotiator. He should focus on the task at hand rather than second-guessing her. 'Go forward, men. Eyes down.'

He forced his feet to march past her. Their eyes met as he accidentally bumped the great lummox of a warrior who had detained her.

'Watch where you are going!'

'I will. I will.' He moved rapidly on.

'We are in. What next?' his men asked after they deposited the worst tempered cow he'd ever encountered in the pen at the side of a barn. Thorkell's men appeared completely disinterested in them. They were either drinking or busy gossiping about the audacity of a woman warrior to walk in and demand an audience.

'We play this Sibba's way,' Cal said, drawing the trio into an alleyway, while the man's attention was distracted by someone offering odds on the woman warrior's longevity. 'Until we play it my way.'

'What do you mean?'

'Sibba wants you to find out where Gettir's remaining men are being held. Free them if possible, but don't take silly chances. I want an alternative way out if we need it.'

The men's eyes widened. 'Does she think the Northmen will join us?'

Cal permitted a grim smile to cross his lips. 'She is determined to give them the opportunity. But I'm not minded to spill your blood unnecessarily. Scout and decide if you can act. Save your own skin, and trust me to do the same.'

'Are you coming with us?' the men asked as he turned away from them in the alleyway.

'Sibba wants me in the hall. I am supposed to look humble and rustic while I am in there.' Cal touched the sword he'd carefully concealed beneath his cloak. A slight change of plan. Sibba had said that after those men were rescued, he could join her in the hall, but his men could complete that task. He was willing to admit that she had a wonderful, strategic brain, but it did not mean she was right all the time. He intended on informing her of that little fact once he had extricated her from Thorkell's clutches. 'Wish me luck.'

Both men laughed. 'Good luck with that. You walk too upright.'

Cal instantly slumped his shoulders and began to walk with a wider, almost rolling gait. 'The hat I was given helps.'

They laughed before back-slapping each other and promising to meet again. Soon.

Cal squared his shoulders and did not look back. 'Trust my plan,' Sibba had whispered to him just before she had kissed him the last time.

He wanted to, but he could not see how they could succeed. Somehow, he'd figure out a way to keep her hide safe. He knew he needed her more than ever. She made him feel like he had rejoined the land of the living, and he had no wish to return to the land of the dead man walking.

Chapter Twelve

Cal made his way with most of the whispering crowd to the hall which served as the centre of Thorkell's power. Expensive tapestries decorated the walls, and at the far end was a raised dais with a stool covered in expensive furs where a corpulent man with dead eyes sat, listening to a bard singing some doleful saga.

The chatter among those present revolved around two topics: the wedding, and the captured woman warrior and what Thorkell would do with her. Several people whispered that the wedding was not going to take place because the would-be bride had got wind of Thorkell's multitude of wives. Some seemed to conflate the two and whispered the new bride had ordered the woman here.

Cal elbowed his way to the front of the assembly and saw Sibba standing in front of the battle-scarred Thorkell. His neck muscles relaxed. She appeared unhurt, but she was flanked by the tattooed warrior he had spotted at the waterfront and a slimmer man who had a tattoo on his left wrist of a snake eating its tail. The design was very similar to the one Sibba had carved on her knife, which made him wonder if there was something he'd missed.

'What are you doing here, Sibba Norrsdottar?' Thorkell thundered. 'How dare you come and disrupt the peace of my wedding?'

Sibba raised her chin, and her blue eyes blazed, but her fists were tightly clenched. Cal realised that she was far more nervous than she wanted to appear. But he couldn't fault her courage. 'I have come to speak with the bride, but these men thought it was best if I spoke with you first.'

'My bride is indisposed.'

'The bride refuses to come out of her chamber. She and her mother have barricaded themselves in,' the warrior standing next to Cal muttered under his breath. 'Thorkell made the mistake of running too many fillies. She got wind of it. Threw something at his head.'

Cal raised a brow. Maybe Rindr was not as biddable as everyone thought. Maybe Thorkell required a broker like Sibba.

'Has the marriage taken place?' Sibba asked, tilting her head to one side. 'Have all the oaths been spoken?'

'All but the bedding,' one of Thorkell's men called out. Much laughter and off-colour jokes followed.

Sibba's face remained a perfect blank as if such vulgarities were beneath her notice. The chatter rapidly died because the men realised the remarks had no chance of piercing Sibba's tone. Cal's respect for her increased.

'Thorkell the sea wolf of Barra, are you claiming her inheritance as yours?' Sibba asked in a measured tone, lifting one brow. 'Are you saying that you are now in charge of her father's felag?'

Thorkell gave a coldly calculating smile. His dead eyes glittered like a blind snake sensing its prey. 'A husband is entitled to his bride's inheritance. North law holds this to be true. I am her husband. She will be my wife in truth before the night is over. Yes, I claim Gettir's felag as mine.'

A tiny smile flickered over Sibba's lips. The hunted had become the hunter.

'Excellent to know.' She banged her fists together. 'I, Sibba Norrsdottar, do hereby challenge you Thorkell the Blackhearted Sea Wolf for your and Gettir's felag.'

A mixture of awe at her courage and terror for her life coursed through Cal. This was what Sibba had meant when she said that she possessed the power to alter things if Rindr was already married and why she wouldn't tell him fully what she intended on doing.

Thorkell threw his head back in mocking laughter. 'You? A mere woman challenges me. For my entire felag? You're not a member of my felag, my dear.'

'I've the right as a captain in Gettir's felag.' She made a cat's paw with her right hand. 'Your felag holds little interest to me, unless it contains Gettir's.'

'He told you that it does. Are you hard of hearing now, woman?' several men called out.

Sibba calmly reached into the pouch she carried at her waist and withdrew several brooches. 'Tokens from the surviving captains that I might speak for them. *I* hold the balance of power in Gettir's felag. Not those poor souls you've locked up and will force at sword-point to bend the knee and kiss your ring.'

'You? But you are a… I mean, your father died.'

Sibba crossed her arms and tilted her chin upwards. 'My father being dead has little to do with my prowess at leading a felag or my skill at fighting. I won my felag because I beat all challengers.'

The entire hall went silent.

A lump formed in Cal's throat. She was doing better than most men in defying the sea wolf. He wanted to go and stand beside her, and it was one of the hardest things he'd ever done to keep quiet and wait until she asked for his help.

'Why did they choose you?'

'I didn't insist on learning their innermost secrets. I simply accepted the position.' She raised her fist. 'My challenge is lawful. Will you accept or not?'

Thorkell blew on his fingers. 'I don't fight women, particularly not misguided women like you.'

A muscle jumped in her jaw, and her knuckles shone white. Cal silently willed Sibba to stay calm. She was winning over the room.

'You won't fight a woman.' Sibba very deliberately tapped a finger against her lips. 'A novel way to speak to someone who is now apparently an important member of your felag.'

'Not my felag.'

'You claimed all of Gettir's felag.'

Thorkell tugged at the neck of his tunic. 'I...I...I...'

'Which is it? Gettir's felag including all its ships now belongs to you because of marriage, or it doesn't.'

'Do you have a death wish?' someone shouted. Another shouted for quiet and that Sibba Norrsdottar had a point.

'Gettir's felag is mine. I claim your ship, Sibba Norrsdottar.' Thorkell slapped his hand on his knee. 'Ha, that is a pleasure I had not thought of. Your ship is mine. Your men are mine.'

'Then, I am part of the felag.'

'I toss you out.' He snapped his fingers. 'Like that, a wolf's head.'

'Not without due process.' Sibba placed her hands on her hips. 'Do you want a rebellion amongst your ranks? Why would any captain fight for you?'

The murmur that the woman spoke the truth became a ripple and then a crescendo. Sibba gave no indication that she had heard it. She stood with her shoulders back and chin up, determined.

'Fine, you are a member of the felag, but I reserve the

right to punish you for your insolence. Your fate is to be a wolf head.'

Sibba raised her chin and stuck her hands on her hips. The hiss of in-taken breaths swirled all around the hall. 'As a member of the felag, I have the right to challenge you. Or have you done away with that right? Must everyone obey you without question?'

'Few have challenged him and lived!' someone called out. 'We prefer to live.'

'Let the challenge happen!' the cry went up. Cal joined in until the rafters rang with the sound.

All the while, Thorkell stroked his chin, watching her with beady eyes. A spider sitting at the centre of his web. 'Did you send that soothsayer to me? To frighten me?'

'How could I do that?' she asked, balancing both hands on her hips. 'Since when have you been afraid of an old woman's mutterings?'

'Why should I take a risk given that prophecy?' Thorkell theatrically rolled his eyes. 'You will have to do better than that, my dear, because all you have done is put yourself into my power.'

Sibba cleared her throat. 'Should I nominate a champion? Then, you'll not be fighting a woman, and the soothsayer's prediction will have no power.'

'I didn't think your men were here.'

'They are not.'

Thorkell smiled a cold and calculating smile. 'I am not minded to wait for their arrival.'

'You believe we are at an impasse.'

'The easiest way is for me to remove you from the felag. You keep your life, but I get your boat. Deal?'

'Another way exists.' Sibba rocked back on her heels,

and a faint smile played on her lips. She'd been expecting that answer, Cal realised. She was a skilled tafl player.

Suddenly he knew where this was leading and why she'd insisted on his being there and in disguise. A huge wave of pride and respect for her surged in his breast. The audacity of the plan nearly took his breath away, but he had to admit that her assessment had been accurate. He knew in that breath that he not only loved her but admired her bravery and her calm under immense pressure. He silently vowed to find a way to save her, because he greatly feared she was intent on throwing her life away if it meant harming Thorkell.

'Your naïveté shows, young Sibba,' Thorkell said. 'Demonstrates why you could never be one of my captains, if that is indeed what you aspire to. Audacious, but ultimately lacking in discipline. Be grateful for my good temper on my wedding day.'

Thorkell's words were designed to humiliate Sibba, Cal realised. The man wanted her angry, but there was something different about Sibba today. Far calmer and more level-headed than the woman who had challenged him to an archery contest.

Sibba paused significantly before responding. 'I think you have been avoiding challengers for years,' she said with a faint, withering smile. 'Always one excuse after another, then a knife in the night for whosoever had the hubris to issue a threat.' She pretended to count on her fingers. 'Is it now fifteen or seventeen challenges you have avoided?'

Thorkell's face drained of colour and then became florid. 'What nonsense are you spouting?'

He fairly spat the words. Cal silently willed Sibba onwards. The sea wolf was very close to losing control and doing something reckless. Cal's fingers itched to grab his sword and issue a challenge in Sibba's name, but he knew Thorkell would find a way of avoiding it.

No, he had to do the harder thing, which was to allow Sibba to continue baiting Thorkell until the man was forced to accept her challenge.

'Wasn't that how you got rid of the last five men who posed a threat?'

She reeled off their names and the manner of their deaths. It was then that Cal realised Sibba knew far more about Thorkell's operation than he'd given her credit for.

Thorkell blinked rapidly. 'Where did you hear about those? I had no part in the deaths of the first three. Ask anyone.'

'Find a champion, Sibba!' Cal shouted, unable to contain his anger. Thankfully, others took up the chant until the rafters shook with the sound.

'What sort of witchcraft is this?' Thorkell asked. 'The woman has no men here.'

'The docks of Constantinople teem with whispers, Thorkell.' Sibba gave a shrug of her shoulders. 'Why do you think my father was making his way back here? He wasn't frightened of you, but he was travelling under a banner of peace, a peace which you broke when you waylaid him.'

Indistinct murmurs and intakes of breaths rippled around the hall. Beads of sweat shone on Thorkell's forehead.

'That is a lie!' Thorkell shouted. 'Norr lost his life in battle. He attacked first.'

Sibba bowed low. 'I travelled in the ship behind him and witnessed the whole thing. Earlier I had attached a flag of truce to my father's ship.'

'I should have your head struck from your shoulders. Or, at the very least, your lying tongue ripped from mouth.'

Sibba tapped a finger against her mouth. 'What if, rather

than insisting on a champion be brought from my crew, I choose a champion from those who are gathered in this hall?'

'I owe you a life debt, Sibba, but you can't ask that of me,' the tattooed warrior who had been at the docks called out. 'Or any of the men who served with your father.'

Sibba's smile quirked upwards. 'I did not intend to ask you, Rekkr. I've seen you fight many times. In fact, I have disarmed you more than once.'

The tattooed warrior said, 'Aye, that much is true.' Laughter broke out in the hall. 'But I suggest taking Thorkell's generous offer and leaving with your life.'

'It would appear you are lacking in this champion of yours.' Thorkell held out his hands. 'As it is my wedding day, I am willing to spare your life. Accept your banishment from these waters, and we shall hear no more of this absurd challenge.'

'I choose that man, that Gael there.' Sibba pointed her finger directly at Cal. 'He looks like he would be brave enough to use a sword to help a lady.'

The men standing near him backed up. Cal pulled his hat so that it was lower on his brow, and he made his shoulders more hunched than ever.

Thorkell sat up straighter. His gaze travelled over Sibba's choice, making Cal's flesh crawl. He hated the small deception, but he figured she had the measure of Thorkell and that the tyrant would back out of any challenge from a warrior.

'Are you talking about me, my lady?' he asked, taking care to speak North tongue badly. 'You want me to fight this here man? If none of these fine fellows from the North will come your aid, surely a poor Gael can help.'

'Can you beat him in a fair fight?' she asked in a soft voice.

'I won't know until I try, but I reckon I will try, my lady.'

She turned towards Thorkell. 'What say you? Will you fight this man, my new champion?'

'That hayseed of a farmer, who probably doesn't know one end of a sword from another?' Thorkell laughed and his minions obediently followed suit. 'Small tip, farmer. Try to stick your opponent with the pointy end.'

Sibba gave him a significant glance. Cal barely inclined his head. 'I believe he knows which end to stick in a man.'

Thorkell shook his head. 'You've tossed away everything, Sibba Norrsdottar. I will beat this man and then grind his bones to make my bread. And then I will take your life and all your men's lives as forfeit as well.'

The hall erupted with a chorus of cheers and stamping feet. Cal noticed Sibba's face was carefully turned away from his. It took all his willpower not to sweep her into his arms and kiss her thoroughly. She'd done it. Thorkell was going to fight him. If the rumours she had heard on the Constantinople docks were true, then Thorkell had not had a proper fight in years, if ever.

Thorkell motioned for quiet. 'I said that I was a generous man, and I am. Farmer, do you still wish to fight, knowing it may be your death? You have never met this woman before. What is she to you?'

'A woman in need,' Cal answered. 'Always had a soft spot for them, your worship. I accept the position of champion.'

Thorkell gave a quick laugh. '*Your worship.* Don't that beat all.'

'Probably has never held a sword,' the skald murmured.

Thorkell's eyes danced at the idea, and Cal willed him to believe it. 'Not a swordsman, eh? You could be right there. Sibba Norrsdottar needs to learn a lesson.'

'What say you? Will you be my champion?' she asked as the noise ceased.

Cal forced his shoulders to become ever more hunched, but every muscle in his body looked tense. In a fair fight, she knew he could take Thorkell. 'My lady, pretty lady from the North, is it what you want?'

'It appears I have need of a champion, and I can't think of a better one.' She held up her hand and slowly lowered her fingers one by one as if she was waiting for Thorkell's next move and was willing him to keep silent. It was as if she had rehearsed this scene in her head several times.

Cal's heart lurched. Sibba believed in him. He silently promised not to let her down. Ever.

'Yes, farmer, you can't back down now, surely. Be big and brave for the little lady.' Thorkell advanced towards him. Close up, Cal spotted the ravages of drink and heavy living on his jowls. Sibba's hunch was correct. He was living on his reputation and preying on the vulnerable.

Thorkell stroked his chin. 'I say we use swords. Do you know how to use a sword, farmer, or would you prefer a pitchfork?'

Much laughter from Thorkell's men. Several started to place bets on how long Cal would last. One threw a broken sword towards him, saying he should use that. Even more laughter.

'Now, now, men.' Thorkell raised his hands, clearly relishing the prospect of teaching an uppity local a lesson as well as defeating Sibba. 'The man should be given a sporting chance. Get him a real sword.' He made a mocking bow to Sibba. 'I won't have it said that I played unfair, my lady.'

'Is that a formal acceptance of my challenge, Thorkell?' Sibba asked. Her words were very precise, and Cal knew she had obviously considered how the scene would play out.

'Aye, it is. If you are prepared to accept your champion's fate.'

Sibba stood very straight. The light hit her cheekbones and showed her steely resilience. Cal found it hard to see the woman who had so recently sighed in his arms, but he knew she was there, and he was determined to protect her to his very last breath. It made the situation more dangerous, but it also gave him someone to fight for. It had been a long time since he felt the deep-down visceral need to fight. 'I am.'

'Then, I gladly accept your challenge, Thorkell.' Cal swept off his hat, allowed his hair to tumble about his shoulder, and withdrew his sword. 'Swords it is, but I prefer to use my own.'

The mocking laughter abruptly ceased, and a distinct murmuring started.

'And you are?' someone called.

'Calwar mac Bedwyr. I believe you may know me by reputation. I have managed to keep my father's islands free from Northern control.' He looked directly at Thorkell. 'The challenge has been offered and accepted. I act as Sibba's champion.'

Thorkell's face contorted into a furious mask. 'That was underhanded and unworthy, my lady. This challenge should not stand. That man appeared to be a farmer.'

'I believe he does work the land, when time permits.' Sibba blew on her fingernails. 'You made the rules. You required me to have a champion. I would happily have fought you.'

Thorkell looked wildly about him. 'But…but…'

'Are you intending to back out?' Cal asked, raising a brow and bringing Thorkell's attention back to him. Sibba had done her bit, and now it was up to him. 'Are you going to show everyone that you are a coward? Not only will you refuse to fight Sibba Norrsdottar on spurious grounds, but you refuse to fight her chosen champion.'

Sweat freely beaded on Thorkell's brow as his Adam's apple worked up and down. He knew he'd been manipulated into this trap and was about to start thrashing.

'Coward,' Sibba said. 'I call you *coward*. You will not fight me, a mere woman. Now you will not fight my chosen champion. Fight, Thorkell, or vacate that chair. Your felag deserves the best.'

Before he could speak, a great stamping of feet and a chorus of *Fight, Thorkell!* rose in the hall. The men were now all looking at Thorkell as if they expected him to come up with an excuse. And the man knew he was backed into a corner.

'Which will it be? Me or my champion?'

Thorkell's tongue darted out and wet his lips.

Cal held his breath waiting, not daring to catch Sibba's eye. In his experience, rats were the most dangerous when caught in a trap with no place else to go.

Finally, Thorkell stood and removed his cloak. 'What is the point of delaying? This is one fight I shall savour winning. A thorn in my side gone, and this so-called woman warrior in the bargain. Today is my lucky day. Written in the runes.'

'Shouldn't we wait on the bride? Surely, she will want to witness this,' the skald said.

'Something to consider,' Thorkell said. 'Rindr can confirm if you are indeed part of her felag.'

Sibba exchanged a glance with Cal. She shook her head. Cal inclined his, indicating that he'd understood her wordless plea.

'We fight now, Thorkell, or you cede the leadership to

Sibba. Those are the Northern rules, are they not?' Cal said, ensuring his voice was hard and unyielding.

The hall went silent again, and he knew he had it right.

'Eager for your death, Calwar mac Bedwyr. Watch well, Sibba, and now your death will be long and painful. A lesson for all who would challenge me.'

The men moved back and rapidly created a ring.

'I suppose I should wish you luck, Cal,' Sibba said, coming up to him and laying a hand on his arm. Her eyes gleamed, and she showed not a trace of fear. He silently promised that they would play tafl as she would be a more than worthy opponent. 'But I think you've the measure of the man. Your skill more than matches his.'

He laid his hand on top of hers. 'You were right. You did know how to get me here, and to have Thorkell accept a formal challenge. Nothing short of amazing.'

'Sometimes you should trust my instincts.' She gave a half shrug, but her eyes danced. 'Thus far, we make a good team.'

He detected a slight wistfulness in her voice, as if she did not expect their partnership to last. He pressed her hand and knew there was much he wanted to tell her about the plans his heart kept making for the future. 'If I—'

She put a finger against his lips. 'Concentrate on the fight. I've faith in your sword arm, but remember Thorkell never plays fair.'

He handed her his cloak and the hat. 'I know.'

Sibba watched Cal stride into the circle with his sword. Behind him, Rekkr appeared to be conferring with several men who she thought she recognised. She dismissed them as men probably wagering. Rekkr might owe her a life debt, but he would not lift a finger to save Cal.

She bit her lip and tried to concentrate on the actual

fight. Thorkell appeared far too confident, flexing his muscles, and waving the sword above his head to the delight of the crowd. She suspected he had several tricks up his sleeve, and it would not be a fair fight.

'You had best have a shield,' Rekkr cried and tossed Cal one. 'Fair is fair.'

Cal caught it midair. Thorkell's face became thunderous, and Sibba knew the risk Rekkr had taken to repay his life debt.

Sibba nodded her thanks and mouthed 'Paid in full.'

Rekkr saluted her before he briefly put his finger to his lips. Maybe there was some hope for her after all. Maybe she had not ruined everything when she'd allowed those men to leave that night. Haakon had often accused her of doing the wrong thing in failing to set adequate guards, but she had only wanted men who were willing to serve them both.

She tried to quell the sudden butterflies in her stomach. When it had been simply her, she had not worried. When she formulated the plan, lying in Cal's arms, she had expected to be the one fighting. Cal was supposed to be backup only. Now she was very glad that he was here.

She had to hope that Cal's men had freed the captives— something to give them a chance if this went wrong. And she wasn't naive enough to think that Thorkell's death would be the end of it either. Whatever happened, they would require assistance to control his warriors, many of whom would have their own designs on the leadership.

The man officiating raised his arm, signalling that the fight was ready to begin, and began counting slowly from ten. But Thorkell abruptly swung his sword before the count was completed.

'Cheat!' Sibba called out.

Thorkell rushed forward, seeking to take first advantage, but Cal raised his shield at the last breath. The blow fell on it with a resounding thump. Cal pushed with his shield, and Thorkell's sword was forced back.

Sibba remembered how to breathe. She should have known Cal would be ready and waiting for any tricks.

'Next time, wait until the count is finished,' Cal said, locking swords with Thorkell.

'Will there be a next time?' Thorkell withdrew his sword and pivoted, forcing Cal off balance.

'In the laps of the saints and angels.' Cal launched his own attack, swinging his sword with great purpose while he thundered towards Thorkell.

Thorkell hastily retreated a few steps and raised his shield. Cal's swing missed connecting by a hair's breadth.

The two men circled each other, testing and probing to find the weakness in the other. A jab here and a parry there. Thorkell moved like a man who used to fight and who expected an easy victory through brute force, whereas Cal balanced on the balls of his feet, moving this way and that. Neither appeared able to land a decisive blow. The highly partisan crowd loudly cheered when Thorkell gained any sort of fleeting advantage and roundly booed when Cal landed any significant blows.

Sibba watched Cal's shield with increasing concern. Was it her imagination, or did the shield appear to buckle? She silently prayed she was seeing things and tried to concentrate on his opponent instead. The man was not as fit as Cal and possibly had been drinking heavily.

Sweat began to pour down Thorkell's face as the stalemate continued.

He suddenly attacked, darting forward and yelling. His sword hit Cal's shield in the middle, and the shield buckled. Cal was forced backwards and half stumbled, one knee hitting the rushes. The flat of Thorkell's sword hit Cal's shoulder and head.

Sibba stifled a scream. A trickle of blood appeared at Cal's temple. He lashed out with the broken shield, catching Thorkell's legs and upending him. Thorkell scuttled backwards. Cal rose but seemed to stagger, disoriented, fighting shadows while he clutched the broken shield.

Thorkell wiped a hand across his face and chuckled. The sound sent shivers down Sibba's spine. Thorkell's warriors started noisily placing their bets on how much longer Cal could last.

Cal made another half-hearted swipe with his sword.

Thorkell gave a laugh and advanced forward. 'I thought you a fearsome warrior. It seems I've given you and your little kingdom far too much respect over the last few years. Know that you are going to lose it all, foolish Gael. You and your family will be dust.'

'I beg to differ.' Cal tossed aside the useless shield, went up on his toes again, and pivoted so quickly that Thorkell did not have time to react. This time, Cal's movements were deliberate and precise, and Sibba knew his earlier action had been a feint designed to lure Thorkell into a false sense of security.

Thorkell appeared to miss it and drove his attack forward. He shouted in anger and bloodlust as he did, leaving his left side open.

Cal pivoted again and drove his sword forward as Thorkell desperately tried to bring the hilt of his sword down on Cal's arm. Cal screamed.

Sibba scrunched up her eyes, unable to watch any more. But the noise of betting ceased, followed by the murmur of *Calwar! Calwar! Calwar!*

She slowly opened her eyes. Thorkell lay on the rush matting, bleeding heavily from his side. But miracles of miracles, Cal was upright. She peered closer. Cal had the point of his sword on Thorkell's throat. 'Will you yield?'

'If I must... You and the woman may go free.' Thorkell allowed his sword to roll out of his hand.

There was something overly practiced about the roll which Sibba instinctively distrusted.

'Don't be fooled. This is no surrender,' Sibba called out. Her heart skipped a beat. 'Keep your guard up!'

Ignoring her, Cal bent down to pick up the sword, and Thorkell lunged at him with a knife he'd concealed in his boot.

'I have you now!'

Cal's reaction was instantaneous. He twisted away, rolling until he could kick the sword out of Thorkell's reach. He stood and faced him again, crouching low.

'This should have been a fair fight, no other weapons.'

'I lied, Gael. What are you going to do about it?'

'Did you have my father murdered?' Sibba cried.

Thorkell half turned towards her. Something fanatical shone in his eyes. 'Will no one shut that woman up? Or will I have to do it myself?'

'Fight me, not Sibba,' Cal roared above the crowd. 'Come on, if you are man enough. Fair or foul, I don't care. I will win in the end.'

Thorkell started towards him, staggering like a giant bear, moved without thinking, and tripped over the sword. His arm went up, and he fell heavily, with a knife embedded in his chest.

Sibba put her hand over her mouth.

'To me, men,' Rekkr cried. 'For Norr. We will not allow

this outrage to stand. We will honour our vow. The time is right.'

At that, seven knives flashed through the air, embedding themselves in Thorkell, one piercing his throat. Thorkell toppled forward, and a pool of blood began to form underneath him. His legs jerked.

Sibba knew that the man who had murdered her father had at last received justice.

'Thorkell tried to cheat,' Rekkr roared. Seven men stood behind him, fierce-eyed and armed. Thorkell's henchmen took a step backwards. 'I couldn't have that. I owe that much to Sibba.'

'I had the measure of him,' Cal answered. 'But justice has now been done. The saints and all the angels have given their answer.'

'If someone wishes to fight me, fight me in the open, not with a knife in the back.' Sibba fell onto her knees and rested her head on her hands. All around her, people were chanting Cal's name and proclaiming him the victor. She watched as one of the men handed Cal Thorkell's sword. And she knew he had done more than win this battle for her. He had captured her heart. And she also knew she could never allow him to know.

'My lord, you have righted a great wrong,' she said, rising instead of confessing the sudden sense of wonderment at her love for him. 'I owe you a great debt. My entire family and felag do.'

The words were too formal for her liking, but they had to suffice. She refused to confess where all might hear and laugh at her.

Cal bowed low. 'I hope I proved myself worthy as your champion. It is your victory, not mine.'

The crowd went wild, stamping their feet, clapping their hands, and chanting Sibba's name.

Despite all the riches he'd showered on his men, few mourned Thorkell. Sibba was reminded of the lesson her father had given Haakon and her years ago: while few may go up against a bully while he lives, the bully is seldom mourned after he has drawn his final breath.

A great wave of weariness rolled over her. They had succeeded, and both had survived. Sibba sank to the ground, stunned, hardly knowing what to do next. Her sacred vow had been fulfilled. Her father's shade could rest in peace.

Cal came over and raised her. She rapidly scanned his face and body to see if there were any major injuries, but other than a few superficial cuts, he appeared fine. 'Sibba, this whole thing could still end poorly. Those knives…'

She nodded and forced her feet to move. She went over to the nearest knife. 'Rekkr told me that besides him, six members of my father's felag had joined Thorkell.'

'And…'

'The nearest knife has my father's device—the serpent chasing its tail etched on the handle.'

She looked over to where Rekkr and a group of men stood.

Several saluted her.

'What do you think—they were biding their time?'

'Sometimes people do not know they can be courageous until they are.'

'Thorkell would have lost without the interference. I had him on his knees.'

'Why are you silent?' Rekkr asked, grabbing her elbow. 'You won. Grab the leadership. You can't allow that Gael to simply take it. He won't be able to hold it. Someone from the North must lead. Take it, and I will pledge my loyalty.'

'Keep this hall for me. I go to fulfil my obligations,' Sibba answered, pulling away from him. 'I gave my word to the other captains. There are people I need to see freed, and their wounds tended.'

Rekkr smiled back at her, the way he used to, before Constantinople and what had happened in the bowels of that house had scarred him. 'You've earned my loyalty. The way you should have had it when your father was murdered. I will look after things here until you return.'

She put both her hands on Rekkr's. 'Delighted to have your service.'

'What would you have me do?' Rekkr knelt. 'I am happy to swear my oath to you, Sibba. I will be a good and faithful servant.'

Sibba put a hand to her head. Her mind had gone blank. She had survived. The oath she'd sworn beside her father's body had been fulfilled, even though most people had told that she'd never do it. Now she had the rest of her life to live. 'I accept with pleasure. Secure the hall.'

Rekkr bowed his head and agreed to keep Thorkell's men in the hall as well ensuring that the body was made ready for its pyre.

'We must give him dignity in death, even though he never gave such honour to his enemies,' Sibba said with a nod. Her stomach seemed a little easier at the thought. It was a simple way to demonstrate that whatever happened next, things had irrevocably altered.

'Are you ready?' Cal asked, handing her Thorkell's sword.

'I'm ready to finish the task we started,' she said, securing the heavy sword in her belt. 'I will prove myself a worthy sea king.'

Thorkell's men created a space for her and Cal to walk through. She caught sight of several hard faces and knew her control of the men was tenuous and that she'd have to demonstrate she was a leader first, not a woman in need of coddling or, worse, a woman enthralled by a man.

Chapter Thirteen

Cal strove to take steadying breaths. His entire body shook, and sweat poured off him as he followed Sibba, who went striding off at a quick pace. A steady rain had fallen when they were in the hall. Now the world glistened as if it had been made anew.

After a few steps towards where Rindr and her mother were supposedly being held, he stopped and put his hands on his knees, struggling to breathe as the enormity of what he'd just been through hit him square in the chest. 'Give me a moment, Sibba.'

Sibba instantly stopped her march. She tossed an apologetic smile over her shoulder, before hurrying back to him. 'Are you up to this? Do you have wounds which need to be tended to? I would not trust any of Thorkell's soothsayers to be able to cure you, but we can send for the priest from where we passed the night.'

'The wounds are superficial. I will live to fight again.' He gritted his teeth, ignored the pain in his side and looked at the empty alleyway. Thorkell's men appeared to have congregated in the hall. He had to trust that Northman who'd sworn his allegiance to Sibba to maintain order. 'I left specific orders that my men were not to take any unnecessary risks.'

'They have trouble remembering orders. Probably take after you.' Her smile melted his heart. 'Have I remembered to say thank you for disobeying me, arriving before I required you and bringing your own sword? For saving me?'

Sibba was being modest. She would have found a way to beat Thorkell if he hadn't been there. He was convinced of that. But he also liked to think she was in his debt.

He struggled to keep his face neutral but could not repress a smile that he knew stretched across his face. 'That is the sort of thing I like to hear.'

'I never had any doubt,' she said. 'You were in command almost from the very start.'

He hadn't been. The fight had been a close call, far closer than he would have wished. He knew he'd relive the entire battle in his dreams many times. But it was kind of her to say.

In the end he'd known who he'd fought for: Sibba. And he suspected Thorkell had forgotten what he was fighting for. He could not allow Thorkell to get his paws on her, and the thought that he cared enough to kill to protect her unnerved him.

At the base of the cliff beside the broken bodies of his family, he'd vowed that he'd never let a woman get that close to his heart again. But Sibba had managed it. Going back to that empty world where he was simply going through the motions of living and feeling numb held no prospect of joy. He had to figure out a way of making her understand how necessary she was to him.

'You did it. This was your victory. We'd never have been here without your vision,' he said instead of confessing his feelings for her.

Now with everyone milling about was not the right time or place. And what could he say to her—that he deeply cared for her? She'd made it very clear at the barn and ear-lier in the hut that the affair was for the duration of the mis-sion only. What was between them was not for ever.

Her brow creased. 'You were the one who fought, Cal.'

'I bow to your expertise on strategy.' Cal wanted to kiss her until her breath came as soft little pants and she was forced to admit her brilliance. False modesty served no one. 'I'm torn between wanting to play tafl with you for the challenge of it, and knowing if we do, you are probably a far superior player to me.'

She tilted her head to one side and gave a sad smile as if she didn't expect the proposed match to ever happen. He struggled not to draw her into his arms and demand to know why she refused to accept compliments. 'I lose as often as I win.'

'We will have to make the stakes worthwhile so ulti-mately it doesn't matter who wins or loses,' he said, already plotting how he could get her into a large soft bed with very few distractions. There he could allow his body to say what his mouth feared to. There he could convince her to inter-twine her body with his.

'Something in my gut told me that we had a chance,' she said and gave one of her smiles which made the world a bright place. 'Not precisely how I planned, but close enough. We adapted and you won.'

'Planned? You mean you thought you'd fight him.'

She made a moue with her mouth. 'Possibly, but not how anyone might have plausibly thought it would happen. Not even the soothsayer.'

'Thorkell accepted your challenge,' he said more roughly than he intended. 'That should be the end of the matter.'

She reached up and patted his cheek. 'You and your father need not worry. This stronghold won't menace the trade route any longer. You tell him that when you next see him.'

'When I next see him?'

'He is hardly likely to travel. I can't leave here, not yet, not until my leadership is secure.'

He put a hand under her elbow. She didn't appear to understand the danger she might be putting herself in, particularly as she seemed to think he was going to leave her here unattended to rule over these Northmen, ruthless pirates to their very fingertips. She needed a consort—him—and he was going to have to find a way of convincing her of this fact. 'Having just saved you, are you expecting me to go and leave you to these men, then? I'm your champion, remember?'

She concentrated on a pebble rather than meeting his eye. 'I knew the odds, Cal, before I embarked on this. My place is here until the Nourns, the weavers of fate, decide otherwise.'

'Thorkell is dead,' he said, trying another tact.

Her eyes became troubled pools. 'One vow fulfilled, and thus it is on to the next oath. Some might say I've been reckless with my oaths, never thinking I'd get beyond the first one.'

He ran a hand through his hair. 'You mean the marriage between Rindr and my father.'

'Gettir died for that alliance. He wanted to see his daughter safe and secure.'

He didn't entirely see why the marriage was necessary now, but he wanted to speak to his father first and get his views. It would depend on how many ships stayed loyal to whoever Rindr married, he supposed. And there was the argument Sibba had used that the leadership had already transferred to Thorkell. Thus, it was Sibba who held the felag, not Rindr. Except he wasn't entirely sure that the other captains would agree with that assessment. He wished he knew the precise terms of Sibba's arrangement instead of her vague assurances about being in charge until Gettir's orders were carried out. 'Suthereyjar will honour its word. We negotiated in good faith. We intend to keep that faith.'

'The waterways must be clear if trade is to prosper in this area,' she said to the pebble. 'I promised the farmer and his wife it would be. You saw the devastation of this land. They need a chance to live in peace, something Thorkell never gave them.'

Waterways to be clear. Live in peace. He hated how his gut twisted. Formal words as though what had been between them had never existed. He wanted to ask about them, their affair and the promises her body made, but he could never speak with flowers.

'Before we go any further, I claim the victor's spoils.' He bent his head and tasted her lips. Warm and luscious, vibrantly alive. He allowed his tongue and mouth to say in movement what he dared not say aloud.

She twined her arm about his neck and kissed him back, pressing her body to his. Fierce and hot. Giving him hope that he could find a way to bind her to him permanently.

Something inside him twanged. She had to accept the bounds and ties voluntarily or he'd lose her for ever.

'If that was the sort of thank you I get, I must find more villains to kill and more ways to help you keep your promises,' he murmured against her hair.

Sibba pressed her hands against his chest. Her eyes were luminous, and he doubted if he'd ever seen a woman look as desirable as she did with a smudge of dirt on her cheek and her hair gently spinning free from the single plait that she'd twisted only this morning.

He knew she wore trousers to demonstrate her status as a warrior, but they accentuated her curves rather than hid them.

'What is it, Sibba? You appear troubled,' he said against her ear. 'Let me take the troubles away.'

'Rindr is locked in. We need to rescue her before someone takes it into his head to secret her and we are forced to start all over again,' she said, pouring cold water over his scheme to take her somewhere and more thoroughly explore this passion.

'She can wait. No harm will come to her there. They must all wait.' He played with her braid in his hand. 'We deserve a few more breaths for us. Savouring our victory.'

He bent his head, intending to thoroughly kiss her again, but she turned her face away. 'I promised the other captains to free Rindr if I could.'

He inwardly sighed and let her go. Her sense of duty and responsibility was one of the reasons he loved her.

The notion that he loved her shocked him, but he also knew how right it was. It was that growing love which had given him the strength to fight Thorkell in the final few breaths of the fight when he thought his muscles would give out. But he knew there would be a time later to declare his love. Do it too soon and she'd run.

He silently prayed to St Michael and all the angels for the patience to wait until the correct time, until he had figured out a way to irrevocably bind her to him, preferably without her realising it as he figured she'd fight against the bonds simply because they were there.

She regarded him with teeth gnawing at her bottom lip and her eyes unfathomable pools. His heart stabbed. She couldn't have guessed why he fought and search for a way to gently let him down, not yet. He had to have time to find a way to make her love him.

'What is wrong, Sibba?' he asked more brusquely than he intended. 'Are you worried about Thorkell's felag?'

She gave a weak smile. 'The head may be gone, but a headless serpent can still do damage with its thrashing tail.'

He smiled at the quaint image, but he knew what she meant. They remained in danger until Thorkell's warriors had sworn loyalty. 'You heard the men in the hall. They were shouting my name, not Thorkell's. They will be on our side when the time comes…if it comes.'

'And you were the one telling me that I was overoptimistic.'

'His felag has splintered, Sibba. It will continue to break.' His jaw tightened. He was not ignorant of the enormity of the task, but the islands, his lands, had suddenly become much more secure thanks to her daring scheme. 'What is troubling you?'

'Rindr deserves an explanation. If your men rescue her or her father's men, things might get muddled.' She placed her hand on his arm as if she was willing him to understand. 'It must be me. You did promise that I would have a chance to speak to her before any marriage.'

It bothered him that Sibba still did not fully trust him. But it really didn't matter who told Rindr and her mother. He was not even sure if his father would still require the alliance.

'My father recovers.'

'Better done sooner. Rindr needs to know the truth about her prospective bridegroom.'

He sighed. The state of his father's health was the last thing he wanted to be thinking about. He wanted to know when Rindr had agreed to the alliance with Thorkell. And how many men any husband of hers would command before he sought to renew the betrothal.

'Are you always this bound by duty?'

She touched his cheek. Her full lip turned upwards. 'It serves me well.'

'Saves you having to think?'

'What would I be thinking about besides my duty?' she asked.

'Maybe this.' He drew her more fully into his arms and started to bend his head the better to kiss some sense into her.

One of his men came skidding around the corner, interrupting them. His face became like a man whose salvation has come. 'Lord, they are after us.'

'What is going on?'

'We failed to find the captives and...' He nodded towards the group of men who were following him.

Cal nodded to Sibba, who held up Thorkell's sword.

'I demand you stop.'

The pursuers suddenly halted. 'Who are you? And what are you doing with Thorkell's sword?'

'The sword belongs to me.' Sibba made a slicing motion with it. She seemed barely big enough to carry such a heavy weapon, but she moved with a quiet authority. 'Will you assist us, or will you stand against us?'

The men jumped back and checked over their shoulders. All bravado gone.

'That...that man was trying to free the prisoners, the ones who refuse to swear loyalty to Thorkell.'

'No one will be swearing to Thorkell. He has met his end,' Sibba said.

'You lie.'

Sibba held the sword aloft above her head. 'Would I be in possession of his sword otherwise?'

Cal was almost sorry for these men whose mouths dropped open. She was playing this exactly right.

'You are the warrior woman who was foretold?' one asked, his eyes growing wide. 'Amazing.'

'I have never put much store into prophecies, but Thorkell did. Now he breathes no longer so the prophecy becomes truth.' Sibba slowly lowered the sword. For a breath, Cal wondered if she would topple backwards, but she firmly planted her feet. 'If you wish to join me, I will not hold the past against you. A fresh start.'

The men glanced at each other. Then one by one they bent their knees until they all knelt and with one voice swore their loyalty to her. They then departed, laughing.

Cal put his hand under Sibba's elbow. 'Those men may yet cause trouble.'

'I know better than to put store in such quick declarations.'

'Spoken like a sensible leader.'

Her eyes danced, sunlight on the sparkling sea. It took all his willpower not to crush her to him and declare that while she might lead men, he intended to see her safe. 'I will go to Rindr. You get the men. We will meet again in the hall.'

He turned his face, and his lips touched her palm. 'Duty first, pleasure afterwards.'

'Always. I take my responsibilities seriously.'

'One day, you will have fulfilled all your oaths.'

She glanced back over her shoulder. 'What is that supposed to mean? Am I to stop stepping up when no one else will?'

'Think on it. You will discover the answer.'

He watched her backside sway as she strode away and hoped she had understood what he was trying to tell her.

* * *

'Rindr!' Sibba pounded on the door and tried to keep her mind on the task at hand, instead of thinking about Cal's cryptic remarks about the fact that one day her oaths would be fulfilled. One oath at a time until the Nourns decided to cut her life thread. Concentrating on her responsibilities meant she had little time to ponder her failures.

She refused to start making halls in the clouds and thinking Cal cared for her or would ask her to make oaths of a more intimate nature. What was between them on this journey was about two warm bodies seeking comfort, nothing more. It couldn't be. She wouldn't allow it. But her heart appeared not to be listening.

She redoubled her efforts on the door. 'Let me in. Open this door now. You are safe. I promise.'

She inwardly grimaced. Another oath.

'Sibba? Is that you? Are you alone?' came Rindr's quavering voice.

'It is hardly anyone else.' She screwed up her eyes, instantly regretting the slight sarcasm. Rindr and Nefja had been through an ordeal.

'Is...is Haakon with you? Please tell him to be careful. I shall always treasure what passed between us, but... I am to be married.'

The hopeful note was very evident in Rindr's voice. Sibba inwardly sighed. She'd hoped that absence had not made the heart grow fonder. Rindr was no good for Haakon.

'He remains in Suthereyjar with King Bedwyr.'

'Doing what?'

'Serving as his bodyguard. Haakon can be very useful in a crisis.' Sibba silently hoped that Haakon's attention had turned to another. Perhaps one of the pretty Gaelic women.

'I'd rather he was here before I open the door, if it is all the same to you. You are the one who caused this problem in the first place.'

Sibba glared at the firmly shut door. They obviously had a different viewpoint on that. 'Open the door, Rindr. We can speak without shouting. Without everyone knowing our business, unless you intend on getting me arrested.'

'Do you know how she has suffered?' Rindr's mother's voice was sharp. 'Not all of us are warriors like you, Sibba. How do we know you come in peace with good intentions towards my daughter? How do we know that the foolish soothsayer spoke true?'

Sibba gritted her teeth. Rindr's mother was one of those women whose mission in life was to make every other woman feel inferior. Sometimes it wasn't deliberate, but Sibba knew she also derived great pleasure in exuding her superiority.

'Why do you think I am here?' Sibba fought to keep the annoyance from her voice but failed. 'Why do you think I would permit Rindr to be used in that fashion? I am here to see my promise to your late husband fulfilled.'

A low murmur of a whispered conversation, but the door stayed firmly shut. Sibba danced on her toes. One part of her wanted to go and be part of the liberation of the captains. Or even back to the hall. Anything but waiting for these two feather-stuffed pillows to open the door.

'Some sense from you at last,' Rindr's mother finally said with withering scorn. 'How have you managed to lure away the guards? How will you manage to get us on a ship? Let alone pilot that ship out of the harbour?'

'Mother!' The sound of Rindr stamping her foot echoed through the door.

'You are both safe. I will keep you from any further harm. I give my word on that. Thorkell is dead. And Haakon will arrive soon, Rindr. Do you think I can keep him away?'

Sibba heard the scraping of trunks, and the door cracked open. Rindr's mother peered out. All that was missing was her holding up a finger to test the wind, but the woman had always been like that, wanting to ensure she had the wind at her back, pushing her towards a successful future.

'Where is Thorkell? He was well enough earlier, bellowing about tonight and scaring poor Rindr half to death.'

Rindr made noises of agreement.

Sibba gritted her teeth. 'Look about you. There has been a change in ownership.'

'All the guards appear to have left. This much is true.' The woman screwed up her eyes tight. 'Be quick about it. Who is in charge now? And none of your usual prevaricating nonsense, Sibba. I am not one to be taken in with your hooded looks like my husband was.'

Sibba stuck her thumbs in her belt. Rindr and Nefja always made her feel like she had two left feet and was incapable of sewing a fine seam, spinning slender thread, or weaving a tablecloth. Haakon always sighed and told her that she imagined things, like Rindr was jealous about how well Sibba could sail a ship and handle a bow and arrows.

'Calwar mac Bedwyr defeated Thorkell,' she said flatly, rather than explaining her part in it. 'Thorkell's body is being made ready for his funeral pyre. You may have been a bride this morning, but you are now a widow.' At the frowns, she continued. 'No one will expect Rindr to join Thorkell in the afterlife. I am not expecting a large pyre, just one big enough to give him some honour. You may attend or not. I've no idea what his other wives are going to do.'

Rindr pushed her mother aside and opened the door further. 'What? Calwar mac Bedwyr killed him for me?'

'He fought him. Others were involved in the killing.' Sibba shifted uneasily, belatedly remembering Rindr's need to be at the centre of any tale. 'Not for you exactly. For the alliance.'

'Pay no attention to Sibba, darling,' Rindr's mother positively cooed. Her face was now all smug smiles. 'She has little understanding about men. Of course Calwar mac Bedwyr did it for you. Why else move now on your wedding day? He could not bear to see you as any other man's bride. A romantic at heart, that man.'

A contented sigh from Rindr. 'What a hero!'

Sibba rolled her eyes. She'd have to apologise to Cal later, but time was precious. 'We need to go. You wouldn't want to keep the hero waiting, would you?'

Rindr flung open the door. She looked infinitely delicate with golden hair and deep sunlit blue eyes. Her figure-hugging gown with its belt of heavy gold chain showed off her figure to its best advantage.

Sibba was immediately conscious of how travel-creased and stained her clothes were and that her braid hung limply over her shoulder. All the shortcomings she had managed not to think about while she was in Cal's arms returned with a vengeance. Despite telling it not to, she knew her heart had been spinning impossible dreams.

Somewhere in the corner of her heart she'd seen Cal and her ruling over Barra benevolently and with great purpose. A foolish dream. She knew wool-gathering never solved anything and nothing happened simply because of it. She needed to be content with what she had.

'We need to go to the hall. You must look suitably solemn and grave. All will be explained.' Her words tasted like ash.

'I knew I was right to put my trust in Calwar,' Rindr positively purred. 'I knew there was something about him and his brooding looks. Sometimes you just know. His feelings for me ran deep.'

'Your mother knew about Calwar's regard for you, my dear.' Nefja put an arm about Rindr's shoulders. 'He is a man going places. He will rule these sea roads for decades to come.'

She stepped from the room, resplendent in a silver-shot gown along with an assortment of golden arm-rings and necklaces.

The woman's glance took in the entirety of Sibba and made her feel like she was something untoward discovered on the bottom of her slipper.

'You did always like to take the glory, Sibba, but you must allow Calwar and Rindr time.' Nefja smiled, baring her fangs. 'Try not to intrude or to mention that brother of yours. Thorkell had spies at Bedwyr's court. He knew all about Bedwyr's affliction and how he was confined to his bed. And I can see from your face that the rumours were true.'

'It wasn't quite like that,' Sibba stammered. The last thing Cal needed was Rindr draping herself across his neck in gratitude. And she'd seen how King Bedwyr was improving.

'What proof do you have, Sibba? None. You've no idea about Lord Calwar's intentions or motivations. You merely talk big. My husband may have been moved to help you and included you in his felag. I was never fooled.' Nefja's voice ran ice-cold and her gaze even colder. 'Your family always makes extravagant promises and assumptions, as my late husband found out to his cost. You should have been with us when we encountered those pirates.'

Sibba concentrated on the rushes, struggling to control her anger. The woman wanted her off balance. For some reason, she saw her as a threat.

'I will hold with no accusation of cowardice, my lady. We all three are aware of why I left and why I chose the route I did. Let us have no rewriting of history.'

'I suppose you may have been right to take the longer route.' Said with a distinct sniff as if Sibba was to blame for everything which had befallen them. 'But events have overtaken us.'

'You see, Mother, I told you—someone did come for us. I was right to resist that man's crude advances.' Rindr's bottom lip trembled. 'I remain important, even if you were unable to negotiate any sort of morning gift except that we would be remain alive.'

Sibba pursed her lips. Rindr had been the one to resist while her mother no doubt required a more pragmatic approach. Proof if she needed it that the mother had actively cooperated with Thorkell. It remained to be seen if it was before or after her husband had died. Sibba rejected the thought as soon as it came.

'Calwar will be happy to escort you both back to Sutherey-jar for Rindr's wedding to Bedwyr. The alliance still holds, my lady, if that is what you are asking.'

'Bedwyr continues to rule?' Rindr's mother asked in a cold voice. 'Remarkable. Thorkell's spies were most specific about his affliction.'

'He was ill, but he recovers. Haakon attends him because Bedwyr wanted someone who could play tafl to an acceptable standard.'

The woman's thin lips turned upwards. Once she had

probably been as pretty as Rindr, but her expression was now one of constant discontent. '*Recovers*? Is that what you call it? You may be naive, Sibba, but do not think I am.'

Sibba tilted her head to one side. 'What misguided rumour have you heard? Bedwyr remains the king. He presided over the council which sent Cal and me here.'

'Since when is Calwar mac Bedwyr *Cal*?'

'Since I came on this mission with him.'

'Play the fool with me, woman, and you will regret it.' Rindr's mother snapped her fingers beneath Sibba's nose. 'You know something. Something about Bedwyr. I see it in your eyes.'

Sibba concentrated on breathing steadily, rather than doing what she wanted which was to ask Nefja why she felt entitled to behave in that fashion. Her only standing was that of mother to Rindr. She was no longer the wife of a sea king. And Bedwyr would honour the obligation. She suddenly wanted him to. She did not want Cal trapped in a marriage to Rindr because of politics.

'My eyes tell you this?' she said when she trusted her voice.

'Bedwyr is an old man. You travel with his son. You will not do my daughter out of her rightful place.'

Sibba kept her face carefully neutral. 'Did I ever say I wanted to? I came here to rescue Rindr and ensure she married the man she wanted to.'

'Calwar has always had an eye for her ankles.' The woman waved an imperious hand. 'I said at the very beginning of our adventure he'd be here to save her, and so it has proved.'

'He came because of her ankles?'

'Stands to reason. Besides, my girl has a substantial inheritance.'

Sibba pressed her lips together and tried to push away
the pang of jealousy and the desire to protest that Cal belonged to her. Cal didn't belong to her. They had simply had
a brief affair. 'I see.'

The woman's eyes narrowed. 'What do you plan on doing,
Sibba, with your future? Going off on some adventure, I
have no doubt.'

'I plan on letting it take care of itself.' Sibba clung to the
door. 'You two are wanted in the main hall.'

'Of course. Come along, Rindr, and be properly grateful to your saviour.'

Rindr stopped and adjusted her gown to better display
her bosom. 'You mustn't worry, Mor. I shall be. I know my
duty. We have spoken of little else for the last few days.'

Sibba bit her lip and held back the scream that Cal belonged to her. Rindr and her mother had been captives.
There would be time enough to sort this mess out properly.
She had to keep calm and think about the prize. Haakon
was going to be upset, but that had always been inevitable.

She inclined her head. 'We should get going. The hall
and your men await, Rindr. Cal has arranged for them to
be freed. They will take their cue from you.'

'I expected no less of him. He is very able. And I will
be in his debt.'

As they started off, Rindr's mother caught Sibba's arm.
'You have altered, my dear.'

'Have I?' Sibba hated the prickling at the back of her
neck. The older woman was up to something.

'I saw how your eyes softened when you mentioned Calwar mac Bedwyr.'

She wet her lips and tried to ignore the faint curl of panic
in her stomach. Who else had noticed? She then remembered they had been entwined earlier, heedless of anyone

who happened past. The woman could not know that. She'd been barricaded in that room.

'You are imagining things.' She winced and knew the words were far too hurried and breathless. While Rindr's mother was many things, she'd never been called a fool.

The woman snapped her fingers. 'Maybe, maybe not. You do realise that the man in question will do whatever it takes to secure the throne.'

'His future prospects have nothing to do with me.'

The woman's gaze narrowed. 'But it has something to do with my daughter. Look at her. Beauty, brains, and excellent peace-weaving skills.'

'Your point?'

'That alliance will stand, one way or another. The Gaels need the North.' The woman's talons tightened about Sibba's arm. 'Do not make a mistake. Do not stand in her way. Go from here with honour while you still can.'

Sibba swallowed her fury. She hated that the woman spoke a little truth. She had no real idea why Cal was interested in her or if that interest extended beyond a few days. She put her hand on her abdomen and knew she had hopes.

'You still think she can marry well.' She permitted her lips to turn upwards. 'I do know what happens to unmarried women when their father dies.' She waited several heartbeats and added, 'Their choices do become more limited.'

'I more than think it, I know it. My husband's men have always been most loyal. They will remain loyal and will give Rindr a chance to marry before any decision about the future of the felag is made.'

The woman gave a distinct emphasis to the word *men* as if she was making a point about Sibba's loyalty. Sibba ground her teeth. She longed to ask who had proved their loyalty the most but held the words back. Deeds, not words, were necessary.

She inclined her head. 'I wish Rindr well. I always have. I believe I've fulfilled my oath to Gettir's felag.'

Chapter Fourteen

The hall had irrevocably altered in the short time it had taken Sibba to rescue Rindr and Nefja. The expensive tapestries lay on the ground, and Thorkell's body was nowhere to be seen. Cal stood beside Thorkell's old stool, speaking to the rescued Northmen, his back towards the women.

Her heart leapt at the sight of him, and she started towards him, Thorkell's sword banging awkwardly against her leg. All the warriors bowed deeply to her, and the women sank to low curtsies as she strode past, but Nefja appeared oblivious to it.

'You were right, Sibba. Lord Calwar is here.' Nefja patted her on the shoulder. 'Leave things to Rindr, please. She knows how to properly express gratitude to her saviour.'

'Her saviour.' Sibba put her hands on her head. 'In a manner of speaking.'

'He is the one who fought for her honour. You should have allowed him to come to her.' Nefja gave a fanged smile. 'You always did like to take the glory, even as a child. They will make a glorious couple. Their colouring even complements each other.'

'Not quite what happened,' Sibba muttered.

'What I say happened.' Nefja inclined her head. 'Until I learn otherwise, it is how it will be for Rindr.'

'But it's not true.'

Rindr rushed up to Cal, prettily made a low curtsy which afforded a good view of her ample bosom and thanked him for rescuing her from a fate worse than death. Cal pulled her up. Inside, Sibba's heart died slightly.

Nefja's talons dug into Sibba's arm. 'You really do need to learn more of the world, Sibba. What virile man can resist a delight like my daughter? Such a handsome couple.'

Cal's inscrutable gaze collided with Sibba's. He lifted a brow. Sibba shrugged.

'As you say...' Sibba murmured.

'Lord Calwar was the one who beat the war-lord, Thorkell,' Rindr's mother called out. 'Everyone says so.'

'You appear to have it wrong, my lady,' he said, stepping away from Rindr. 'I played no real part in your or your daughter's rescue. My purpose was very different.'

Rindr's mouth dropped open, and her face turned bright pink. 'Wrong? But you won!'

'I fought as Sibba Norrsdottar's champion.' He made a low bow in Sibba's direction. 'It is her you owe thanks to, not me.'

The implication that they could have rotted for all he cared hung in the air.

Rindr's mother tightened her talons. 'Is this true?'

'I am in possession of Thorkell's sword and therefore his felag. This stronghold now belongs to me,' Sibba said, pulling free. 'Shall we say the rescue was a joint enterprise and leave it at that?'

Scorn fairly dripped from the woman. 'And you as a woman think you can hold it?'

'I make it a point not to predict the future,' Sibba said. Having a public argument with the woman was the last thing she needed. She had to make allowances as Rindr and Nefja had endured captivity.

Without waiting for an answer, she strode across the hall towards where Cal and Rindr stood. It took longer than she anticipated as people kept stopping her to congratulate her and pledge their support.

'I would see you treated with proper regard,' Cal murmured in her ear when she arrived.

'Proper regard? The warriors have been most generous.' She pretended ignorance, but her heart warmed. He'd noticed the disrespect Rindr and Nefja displayed. 'They appear to want someone from the North leading them.'

'Where you need to sit from now on.' Cal gestured to Thorkell's stool. 'No more hesitating at the back.'

'Mor, what is going on here?' Rindr asked, rushing over to her mother. 'Why are those people greeting Sibba in that fashion?'

'I'm sure I don't know. My head is in a muddle.' Her mother pasted a smile on and made a low curtsy. 'All will be explained now that we have reached Lord Calwar.'

'Sibba Norrsdottar challenged Thorkell for the leadership but was forced to use a champion,' Rekkr proclaimed, stepping forward and glaring at the pair. 'You would do well to show her some respect.'

'Who are you?'

'Sibba's second-in-command, currently. Formerly a captain in Thorkell's felag.' Rekkr's smile somehow made his tattoos seem fiercer. 'I'm not sure I like your attitude.'

'Rindr and her mother are our guests, Rekkr,' Sibba said in a loud voice. 'I trust you will give them proper courtesy.'

'As long as they extend it to you, Sibba. You are now the leader of the joint felag. Sea King, in truth.'

The men in the hall began shouting Sibba's name.

Rindr's mother looked as if she had swallowed a bitter plum. 'I had little idea.'

'I believe there is some question about which former warriors of Gettir's felag have actually sworn allegiance to Thorkell and thus to me.' Sibba inclined her head, knowing she could afford to be gracious. Honey worked better than vinegar. 'I have no wish to do Rindr out of her inheritance. All who wish are free to swear allegiance as they see fit.'

'How gracious of you,' Rindr's mother murmured, but her eyes were cold rocks.

'Better than you deserve,' Cal answered. He cleared his throat. 'I understand, Sibba, these men expect a feast.'

Sibba frowned trying to understand his mood. She accepted the change of subject. 'There is going to be no wedding. The marriage between Rindr and Thorkell was not properly concluded, and thus Rindr is neither a bride nor indeed a widow.'

Cal shrugged. 'Wasting food when so many are hungry goes against my grain, but it is your choice.'

'I believe any feast of thanksgiving and celebration needs to wait until we can send word to all parts of the island, as well as to Suthereyjar, inviting everyone to partake.' The knots in Sibba's stomach eased. She wasn't going to have to watch Rindr and her mother being supremely elegant while she was dressed in her battledress. 'Anything which will perish can be consumed today, but we have much work to do before our guests arrive.'

Cal nodded and gave a smile which warmed her down to her toes. Sibba dug her nails into her palm to keep her warm feelings about him from appearing on her face.

'Does that mean Haakon will be coming here?' Rindr asked. Her voice trembled slightly.

'We will invite Bedwyr as well as the remainder of your

father's felag. The danger has passed, and hopefully we can all celebrate our new friendship.'

'I suspect you will need someone to assist with the hospitality,' Nefja said. 'If you wish to have the respect of a sea king, Sibba, you cannot be the one offering mead and ale. My daughter and I can assist you with this.'

Sibba hated the slight twist in her stomach. But she had to admit that Nefja was right: she could not do both. She could not afford to be seen as a peace-weaver when she was a sea king. 'I always welcome help thoughtfully given.'

'My daughter and I will be honoured to help with the hospitality. After all, you did all this under the auspices of my late husband's felag.'

Sibba hesitated until she caught Cal's eye. He gave a slight nod. Honey over vinegar, even though she kept remembering how the woman had belittled her the last time they clashed. 'What a splendid idea. It will be good for the North to show a united front.'

The woman's mouth worked up and down. She had obviously expected Sibba to refuse.

Rindr grabbed her mother's arm and whispered something in her ear. The woman smiled, shook her head, and patted Rindr's shoulder.

'Is there a problem, Rindr?'

'I merely wanted to know if I could change. I've no wish to spoil my best gown. I shall need it for the new feast. Haakon—'

'My daughter is overtired. The day has been traumatic. I trust you understand and forgive, Sibba. May we retire?'

Sibba waved her hand. 'Certainly. You are guests, not prisoners.'

Rindr and her mother hurried off, whispering.

'I suspect there will be problems,' Sibba said, tapping her finger against her mouth.

'You don't trust them,' Cal murmured, his voice tickling her ear. 'But your generosity has been noted.'

'They were badly frightened.' Her gut told her not to trust the women, but she also knew how wretched it had been for them, and Cal being in charge was a natural assumption. 'It is an unusual situation for them.'

'They attempted to undermine you from the instant they walked into this hall,' Cal said.

'They didn't listen to my explanation, that is all.' Sibba attempted to silence the butterflies beating her stomach. All she really wanted to do was to put her hands about her middle and curl up into a ball.

Cal put his hands on her shoulders. 'I told you that I wouldn't allow it to happen. Rekkr agrees with me.'

She looked up into his face. Her instinct was to melt into him, but far too many people were watching. Nefja had been right: she couldn't retain the men's respect if she deferred to a man. And Rekkr should have approached her first. She was a leader before a woman—her father's advice was always sound. Even if her heart panged slightly and wished it wasn't so.

She forced her feet to move away from him. 'Still being my champion, I see.'

His hands returned to his side. 'Is that a problem?'

'Thorkell is dead. I can stand on my own two feet. I will fight my own battles.'

His smile warmed her down to the tips of her toes, but she resolutely ignored the feeling. 'Why fight when others will do it for you?'

'Next time, ask.'

He tilted his head to one side. 'I will. And I apologise if I usurped your role.'

'I won't become a vassal. It is the surest way to lose my newly won power.'

A muscle jumped in his cheek. 'What are you saying?'

'You were right about one thing earlier. I do mean to hold this, and I shall do it, but I can't do it if people consider me your puppet.'

His eyes assessed her. 'There are reasons that I am in awe of your skills.'

'I shall take that as a compliment.' She pinched the bridge of her nose. 'I suspect in the days and weeks to come, I am going to require every last particle of my diplomatic skills.'

He put his hand under her elbow. The temptation to lean into that touch was great, but Sibba resisted. Too many people were watching, and she needed to seem strong. That was the excuse she gave herself, but she knew it was only that. She also knew she couldn't go on like this, hoping to feel his lips move against hers.

'If anyone can do it, you can,' he said in a low voice.

'At least one of us believes in me.' Her laugh came out strangled.

'Always. Shall we go somewhere, and I can demonstrate?' His low voice rippled over her shattered nerves.

To go somewhere and sink into Cal's body was precisely what she wanted, but it would be a mistake. She needed to prove that she could lead the Northern warriors.

She looked up at him. 'We can't do that. It happened, and now it finishes.'

'It's over?'

'We agreed.' She swallowed hard and made sure her voice was steady. Even if her entire being ached with the wrongness of it. But it was her only hope of fulfilling this dream. 'I need you to speak with the Barra Gaels and get them to come to the feast of celebration. They will listen to you. Get that banner out of the trunk in the hut. I discovered it when we were so cold. I assume it belonged to your late wife.'

He tilted his head to one side, and his eyes became inscrutable. 'As you wish.'

She drew a deep breath. 'Thank you.'

His hand closed about her elbow. 'What is going on? Why are you sending me away?'

She pointedly looked at his fingers, and he released them one by one. 'Because you are the only person that I trust.'

Her heart ached. A clean break was better. She had to make sure Barra was safe. And it would make it easier than to see the inevitable. How could she compete with someone like Rindr? How could she afford to be a woman?

'Talk to me, Sibba.'

'We have done all the talking we need to. You know what is required if you are not too afraid to do it.'

'I'm not afraid.'

'Then, do it. Many matters command my attention.' She turned on her heel and marched straight up to several warriors and engaged them in conversation, trying to ignore the ache in her heart.

When she finished, she glanced over at him. He was regarding her with dark brooding eyes. He beckoned to her. She held out her hands and shrugged. 'Are you waiting for something?'

'To say goodbye. I will do as you suggest and see the Gaels of Barra. We will speak then when matters are more settled.'

Sibba closed her eyes as all her fears washed over her.

She clenched her fist and swallowed hard. She refused to weaken even if she was dying on the inside. 'I see.'

'I hope you do.' He turned on his heel and strode away.

Bittersweet pride washed over Sibba when she saw her longship, followed by the remainder of Gettir's old fleet plus several Gaelic ships arrive. She'd expected to feel giddy relief or a quiet sense of accomplishment, standing there watching the ships come in, not this crippling sense of responsibility with no one to share it with. For once even the weather appeared to be cooperating, with bright sunshine and a dark blue sky. Her men stood in formation with Cal and the Barra Gaels to the right of them. The banner from the trunk waved in the breeze.

He'd done as she asked, but he had not sought her out to be alone since his return. That simple fact hurt more than she expected. She'd missed his voice, his challenges to do better, and his gentle laughter, but mostly she missed him. She knew she'd been the one to push him away, but the fact provided scant comfort.

Sibba knew the rumours about Cal and Rindr's betrothal being imminent had stemmed from Nefja, but he'd done little to dispel them as far she could tell. She hated to think how in years to come, whatever happened, whoever he married, she'd have to pretend that there had never been anything between them. She wished there had been some way that she could have been both a leader and a woman. She wished the world worked in another fashion. She wished she had figured out how to make that happen before she'd irrevocably broken with Cal.

All should be fine, except her stomach, neck, and shoulders ached. She had not realised how tense she was until that tension vanished, leaving only the pain and faint nausea that this was real, and many people now depended on her for their security.

From here on out, she stood alone and dedicated herself to the service of the felag. She wished the prospect didn't feel so lonely.

She curled her fists and attempted to ignore how delicate and lovely Rindr and Nefja looked as they waited to greet the new arrivals, the very picture of what she'd always been instructed Northern women looked and acted like.

Sibba wore a carefully selected tunic and trousers, set off with a fur-trimmed cloak to give herself the apt gravitas. She'd discovered the cloak and the embroidered tunic in an iron-bound trunk in Thorkell's old chambers and had been proud of the ensemble until she spied Rindr and her mother in gowns which flattered their figures.

She overheard the whisper of *dressing up* and the hastily stifled giggle, and all the pleasure she had felt vanished. She wished she could catch Cal's eye for reassurance, but that would feel like weakness. And yet somehow, knowing he was there made her breathe easier as if all was right with the world.

When the boats had docked, she gave a little speech of welcome. The wind whipped most of the words from her throat, but people cheered loudly enough. The Barra Gaels screamed her name the loudest, prompting the Northmen to shout all the louder. A quick glance at Cal showed him smiling broadly. The knots in her stomach relaxed. He believed in her, and that made everything better.

Haakon was one of the first off. He ran towards her and caught her hands, spinning her round and round.

'You look every inch the queen you are supposed to be,' Haakon cried. 'And isn't that one of our father's old tunics that he had made in Constantinople?'

'I thought I recognised it when I discovered it amongst Thorkell's things,' she said, hoping Haakon wouldn't ask about Rindr and she wouldn't have to lie.

'It suits you.' Haakon hugged her again. 'My sister, the undisputed Sea King—or is it Sea Queen?—of the North in Lochlann.'

'Careful,' she said. 'I am supposed to be dignified. The title is Sea King, and my sex makes no difference.'

'Dignity be blown.' He hugged her tight and then let her go. 'If our father could see you now, he'd be proud, truly proud. Nobody else could have done it.'

'Lord Calwar helped.'

Haakon's gaze narrowed, obviously noting that she ascribed Cal his full honour. 'You alone lead. Our father always said women can only lead if they are alone.'

'It worked out that way.' Sibba shrugged and scuffed her boot. 'I kept my promises, and my oath-bonded warriors have responded. They like the thought of being fed and warm. Discipline is already better. A few have left, but that is to be expected.'

'But most stayed...' Haakon touched her arm. 'I must help Bedwyr get off the boat, but I wanted to see you first.'

A great cry went up where the women were standing. 'Rindr has collapsed! Rindr has fainted!'

'Can someone help us, please?' Nefja cried. 'My daughter! She is unwell. Lord Calwar?'

At Cal's questioning look, Sibba nodded and indicated that he should help. Cal crossed over and scooped Rindr up. He started off to the hall, with Nefja bleating behind.

He stopped and gave Nefja a hard stare. 'Nefja, you need to see the guests as you promised Sibba.'

Nefja's mouth open and closed. 'Of course, my lord. I trust you to look after my daughter.'

'You won't regret those words.' Cal strode away, carrying Rindr in his arms with her head resting prettily against his chest.

'Rindr is here and safe,' she said around the ashes in her mouth.

Haakon winced. 'Lord Calwar and Rindr? When did that happen?'

Sibba kept her face carefully blank. 'Rindr and her mother have been in seclusion since Thorkell's death. They only came out to welcome the fleet.'

She did not add that they had gone directly into seclusion after Rindr discovered there were several more so-called wives of Thorkell who had superior claims to any remaining fortune.

'Sounds about right.' Haakon looked about him. 'Shall I go see how Rindr is?'

'I will send someone else to help Bedwyr off the boat.'

Haakon made an annoyed noise in the back of his throat. 'His father fears Cal is getting bored, but Bedwyr has no intention of dying or retiring.'

'Why are you telling me this?'

'I thought you might like to know.' Haakon widened his eyes. 'I thought there might be something between you two. The way you were with him before you left. That you might be able to find a role for him here. Our father wasn't right about everything, Sibba. You must remember that.'

'You were spinning webs with moonbeams and starlight, Haakon. Nothing exists between us. Nothing at all.' She caught her bottom lip between her teeth, knowing that she'd been the one to push Cal away. 'Cal wants to help his father. They gave their word about the alliance.'

Haakon raised a brow. 'I shall leave it there now, but I will have my say.'

* * *

Cal placed Rindr on the bench. He struggled to contain his annoyance. The last place he wanted to be was here with this woman, but she also held the key to his future happiness. It had been obvious that she was going to try something. He knew what her mother was hoping for and that wasn't going to happen: he had no intention of marrying the milksop woman. Neither was he about to force Rindr to marry his father.

He silently prayed his scheme would work and he could begin to repair the chasm which had developed between Sibba and him.

Rindr struggled to sit up, her pale blue eyes were wide, and her mouth turned down in a pout which some men might enjoy but Cal found deeply unattractive. 'What happened to me? Why have you brought me here? Why are we alone?'

Cal crossed his arms and glowered at her. 'Suppose you tell me what is going on. Your collapse was far too well-timed.'

Her lashes fluttered, and she put a hand to her ample bosom. 'Haakon is here. It was a shock.'

'Do you love him? Speak now, and I may be able to help,' Cal said. Any second now her mother would barge through that door and accuse him of something, seeking to force a marriage—something he deeply wished to avoid.

Her lashes swept down before she briefly nodded. 'But my mother says—'

He clenched his jaw and struggled to keep his temper. 'Your mother isn't you. You must do what is right for you. I believe you have earned that after your ordeal.'

Her eyes went wide. 'Do you think he cares for me? Do you think he will have me? My mother says I will be penniless if Sibba has her way. Haakon will never want me, not now. All I have is the treaty you negotiated.'

'You must ask yourself that question, not me. However, I know Sibba has a generous heart.'

The flash of relief mixed with a promise of salvation which flickered across her face, before being replaced by a faintly depressed frown, told Cal all he required about Rindr's hopes and dreams. He also knew that she would not tell him the truth unless Haakon was there. He silently prayed that he was right about Sibba's brother.

'My heart tells me nothing of any import,' she whispered. 'He didn't even look for me.'

'But I do know that he wanted you rescued. He argued for it. Threatened to go on his own.'

Rindr sat up straighter, and something akin to hope flickered in her eyes. 'He stayed with your father. If he was interested in me, he'd have come, or so my mother says.'

A vague sense of pity for Haakon swept over Cal. He hoped the man would be equal to the task. 'He paid a price for the rescue. The best people went because he wanted to ensure your safety.'

Rindr put her hands over her mouth. 'I'd never considered that. Oh, dear. My mother has been lying to me.'

The hall doors crashed open, and Sibba's brother strode in, bristling with anger.

Cal's shoulders relaxed. Haakon was behaving precisely as his instinct told him he would—how he'd have behaved if someone carried Sibba off.

'Calwar! Where are you hiding Rindr? Produce her. Immediately,' Haakon thundered. 'I will not have her abused!'

'Oh, Haakon!' Rindr trilled, clapping her hands together.

His hand tightened on his sword, and his jaw clenched. Cal made a low bow and hid his smile.

'I believe you and this lady need to speak. Alone and in private. I'm merely the facilitator of the situation.'

Haakon's mouth dropped open. 'Rindr and me? Alone?'

'You are the reason she fainted.' Cal put a hand to his heart. 'She saw you and—'

'She did?' Haakon stood up a bit straighter. 'Why, yes! We are fated to be together.'

Rindr held out her hand, and her face became meltingly sweet. 'Oh, Haakon. How masterful you are.'

Haakon stuck out his chest. 'Masterful? Why, of course I am.'

He went over and gathered her to his chest. Their mouths met, and it became clear a third party was superfluous.

'Don't worry. I will see myself out. I believe your mother has other things to occupy her, Rindr.' Cal cocked his head to one side. 'Was there a specific reason you came to find me, Haakon? Besides saving me the trouble of reuniting you two.'

'Sibba needs you,' Haakon said in a fierce voice, turning from Rindr but keeping hold of her hand. 'You must not abandon her, not even for your father. He is getting better every day.'

'Sibba has everything under control. Thorkell's men have pledged their loyalty. She commands Barra. The Barra Gaels welcomed her intervention.'

'If you knew her like I do, you could see how nervous she is and how much she tries to hide it,' Haakon continued in a calmer tone. 'She is terrified.'

'Why are you telling me this?'

Haakon let go an exaggerated sigh. 'Because my sister sometimes likes to cut her nose off to spite her face. Sibba is a very stubborn person and determined, but she needs someone strong with her. Our father drummed into her that she had to stand alone if she was to lead.'

Cal tensed. He wanted to support her, but she didn't want his support. It hurt him far more than he would like. And she was slipping away from him. He should have told her before they left about his feelings for her or directly after the fight. Now any declaration would look like he had designs on the felag. 'Rindr must decide who she wishes to marry.'

Rindr widened her blue eyes and declared that the only man she wanted to marry was Haakon.

'Why did you fight Thorkell, Calwar?' Haakon asked, rather than answering.

'Sibba required a champion,' he said, shaking his head. 'I fulfilled that role. Nothing more, nothing less.'

'She still does.' Haakon nodded. 'She can't hold her drink very well, in case you need to break down her defences.'

'Why are you telling me this?'

'Because you are someone I would welcome as a brother-in-law, and I must look to supporting the woman I love instead of my sister.' He turned back to Rindr and clasped her to his chest. 'Now, shall I show you how much I missed you, my darling moonbeam?'

Cal let himself out because he knew he would not be missed for a long while.

'There you are, Lord Calwar!' Rekkr strode towards him. 'I trust all is well with that young woman. Her mother has been wondering what is taking so long.'

'Sibba's brother is with her. I believe the reunion is going well.'

The tattoos crinkled about the man's eyes. 'Haakon and Rindr. Nefja will be unhappy, but I suppose she can cope.'

'Suthereyjar will not stand in their way.'

Rekkr nodded. 'What about you and our commander?'

'What about it?'

'You acted as her champion.' The man's tattoos quivered, and Cal didn't know if it was supressed amusement or anger. 'I think you would like to continue to be that.'

'I fully accept that a Northerner must govern here,' he said, playing for time.

Rekkr frowned. 'Sibba needs someone to look after her. Someone who understands her. I've known her since she only came up to my waist. She can't do it alone, not if her brother is otherwise occupied.'

'Why are you telling me this?' Cal clenched his jaw. No one dictated who he should love or indeed who Sibba should love.

'Because the woman can be as stubborn as all get-out.' Rekkr leant in and lowered his voice. 'My advice to you is to ply her with mead and then see. She likes you, and I want her to be happy. My men and I took a vote on it.'

There was an implication of unimaginable tortures if he hurt Sibba. 'And if I should make her unhappy?'

'It depends on what she is unhappy about.'

'I will bear your words in mind.' Cal kept a straight face. Two people, three if you counted Rindr, were advising him to do something underhanded. He had no wish to secure Sibba that way. She needed to come to him freely and realise on her own that they belonged together.

One thing he'd learned was that trying to force anything with a woman never worked. And he wanted everything to work with Sibba.

Sibba pinched the top of her nose and tried to concentrate on everything but Cal's disappearance with Rindr. The fact hurt more than she thought it would, sucking the joy and pleasure she had from successfully negotiating a treaty between the Barra Gaels and the North as well as

Bedwyr. It all seemed hollow because Cal wasn't there. She stuffed the feelings down and tried to focus on the middle distance while she listened to King Bedwyr delivering his address, welcoming the new alliance.

'Sibba,' Rekkr said, coming to stand beside her, 'all seems to be in hand, thanks to Lord Calwar.'

Sibba tilted her head to one side. 'What do you mean? Calwar took no part in the negotiations. He left me to it while he ministers to Rindr.'

Rekkr's eyes crinkled. 'Would you have him undermine your authority, particularly after you told him that you intended to take control?'

She bit her lip. 'I suppose you are right. What has he done that is praiseworthy?'

'He has allowed young Haakon and Rindr to spend time together. Alone.'

'Alone?'

'I had a quick peep in, and I doubt that they will notice anyone or anything, if you catch my meaning.'

Sibba put her hands over her mouth. Cal had done something he said he never would. He had given Rindr a choice. And he'd carefully stayed until Haakon was there, and Rindr had to acknowledge her love for him—something she would not have thought of. 'And Cal left them?'

'The Gaels won't stand in their way is what he told me. With you in charge, they have the peace they craved.'

Sibba forced a nod, but her heart raced. With her in charge? The only way that could happen would be if she gave up all hope of Cal and her.

'And Nefja?'

'Her daughter will be married to the brother of one of the most powerful sea kings in Lochlann. How can she object? All the captains support you.'

A wave of tiredness washed over Sibba. All she could see before her was loneliness and never being able to share her thoughts with someone who instinctively understood her. She pressed her hands against her eyes and willed the feeling away. She'd made that choice. A little voice asked her if her father's way was the only way. She had found her own means of dealing with Thorkell, so maybe she could navigate a path through. 'I suppose you are right.'

'If you thought throwing Rindr at Lord Calwar would solve your problem, you have another thing coming.'

'Excuse me?'

Rekkr sighed. 'I've known you a long time, Sibba. You never let people get close. You try to push them away. Ask your brother. You use your father's words as a shield. If he'd allowed people to be closer, then maybe he'd have survived.'

'Me? I have been busy trying to forge alliances.'

'Do I have your permission to direct Nefja to where Haakon and Rindr are currently?'

'You appear intent on doing that,' Sibba said with what she hoped was withering scorn. It bothered her that Rekkr was right. She had been very busy and had little time to seek Cal out after he returned with the Barra Gaels. Had she quit the battlefield too quickly? Had she used the necessity of her being seen to be a strong leader to push Cal away? Could she seduce him?

'All I'm saying is don't wait too long. Lord Calwar will be returning to Suthereyjar, and then what will you do?'

'Lead this felag to peace and prosperity,' Sibba responded in what she hoped was a cool voice.

'Lie to me if you like, but you are the one facing a life of loneliness, not me.'

'Some day you will go too far.'

'Some day you will see what you casually threw away.

You showed me what I'd tossed away when you challenged Thorkell. It was you and Lord Calwar working together which brought it about.' Rekkr bowed. 'Your servant, my lady. Always.'

Chapter Fifteen

The entire hall teemed with people enjoying themselves, laughing and joking. The huge contrast with when Thorkell presided forcibly struck Sibba. The happy couple sat at the high table to the left of Sibba, with Bedwyr on the right. At the sight of the couple's devotion, Bedwyr immediately released Rindr from the betrothal and bestowed his blessing on Haakon, the most skilled tafl player he had seen in a long time. Sibba tried to concentrate on the joyous mood of celebration rather than the sinking pit in her stomach that all was going to go wrong tonight with her scheme to seduce Cal and why she should postpone it.

Perhaps it was better for everyone if no one knew about her growing love for Cal or her desire to be held. Maybe it was better for everyone if she did choose a strict life of dedication to duty. A little voice in the back of her mind called her a coward.

'Tomorrow, I return to Suthereyjar confident in the knowledge that my brothers and sisters on Barra are now safe,' Bedwyr said, rising and interrupting her thoughts. 'A toast to Sibba Norrsdottar. Long may we be allies and, most importantly, friends!'

Everyone in the room, even Nefja, rose and toasted her. The Barra Gaels cheered and pledged their loyalty to

Sibba while the contingent from Suthereyjar pounded the table.

Sibba knew from the look which passed between Cal and Bedwyr that Cal no longer had any reason to stay on in Barra. She had to do something. Tonight. The decision had been taken out of her hands.

She swayed slightly, fumbling for her words. She opened her mouth, but no sound emerged; she swallowed hard and managed to choke out her gratitude, including her hopes for a peaceful and prosperous future. Her words sounded high and strained to her ears but were well received with much stamping and cheering.

'Is something wrong, Sibba?' Cal asked in an undertone, coming to stand beside her. 'You went pale. Your voice betrayed your strain.'

She forced her lips to turn upwards. Cal would have to notice. 'Working too hard. But people enjoyed it.'

'Then, I suggest you quit the feast and go to bed.'

She tilted her head to one side. The mead flowed warmly in her veins. She knew she had to take the risk. 'With you as my...protector?'

Her heart pounded, and she could scarcely credit that she'd said the words.

A gleam appeared in Cal's eyes. 'When someone like you asks such a thing, who am I to say no? It would be my pleasure to see you to your chamber.'

She put her hand to her throat. 'On second thought, remaining here might be better.'

'If you go, my father can retire,' Cal said quietly. 'He remains unwell, despite his recent improvement. Haakon and Rekkr can see to the feast.'

She twirled her goblet. Cal was right. If she left, she'd give Bedwyr the opportunity to withdraw as well. He was looking after his father's welfare, nothing to do with any desire for her.

'When you put it like that…' she said, deciding to try. 'I trust the hall will be standing in the morning. Come if you like, but I am sure I can make my own way.'

She walked quickly towards the exit without turning around, but she fancied she heard his footsteps behind. She'd cast her die, and now she had to hope she could discover a way to explain to Cal how she felt about him.

Sibba's private chamber with its flagon of wine, dish of sweetmeats, and large bed was better appointed than Cal had hoped. With its strategically placed torches, the room could have been designed for seduction. Who had done it—Sibba or, more likely, someone like Rindr, intent on helping?

He rejected that idea as the hope of a desperate man. Sibba would not do that. Instead, he had to hope that Haakon was right: Sibba did care for him but was too stubborn to say it, and this was the slightly misguided work of Rekkr or Haakon and Rindr who appeared very cosy at the feast. All three had been quick to ensure Sibba left with him. The excuse that his father needed his bed was a convenient one, and he was glad Sibba had accepted it without question.

She nestled nicely into his chest with his arm about her waist. He suspected that Rekkr had somehow managed to keep her drink full, despite him trying to ensure that she did not drink more than she wished.

'Back safe and sound as I promised,' he said, loosening his arm. He knew he should walk away and think no more about it. He knew forgetting was a lie, however. He would think of Sibba and what they had shared every day until he died.

She put a hand to her head. 'Did you promise? It is all muddled.'

'I did. I intend to keep you straight. No jeopardising the new alliance. It was kind of you to realise that my father would not depart while the host remained at the high table.'

She looked up at him with deeply pooled eyes. The tiredness fairly rolled off her. 'Your father didn't come into my considerations before that. I will try to do better next time. A leader must always try harder to be deserving of her men's regard.'

He lifted her chin, enabling him to see her face more clearly. The torches sent strange shadows across her face, making it all hard planes and sunken, bruised eyes. His heart clenched. He should have done more to take the pain. He shouldn't have stayed away. 'Eight of your men made a point of telling me that you push yourself beyond the limits any person can endure for long. Why they think I have any power to do something about it I don't know, but they want you leading them for years to come, not just for a few weeks.'

She shook her head. 'They don't seem to realise that I don't require a champion. Never did. I can lead on my own without deferring to anyone.'

'You are more than suitable to the task of leading a felag, Sibba. Never allow anyone to tell you differently. But being able to lead means ensuring you are ready to.'

She reached for the goblet, taking care to fill it to the brim. His words echoed the thoughts she'd had earlier about doing things differently, doing things her way rather than how her father had governed. 'You are free with your advice.'

Before she could drink it, he took it from her. 'Why drink more mead when you require a friend?'

'Are you my friend?'

'I'd like to think I am, if you will let me be.'

'Maybe I need courage,' she said in a small voice. She put her hand over her mouth, unable to believe she had said that. And she did know Cal was her friend. Possibly the most faithful one she'd ever had. But she also knew she wanted something more than friendship. She had to find a way to explain that she'd made a mistake and she wanted to continue with whatever was between them.

'You need more courage?' Cal shook his head. 'You have more courage in your little finger than most men have in their entire body.'

She tucked her head into her neck. 'I wanted to ask you something earlier but…'

Cal raised her hand to his lips, brushed her palm, and then folded her fingers about the kiss. His heart knocked loudly in his ears. He knew he had to get this right, because his entire future depended on it. He refused to go back to that half-life he was leading before he met her. 'You've had too much to drink. All these fears about your ability to lead will vanish when the sun rises.'

She blinked at him. Her tongue moistened her lips. It was all he could do not to draw her to him. 'Why do you say that? About the drink.'

'You asked me to take you to bed in a very roundabout way. Something you'd never do without drink. I won't take advantage of you, Sibba. I have far too much respect for you for that.'

Her cheeks coloured before she buried her face in her hands. 'In front of everyone?'

'Pretty much.'

'How loud was I?'

He pretended to frown. 'I believe you were loud about it. Haakon, Rindr, and her mother certainly heard you say it.'

Sibba sat heavily down on the bed. 'You're right. I may have had too much to drink. You can always say it was a mistake later.'

'A mistake later? What are you on about, Sibba?'

'You're going to go back to Suthereyjar on the next tide. Leaving me alone.' She clasped her hand over her mouth and gave a soft hiccup. 'I didn't mean to say that.'

'You are not the first person to tell me this. Even my father has noticed and is concerned. He lives yet and has little intention of dying anytime soon. I need to live.'

'Is that what you are doing—living?'

'Before I met you, I was living a half-life, sleeping, walking, and making decisions which might have been sensible but lacked heart or compassion. You reawakened those feelings in me.'

She banged her hand against her ear. 'What is this?'

'I like to think of it as protecting my interests.'

'Am I your *interest* now?' She made a cat's paw with her hand. 'I'm nobody's interest, Calwar. Can't be. Not ever.'

A lump developed in his throatShe didn't believe in him.

He had to make his move tonight and bind her to him. He had to show her how good they were together.

'I arranged for Haakon and Rindr to speak alone, not because I suddenly believed in Haakon's devotion but because I wanted to do what was right for you,' Cal said, putting his hands on Sibba's shoulders. 'I wanted to do something you couldn't do, and that was to show Rindr her choices. She made the correct one.'

Sibba's mouth trembled. 'Did she?'

'She chose love.' Cal allowed his mouth to brush Sibba's. 'Now, stop inventing reasons why I should not desire you.'

Sibba's brow knitted. 'Trying to be strong is hard.'

'You don't have to be with me.' He put his arms about her. 'I promise. You can lean on me.'

Sibba laid her head against his chest, listening to the steady thump of his heart. One last time, Sibba promised her heart. One last time, and then she'd be the hardened warrior her men required, the way her father told she had to be.

'Sibba?' he whispered in her ear. 'Don't give me hope if you don't mean it.'

'Is this enough hope?' Her hand curled around his neck, and she drew his lips to hers.

The kiss instantly deepened. She allowed her tongue to say all the things she didn't dare whisper.

'Sibba,' he murmured against her hair, his hands roaming down her body, sliding over her breasts. 'We should—'

She dragged his mouth back to hers. 'Let's not speak. I want to feel.'

'As my lady commands.'

He picked her up as if she weighed no more than a feather and carried her over to the bed piled high with luxurious furs.

'This time, a bed, my lady. My sole condition.'

He placed her gently on the silky softness. She smiled back at him. The pain and loneliness forgotten in the heat of his look.

'Only one?'

His lips quirked upwards. 'I know better than to ask for more.'

'Sometimes you don't ask enough.'

She reached up, buried her hands deep in his hair, and held him. Their tongues touched and tangled. Devoured.

He ran his hands down her chest and palmed her breasts,

rubbing his knuckles against her nipples, making them hard and tight. The heat flared within her.

Her breath caught in her throat, and her body bucked upwards, seeking his questing hands and the release they offered.

'Allow me to undress you,' he rasped against her ear.

At her nod, he slowly removed each of her garments, stroking each particle of skin he revealed until she lay naked against the soft fur. She watched as his garments hit the floor with a thud and he loomed above her, skin gleaming in the flickering torchlight.

He lowered his mouth and traversed down her body, lapping at her skin until he stopped to feast at the apex of her thighs. His tongue circled round and round until her senses trembled on the brink of the release that must arrive soon. She clawed at his shoulders, crying his name.

'Do you want me?' he asked, lifting his head.

She forced the word from her throat. 'Yes.'

'Then, you may have me. Slow and gentle, as I promised for our first time in a bed.'

'Slow and gentle? But—'

He caught her chin between his fingers, before dropping a kiss against her swollen lips. 'You must understand the possibilities, Sibba.'

His hands roamed over her body, delicately touching her as if she was made of the most precious glass, taking his time with exquisite tenderness until she knew he had spoken an important truth. The brink where she had trembled earlier was a low hill compared to the gigantic precipice she now teetered on. She whispered his name again, stroking his back.

He levered his body and slid himself in. Her body expanded to welcome him before clenching tight about him and joining the two into one. She knew she wanted to hang on to him for as long as possible until he said his goodbyes. Just one night, she silently prayed before she gave herself up to the maelstrom that engulfed them both.

Sibba lay in Cal's arms, looking up at the ceiling. The torches were guttering to their last gasp of light.

All the mead had flowed out of her veins, but her mind still fizzed. She wanted this to have meant something to Cal, but she greatly feared she'd trapped him into it, demanding that he make love to her. What had she been thinking? Had she truly discarded every shred of self-respect? She groaned softly.

'What are you thinking about?' he asked, drawing a line down her face.

'I could say I was thinking about setting up the archery targets,' she said, concentrating on the darkening rafters and willing the feeling of utter humiliation to go.

'You could, but it would be a lie.' He nipped her chin. 'You were thinking of me.'

She raised herself up on her elbow 'Was I? Or are you merely saying that because you need to leave and catch the next tide?'

'I'm not going to go that easily, Sibba,' he said. 'I'm tired of lying to you, and most of all to myself. When I volunteered to be your champion, it had nothing to do with my duty towards my father or my country, and everything with my desire to protect you. I want to be your last line of defence, the person you can always turn to when the night seems the blackest, Sibba, if you will let me.'

Sibba tried to ignore the sudden pounding of her heart. He hadn't denied the need to go back with his father. 'Is that what you are—my final hope?'

He wrapped her hair about his hand. 'When my wife and son died, I thought the light had gone out of my world and would never return. Then I met you, and you showed me that such things as hope, decency, and kindness existed in this world. Unexpected from a Northern war leader.'

She froze. 'What are you saying? You are going to return to Suthereyjar with your father. Tonight was your way of saying goodbye. Your wife's people are safe.'

He kissed her temple. 'Tonight is my way of demonstrating how much you mean to me. How much I want you in my life. How much I need you. Not lust but love, Sibba. Not duty but desire.'

Sibba found it impossible to prevent her heart from soaring. He wanted her in his life. But she also had to be practical.

'How is that going to be possible? Your father needs you.'

'But I need you more.' Cal smoothed her hair back from her forehead. 'Because this is where my heart tells me to be. Everyone else can go hang.'

She forgot how to breathe. Cal wanted to stay here with her, in her bed, not because it was his duty or a necessary alliance but because he cared about her and what happened to her. She had to pinch herself to ensure she wasn't dreaming. 'When did you decide this?'

He took her face between his hands. 'I love you, Sibba. I started falling for you when you put those arrows in the loaf of bread, and each day my love for you grew. Your strength, your resilience, and your determination were the only reasons we succeeded against Thorkell. But I didn't realise how important you were to me until you decided that you were going to go alone. I had to figure out a way to show you that you need me in your life just as much I need you.'

He loved her. And had loved her since that first day. Sibba's heart knocked in her chest.

'It took me a little longer... When you stole that kiss, you stole my heart, and I've no wish to get it back,' she said, bringing her hand up to the side of his face. 'Without you, none of this would have been possible. Without you believing in me, I'd never have been able to face Thorkell. My father was wrong—I can be a leader and a woman at the same time, if I have you by my side. We will make our own rules and not be governed by other people's.'

'I meant what I said. I am your champion. Then. Now. And for always. Will you have me as your life's partner?'

He was giving her a choice. Just when she thought she couldn't love him more, he found a way to wrap new strings about her heart.

She drew his face closer. 'I accept your marriage proposal because you are as necessary to me as breathing.'

He nipped her chin. 'My proposal? Are you certain that is what it is?'

'We will marry,' she said, looking up at the shifting shadows on the ceiling. 'Both in the North way and in the Christian fashion. Any child of ours will inherit both kingdoms, if they prove worthy. It will be a kingdom of Gaels and the North. And we will hold it against all who mean us harm. We look for peace but are prepared to defend. Together.'

'I do like your way of thinking.' Cal recaptured her mouth, and for a long time, there was no need for words.

Eighteen months later, Barra

Everything in the chamber was still except for the soft breathing of his baby son. Cal stood for a long breath drinking in the scene: Sibba asleep on the bed, her hair splayed and young Amlaib in the cradle, blowing small sleep bubbles. Perfect peace, something he had never truly considered that he would have.

He cleared his throat.

Instantly her eyes sprung open. Her lips turned up in a sleepy smile. She patted the bed, inviting him to join her. 'You've returned.'

'I came in on the tide. All is well with my father. Haakon was overly concerned. He and the priest make a pretty pair, clucking and cooing over my father. Not that my father has any objections. He enjoys the attention and takes every opportunity to lecture me about looking after you better. Imagine!'

Sibba's eyes crinkled in the corners like they always did when she was amused. He was surprised and pleased how attuned they were to each other. He never felt like he had to explain a joke.

'You look after me well enough. I've no complaints.' Her brow furrowed, and she pretended to think. 'Actually one, now that I consider.'

'What is that?'

'We've yet to pit our archery skills against each other. Again.'

'Do you think I would risk losing to you?'

'But you enjoy losing.'

'Only when the wager means we both win.'

Sibba smiled and patted the pillows beside her. Cal needed no further invitation to go and sit beside her. 'It is good that Haakon has found a place with your father. How is he, truly?'

'He thrives. He appears to understand my father's many moods far better than I ever did.'

'Is that all? You are keeping something from me. I see it in the way you tilt your head.'

'No secrets from you.' Cal took a deep breath. 'The big news is that Rindr is pregnant. Nefja and Father Aidan remain at loggerheads over the best way to treat her, but my father thinks they secretly enjoy the sparring.'

Sibba gave a heart-melting smile at the news.

'I hope she has an easier time of it than I did.'

Sibba had been ill at the very start of her pregnancy, but her labour was straightforward. Amlaib was a fighter and as determined as his mother. He'd thrived and was growing stronger each day.

'She appears to be.' He pushed her hair back from her temple. 'And now, wife, we have spent quite enough time discussing your brother and his wife. I think we can safely discuss us.'

'Yes, a most interesting discussion to have,' she breathed, curling her hand about his neck. 'We can indulge because our baby is sleeping peacefully and all is right with our world.'

* * * * *

*If you enjoyed this story,
be sure to read Michelle Styles's
latest Historical romance*
A Viking Heir to Bind Them

*And why not pick up her
Vows and Vikings miniseries?*

A Deal with Her Rebel Viking
Betrothed to the Enemy Viking
To Wed a Viking Warrior